A CHAMBER OF DELIGHTS

Todd bit Sophie's neck and skimmed her buttocks with his fingers. Sophie began to quiver and set her legs apart to give him unrestricted access. Now he raked her body with his fingers, drawing them down her flanks, from the hollows of her armpits to her thighs.

'Beg,' he whispered. 'Beg and I'll give you this.' He stroked his shaft, making it swell. 'You know how much you want it.'

By the same author:

A CHALICE OF DELIGHTS
VIRGINIA'S QUEST

A CHAMBER OF DELIGHTS

Katrina Young

Nexus

This book is a work of fiction.
In real life, make sure you practise safe sex.

First published in 1997 by
Nexus
332 Ladbroke Grove
London W10 5AH

Copyright © Katrina Young 1997

The right of Katrina Young to be identified as the Author
of this Work has been asserted by her in accordance with
the Copyright Designs and Patents Act 1988.

Typeset by TW Typesetting, Plymouth, Devon

Printed and bound by
Caledonian Books Ltd, Glasgow

ISBN 0 352 33213 1

Contents

Prologue

As a consort to an English earl, Gael led a life of luxury and ease. Her duties, apart from pandering to the Earl of Grymwell's lascivious demands, were to host week-ends of debauchery and lust at Grymwell Hall. But the earl tired of playing with her and sent her upon a mission to deliver a valuable antique – the chalice of delights – to a millionaire collector in the south of France.

Too late, Gael realised that she had been dumped by the earl, and was shocked to find that the French millionaire believed that she was his to enjoy in any way he chose. After a series of erotic experiences with servants and their master, Gael escaped from his chateau and made her way to Paris. Penniless and dejected, she met up with a former lover, the elegant Melindi Mocambo, and quickly found herself sexually involved again.

The story begins with Gael wondering what she will do with her life away from the luxury and sophistication of Grymwell Hall.

1

The French Mistress

Standing on the balcony with her legs set wide apart, Gael delighted at the caress of a balmy breeze upon her breasts. Then she closed her eyes and sighed as she felt a different kind of heat upon her back.

As a long, black hand eased between her legs, she murmured with the pleasure that it brought her. A thumb slipped up inside her, widened her and searched her. It pressed against her G-spot. It sent a wave of pleasure through her belly to her breasts, and then withdrew.

The hum of Paris came up on the sultry air. Streamers of bright car lights stretched along the avenues and wound around the floodlit Arc de Triomphe.

As the hand explored the inside of Gael's thigh, she sighed again. 'My God, Melindi, you're a devil with your fingers. Please don't tease. I want to feel your tongue.'

Melindi thrust out her breasts against Gael's back. Full and firm, the nipples pressed against naked skin. She held her head up regally and smiled.

'And you, my little pink morsel, are very naughty, standing here stark naked for all the world to see. I'm going to have to spank you hard. Bend down.'

On the benches in the park below, lovers kissed and petted, too intent upon their touching to glance up.

3

They didn't see the black-haired young Englishwoman silhouetted against the glow of the plush apartment's lamps. They didn't see her grip the balustrade and thrust herself out needfully to the Nubian princess. And neither did they hear her gasp with pleasure as the elegant hand struck her bottom, making her body jolt, bringing her secret lips tingling into life.

Gael's nipples burgeoned swiftly. Her prominent labia swelled as she thrust them out for more. The long hand struck her smartly, building up a rhythm. Then, deep inside her body, she began to sense that fluid warmth which a spanking always brought.

Melindi knelt. She licked Gael's thigh. She snaked her hand between Gael's legs once more. She plunged her thumb into Gael's cleft and massaged at her nub.

Gael whispered, 'My God, Melindi, I love it but I need it harder. Please.'

The black girl's frotting action became more urgent still. Beads of perspiration welled up on Gael's forehead and ran down to her cheeks as she widened her stance to stretch herself as tautly as she could.

Melindi sank her teeth into Gael's buttock and raked her thigh with scarlet nails.

Gael yelped. Then she pushed back on to the intruding thumb, desperate for fulfilment, delighting in the sheer abandonment of the act.

It had been a strange few weeks.

Melindi had been her saviour when she had arrived in Paris with only a few francs in the pocket of her kneed-out jeans. After they had last made love in England, Gael had never imagined that she would see the Parisian model again. Now here she was, free of men and free of domination. She had exchanged all that for the gentle caresses and intelligent tongue of a woman – a svelte-skinned, nubile creature whom she loved to lick and suck.

As she pushed herself backward, Melindi's tongue

4

began to lick her. The tip of it worked in tight little circles around her anal ring while fingers stroked her clitoris exquisitely. As her nipples touched the railing Gael rubbed them on the iron, delighting in its coldness.

The fingers stroked her nubbin, sensitised and needing to be sucked. When the walls of her vagina began to quiver with pre-orgasmic tension, Gael bit her lip and drew a long, deep breath. Why wouldn't a man do this to her? Men had always wanted to spread her out and take her hard – to fill her and to sate themselves inside her. In the future she might need just that, but now it was the furthest thing from her mind.

The surfaces of her inner thighs began to flutter nicely. The tremors rippled upward through her core. The tip of Melindi's tongue pressed hard into her anal ring, and her skin became alive with the tingling which that brought.

Then her climax came. She loosed a deep moan which echoed off the stone façade and over leaded rooftops. She rotated herself upon the phallic thumb, seeking even greater satisfaction.

Melindi did not stop. Her fingers caressed Gael's clitoris, massaging it slowly, keeping the orgasmic pulses surging in small waves. Five minutes passed before the pulses ceased.

As Gael stretched herself and turned, her lips met Melindi's succulent, red bows as the model stood. Their nipples touched and kissed as well when Melindi held her close.

'You're a temptress, but I love you, Melindi Mocambo,' Gael whispered as she kissed the slender neck and ran her palm down the sleek back. 'What am I going to do without you?'

Melindi pulled away and brushed Gael's brow. 'Don't worry, Pinky, my sweet. I'll see you when I come to England. With my house near London as your base, you'll have your new career to occupy your time.'

Gael smiled thinly. 'Do you think I'll be a good facilitator?'

Melindi set her head back and laughed. 'What a lovely word for it. Yes – I think you'll be marvellous at it, darling. What better way to spend your time than making people's wildest dreams come true. And think of all the "presents" you'll attract.'

That was all Gael had thought of for weeks. 'But I'll need capital, Mel.'

Melindi shrugged. 'So – hock those expensive baubles I smuggled out of Grymwell Hall for you before the earl chucked you out.'

Gael had resigned herself to using her jewellery as security for loans. The diamonds and rubies and gold were all she had in the world. She shivered. She'd thought herself secure at Grymwell Hall. Accustomed to the soft life as the consort to an earl, she had now to make her own way in the world.

Melindi lifted her chin and kissed her lips. 'Bunny Grymwell was a bastard, darling. You're well rid of him.'

'But I loved him, Mel.'

'You loved the way he tied you up and spanked you before he teased you with that enormous cock of his. It never seemed to tire.'

'How do you know about that?'

Melindi grinned. 'You weren't the only recipient of its ministrations, sweetie. He kept it up for hours. I must have come a hundred times, at least.'

Gael pushed her shoulder playfully. 'He never made me come like that. He always kept me on the edge.'

'But you were his slave.' Melindi pushed her tongue into Gael's mouth, toyed with Gael's tongue then withdrew.

Gael threw her head back. 'I could have left him if I'd wanted to.'

'But you needed all those horny men which Grymwell

plied you with, sweetie. Surely you haven't forgotten them already.'

'Bunny only let me have them so he could watch them strip me bare and have me in a dozen different ways.'

'But you loved every second of it, darling. You loved the way they chased you and ripped your knickers off before they pinned you to the bed. You told me so yourself.' Melindi sent her tongue into Gael's ear, whispering, 'And what about the women?'

Gael snuggled up to Melindi's neck. 'You were my first.'

'And am I still your only girlfriend?'

'Of course you are.'

'Then come into my boudoir, you wicked creature. I want to feel your tongue between my legs.'

Melindi took Gael's hands and drew her to the bedroom. 'And don't worry. You'll be a huge success. You were a marvellous hostess at the Hall. At least Bunny Grymwell trained you well for that.' As Melindi sat on the edge of the bed, she pulled Gael to herself, setting her lips to Gael's nipple and closing her eyes as she sucked.

Gael also closed her eyes as the nipple came alive and sent little tingles down to her clitoris. 'I shall only take money for organising parties, Mel. What people do there will be entirely their own affair.'

'But I take it you will participate freely if they insist, my little marshmallow.' Melindi lapped at Gael's soft, pink breast. 'I can't imagine those devils being unable to keep their great horns out of here.' She ran the flat of her hand between Gael's legs. 'You won't deny yourself the opportunity to have that kind of fun, will you?'

'Perhaps.' Gael took a deep breath as her thighs closed on Melindi's hand again, already needing more.

Melindi lay on her back. She pulled her legs right up. As Gael knelt and put her head between them, the vista made her tremble. Melindi was the most sensuous of women, her full breasts tight, her figure sleek. Between her strong, taut legs nestled a purse of flesh so large and so succulent that Gael wondered how it felt as the woman strode the catwalks. She was successful because she was so sexy. She was sexy because she could feel herself all the time. Whatever the situation, Melindi was always ready – always randy.

'And don't forget,' Melindi continued as she placed a pillow under her hips to raise herself for Gael, 'you're very well connected. Think of the rich and famous people you know. And with my list of clients from the fashion houses, you've got it made, girl. The idle rich are always lusting to fill their lives with excitement in some way.' Now she widened her legs, opening her vulva, the sinews of her loins taut, their hollows stretched.

Gael ran her tongue through the hollows and looked up. 'Don't you think Bunny Grymwell will be mad at me if I poach his cronies?' She ran her finger over the tight little black curls of Melindi's pubis, and down the fringes of the open vulva. She worked the clitoral nub in circles until it rose from its protective hood.

Melindi wriggled and sighed. 'Sod Grymwell, darling. Anyway, you should have left him sooner.'

'I know,' Gael said dreamily as she toyed at Melindi's clitoris with the warm tip of her tongue. 'But he excited me.'

'He excited you beyond all reason, sometimes.'

'I suppose he did.' Gael eased her tongue through the leaves of distended flesh between Melindi's legs. 'I hated him at times.'

'Isn't that why you rebelled?'

'And the reason why he chucked me out.' Gael lapped hard in the hollows of Melindi's groin.

'Then get your revenge by inviting his cronies to your parties and exclude him. Take them to my chamber of delights. He's got nothing like that at the Hall. They'll soon desert Grymwell for you.'

'What "chamber of delights"?' Gael looked up, across the prominent mons, between the firm breasts and into Melindi's eyes.

'There's a large room in the basement of the London house which holds a lot of secrets.'

'What sort of secrets?'

'You'll have to wait and see, darling.' Melindi pulled Gael's head into her crotch, rotating her vulva against Gael's lips. The nectar of Melindi's arousal welled as she squeezed herself shut. Then Gael put her mouth to the soft, moist flesh and kissed it gently. The sweet musk sped her heartbeat as it filtered up her nose, satin-soft legs warm upon her cheeks. And Melindi's inner core was hot as Gael pulled apart the long, smooth lips and drove her tongue between them.

Melindi moaned and pressed down on Gael's mouth. Her clitoris rose and fell as she flexed her hips. Now Gael reached up and pinched the dark nipples gently. The breasts rose too, and bounced with Melindi's heaving. This tugged the nipples more.

Melindi pulled her legs back further still. Gael raked her flanks, leaving pink trails on the blackness of the skin. Melindi began to pant. She kneaded at Gael's hair and clawed her scalp, making Gael rasp her harder.

As Gael traced Melindi's anus with her tongue, her lover wriggled herself against it and whispered, 'Yes. Oh yes, I've always loved the way you do that.'

Gael bit the hollow of Melindi's groin and made her yelp. She bit the taut skin where the roundel of her bottom met her anus. She nipped and licked and scratched her lover into a frenzy until Melindi let out a cry and the lips of her vulva began to open and close rhythmically. Gael pulled away and watched, fascinated by the pulsing form. She kissed it tenderly, delighting in the way it moved beneath her lips just as Melindi's other mouth would kiss.

Afterwards, they lay side by side, each of their heads

9

to the other's feet, each with an arm between the other's legs, and a finger deep inside the other's vaginal sheath, feeling its moistness, toying with its sensuous folds. And then they slept.

2

A Naked Affair

The English house was everything Melindi had promised. Set in spacious grounds, surrounded by thick hedges, the top storey looked out across a heath on the southern fringe of London. Extensive gardens were fringed by woods, bordering a lake. On the edge of sweeping lawns, a summer-house stood, glinting in the morning light. Bought some years before by Melindi's father when he had been an ambassador to Britain, this house and grounds was the perfect place in which to execute the plan.

Gael stood at the window of her bedroom, looking over a lingering mist, drawn up by morning sunshine. Below her, a strong young gardener rode a mower, cutting perfect stripes in a large expanse of lawn. Melindi had not told her about him. Gael half wanted him to see her, naked at the window, her breasts so firm and tingling from the shower, her black hair shining as she brushed it out. But she had resolved not to draw this man into her bed. She didn't want the slightest whisper of impropriety going around the district.

Now she turned to the mirror. Lifting her breasts, she pulled the nipples gently into stiffness. A week had passed since they had felt a mouth. Melindi had flown off to New York. Alone in the world at 22, Gael had no one else. She smoothed her pubis with her fingers. The bristles had grown longer and softer since she had stopped shaving it. With no one to see its nakedness, there had seemed to be no point. Now the black hair was beginning to obscure its dark pink crevice. A fringe of bristles down the edges of its lips had started tickling. It made her very conscious of herself as she walked, fixing her attention there.

Now she took an eight-inch ivory form, shaped like an erect penis. She squatted and eased its mushroom head between her secret lips, deep into the sheath of her vagina. She smiled. Men were always so surprised at her depth and at the strength of her muscles. As they plumbed that depth, none but the very largest were able to fill her fully. They moaned as she engulfed them and clamped as they withdrew. And they growled when she shut herself tightly as they tried to penetrate her, triumphant when she let them in, thinking their insistent strength had overcome her resistance.

A sheer, white thong now barely hid her pubis as she drew the tapes up over her hips and passed the centre one back between her legs. It parted the cheeks of her bottom and rubbed upon her anus.

Some strutting strides around the room made sure that the ivory cock was tight enough to give her constant pleasure. She loved the feel of the man-shaped thing deep inside her sheath. It gave her an air of superiority as she viewed a man when he scanned her mount and her breasts, presumably imagining how she would look when stripped bare. Then she could say to herself, I know what you want to push between my legs, but I already have one of my own. Although – if she were truthful – it was no substitute for the real thing. Apart from that, it was the excitement of the chase and capture which was so important to her. She never gave in meekly. She made them fight for what she wanted.

Fighting brought her on so much more violently than if she lay with her legs held back and let them rip her panties off. Having a man view the moistened purse of her sex never ceased to thrill her. She loved the way the sight of it made them hard. But then they knew she wanted them, so she'd close her legs and make them force her open under loud but playful protest. It made her eyes blaze. It made the nimbuses of her breasts rise proudly. The little rings of bumps would stand prominently. Her teats would poke out, yearning for his mouth.

Now she slipped into faded jeans. The belt hung low upon her hips and the cleft of her sex showed clearly in their tightness. A pale pink crop top, pulled tightly over her breasts, left her navel free, a delicious dimple in a soft marshmallow, as Melindi fondly called it.

A lick of ruby lip gloss and she was ready for the day.

The sweeping staircase led down to the foyer of the rambling house. As she descended, the dildo worked deeper between her legs, each step giving her more and more pleasure.

'Good morning, Miss Gael.'

Gael looked down on the red-haired young woman polishing the brasswork of the large front door.

'Morning, Sophie. Is my breakfast ready?'

The girl looked slightly petulant. It was as if she did not like being at the beck and call of someone only a year or two older than herself. She thrust out her breasts under their cover of a thin white blouse.

'The cornflakes are in the pantry and the coffee's on. If you want an egg, you'll find them in the fridge.'

Gael nearly scowled but stopped herself. At Grymwell Hall, she had been used to having servants running round her. But that time was past. Now she was only the temporary mistress in this house, and she would not cause an upset by being strict with the little help she had.

Sophie stopped her rubbing and looked Gael up and down. Gael thought that her eyes rested on the V in her

13

jeans for rather longer than they should. Was the girl inclined to like a woman in her bed?

Tall and slim, Sophie stood up straight, her nipples showing darkly through her blouse. Her jeans hugged every curve of a softly rounded bottom, and as she walked, Gael had noticed how she wiggled it provocatively.

As they studied each other, Gael was drawn to the sensuous lips. Devoid of lipstick but shining wetly as Sophie ran her tongue over them, Gael wanted to put her mouth to them and experience their softness.

The green eyes were clear as they studied Gael's lips, making them tingle nicely. But Gael turned away. There was no way she was going to get sexually involved with servants, even though the nineteen-year-old siren was becoming more appealing by the minute.

Gael ate a bowl of cornflakes and wandered into the drawing room with her coffee. The large room was plushly furnished in Victorian style, the French windows leading into a sunken garden enclosed by a high wall of weathered brick. She might run naked in the moonlight there and nobody would see her. Her guests might do the same, if they were so inclined. The house was ideal for discreet parties. Large enough for people to spread into its spacious rooms, it was not too large to be unfriendly.

Then there was the secret in the basement. Melindi had hinted that it held something that would surprise Gael. It was securely locked and Gael had not yet found the key. She was reluctant to ask Sophie in case that showed too much interest in the place. But then, Sophie might be quite innocent of what that basement held.

Gael stepped down from the terrace and walked through the garden. She brushed past a riot of flowers and sauntered through a gateway into the grounds. She peeked into the summer-house with its wicker chairs and plump floral cushions. She walked to the crystal-clear lake, among the trees and turned back towards a little chapel. Though it was deconsecrated and overgrown, Gael had plans for it.

'Good morning, Miss Gael.'

Gael spun at the sound of the voice, her heart speeding at its rich and mellow tones. She flung her head back, letting her hair whirl around her shoulders as she faced the gardener. Naked to the waist, his smooth chest shone with perspiration. A whorl of tiny, golden hairs spun around his navel.

'Good morning, Todd. What a lovely day it is.' She tingled as he studied her mouth, scanned her breasts and then her mount. He smiled as his eyes reached hers once more. Her nipples swelled. She swallowed hard. Todd Flanders was a hunk. And the large bulge in the V of his shorts told her that he was rising at the sight of her.

'Yes, miss, it's a very nice day. And it'll be a hot one again, for sure.' He changed his stance self-consciously and Gael was certain that the bulge in his shorts had grown. It always gave her such a boost to do that to a man. She squeezed the dildo between her legs and smiled demurely as it slipped up inside her and then down again as she relaxed her vaginal muscles.

She fixed her gaze on the gardener's blue eyes. 'Have you finished the lawns?' She could see that he had but she needed to break the tension growing between them. How old was he? Twenty-eight, give a year each way. Surely much older than herself. Old enough to be experienced with women. A man like that would have plenty of them to choose from. He had probably started at an early age, taking them to the woods, sucking on their little breasts before stripping off their knickers. Slipping his youthful finger through their virgin lips, he had probably . . .

She stopped her fantasy. He might even be a virgin himself for all she knew.

'What do you want me to do now, Miss Gael?' He

15

shifted his stance again, his legs apart, his hands upon his hips.

What didn't she want him to do? He made her feel so horny. She wanted him to take her somewhere quiet and lay her down in the sunlight among soft, green grass. She wanted him to run his hand up the inside of her leg as she slipped her zip to show him she was naked inside the tight, blue denim of her jeans. Then she would slip them off. She would open her legs and show him how wet she was. Pulling out the ivory dildo, she would work it in and out of herself as he watched. Then she would cast it aside, pull apart his fly as he knelt between her legs and put her mouth over the swollen head of his cock as it sprang out. When she had it wet, and red from the scarlet of her lips, she would guide it to the pulsing hole between her thighs and feel its heat. She would . . .

He coughed at the silence which hung between them. She shook herself out of her daydream and gulped out, 'Have you cleaned the chapel as I asked?'

He nodded. 'Want to look?' Without waiting for an answer, he strode off to the chapel. She followed, feeling meek as she watched the muscles of his back and the firm cheeks of his bottom working beneath the smooth, tanned skin.

When he pushed the chapel door, it groaned. As he lifted a strand of ivy for her to duck under, she scented his perspiration. It sent her pulses racing, his heat radiating to her as she sidled past him. The scent of a man always drove her to irrational action. Add the aroma of an erect cock as she pulled it from his trousers, and she was lost.

Gael resolved anew not to make a move on him. She would not risk it, no matter how tempting he might seem.

The stone-flagged floor felt cold to her sandalled feet. Flanders had cleaned the pews and swept up a carpet of crinkled leaves. A confessional box stood starkly against a whitewashed wall.

16

'Were they very devout?' As she looked up into the gardener's eyes, his presence made her tremble. My God, she wanted him. By the way he looked and pursed his lips she sensed that he wanted her.

'Who do you mean?' He ran long fingers through a shock of blond hair.

'The people who had this chapel built. Were they very religious?'

He shrugged. 'Don't know, miss. It was only when Miss Melindi inherited the house that I came to do the gardens.'

Now as he said Melindi's name, Gael thought she saw a glint of lust in the blueness of his eyes. Although it quickly died, she wondered how Melindi employed her gardener while she stayed there. Then she wondered if she was being silly by denying herself the pleasure of such a horny male. But perhaps he was shy after all. Perhaps he'd never had a woman. Perhaps she could be his first. Her hands itched to undo his belt and open up his shorts. His penis looked so huge. Large ones always . . .

'I cleaned up that confessional, as you asked, miss. You can inspect it if you like.'

That shook Gael out of her second fantasy and she opened the priest's door of the box. He'd polished the brass grille, and the wood smelled nicely of beeswax.

'That's excellent. Thank you.' She gave him a genuine smile.

Now he studied her closely, a serious look on his face. 'Are you devout as well, miss?' The question took her off guard. Was he thinking that she was too pious to risk a pass? Damn. She wanted him more every second that he stood there. But it was probably best for him to think she was above such things.

'I'm having some guests tomorrow night. Some very devout friends.' She gave him a wicked little smirk and turned to go. 'Leave the door unlocked, will you. I shall need the confessional.'

As she strode across the lawn, pictures of the gardener's taut belly and his swelling bulge filled her mind. He clearly hadn't known whether she'd been joking about the confessional or not. But she'd never been so serious in her life. As soon as she'd seen it standing in the chapel, she'd had an inspiration. That was the one thing she had needed to give her role of 'Facilitator of Fantasies' the spark that could make her parties a wild success.

The day passed very quickly. The evening air was hot. Gael slipped on a blouse and a wrap-over skirt that would keep her body cool. From her bedroom she could see the clear, sandy-bottomed lake shimmering through the trees. It was so long since she had swum naked on a hot summer's eve. She grabbed a towel and skipped lightly down the stairs.

As she neared the water, she opened her blouse and ran, delighting in the coolness of the breeze against her skin. Then she heard a laugh. She saw clothes strewn along the shore where a young woman sat naked upon a log. Gael slipped behind a tree trunk as a man swam strongly towards the girl. She giggled when he splashed her.

Now Gael recognised the gardener. And surely that was Sophie. A flash of anger went through Gael. Her pulse began to pound as Flanders pulled the redheaded maid into the water. They fought, she splashing him and trying to duck him under; he grabbing her breasts from behind and pulling her backwards.

Then he dived.

Sophie tried to find him.

He came between her legs, his face upward. She shrieked and wriggled as his mouth closed on her sex. Then he turned, hoisted her over his shoulder and carried her to the grassy shore.

Now Gael saw what she had been imagining all day.

His penis erupted strongly from a mat of golden hair, curving up against his panting belly. His testicles hung heavily as he walked towards Gael's hiding-place. With Sophie's bottom towards her, her legs apart, the crevice of her sex showed plainly in the golden light, the ginger hair that fringed it streaming drops of water.

'Let me down, you brute.' Sophie hammered at his back.

Gael stayed behind her tree trunk and peeped through the lower leaves. Now the girl wriggled to get free, but he held her fast. They were so close now that Gael could hear their breathing. She prayed they wouldn't hear hers. Her heart was thumping loudly. Her abdomen pumped hard.

'Let me down, I said, Todd Flanders.' Sophie's tone was full of fun as she wriggled to no avail.

He slapped her bottom. 'Not until you grovel.' He slapped again.

'Ouch, you brute. Now I won't play your silly game.'

'You will, or I'll spank you hard.' He slapped her again, making red weals rise on her freckled flesh. Then he raked her with his fingers, drawing them down through the crevice of her bottom, parting her sex lips wetly.

Sophie cried out, half in frustration, half in pleasure, Gael thought. And as he spanked the girl, his phallus jerked.

Gael swallowed hard. In the flesh, that cock was even bigger than she'd pictured it. She began to feel she'd been a fool not to let him know that she'd wanted him. But perhaps he was committed to Sophie. Perhaps he wouldn't be interested in anyone but the maid. They were clearly lovers. Gael knew she'd been a fool to think he was a virgin and even more so to think he was available to her.

He spanked Sophie's bottom again. Particularly well-rounded, it bounced as he struck it with the flat of his

19

hand, making sure that the tips of his fingers just caught the hairy fringes of her vulva. Through a mass of ginger hair, the lips had risen plumply, more rosy than the pale pink of her thighs.

The purse of flesh between Gael's own legs was more than moist inside. Her legs were trembling violently, half with the fear of being caught, and half with anticipation of Flanders' next move.

He stood the housemaid on her feet. He picked up his shorts and drew the belt out slowly.

Sophie yelped as he thwacked it into his palm. 'Don't you dare touch me with that, you brute.' She turned to flee but he tackled her to the ground, sat astride her and forced her arms above her head.

She wriggled under him, his phallus between her breasts, the helmet of it swollen as he thrust up. He tied her wrists together and, with apparently little effort, hoisted Sophie up and hooked the belt to a tree branch above. Springing on the balls of her feet, her breasts were taut, her armpits deeply hollowed by their tension.

She wriggled hard but Gael could see that her eyes were lit up with fun. When Flanders found a slender, whippy branch, they lit up even more. But she spat, 'And you can drop that, you brute. I shan't grovel if you whip me.'

He grinned, flashing perfect teeth. 'You know how much you like to be whipped, Mrs Sones.' He thwacked the switch into his palm. 'You'll beg me to fuck you or I'll leave you hanging here all night.' As he laughed, his phallus wagged to the movements of his belly. His testicles swung freely.

'You wouldn't dare leave me here,' she pouted.

'Try me.' He brought the switch down on her bottom, making her arch and thrust her breasts out more. The teats were hard, erupting from dark rings. They were the nipples of a nursing mother. So, Gael thought, she wasn't such an innocent after all. Was she having the gardener on the side while her husband stayed at home?

Flanders swiped Sophie's bottom and made her yelp. He spread her legs and drew the switch between them very slowly, making her writhe at every little touch.

Gael put her hand inside her skirt. It found her open crevice as she crouched. As her finger slipped into her moistness, she wondered what it would feel like to be hung up naked and so helpless. Something in being tied and unable to resist the ministrations of a man had always made her horny.

As Flanders whisked the switch between Sophie's legs, Gael, breathing heavily, began to work her dildo, squatting lower to open herself up wide.

Flanders walked around his prize, chastising her lightly with the switch, bringing lines of colour to her skin. She glared at him defiantly until he put his hand between her legs and began, slowly, to rub her. Then she started to moan, and wriggled on his hand.

He nipped her neck.

She yelped and tried to nip him in return, but was too securely tied. He was her master – she his slave.

Gael wondered what he'd do with the girl. She could see the wetness on his hand as he drew it between her legs. And little beads of milk were rising from her nipples. He sucked them, making her set her head right back. Panting deeply, she thrust a nipple deeper into his mouth.

He bit her neck and skimmed her nubbin with his finger. Sophie began to quiver and set her legs apart to give him unrestricted access.

Now he raked her body with his fingers, drawing them down her flanks, from the hollows of her armpits to her thighs. 'Beg,' he whispered. 'Beg and I'll give you this.' He stroked his shaft and made it swell. 'You know how much you want it.'

She shook her head. 'Shan't. You're a bastard and I hate you.'

'And do you hate me doing this?' He crouched and

spread her legs so that her feet were on his knees. Hanging from the branch, all she could do was bounce on him.

He yoked her under her knees, lifting her legs and making her sex lips taut as she swung.

Looking up into her crotch, he parted her labia with his tongue. Then he sucked her very slowly, like he might suck an orange, drawing out its juice; he closed his eyes and savoured its aroma.

As he sucked, she began to whimper softly. 'Bastard. You bastard. For God's sake do me properly.'

'Are you begging me, Mrs Sones?' He drove his tongue between the thick lips of her sex, tickling at her clitoris.

Gael felt a tremor of intense lust. She wanted to be tied and hung and spread and licked like that. She wanted him to force her legs apart and bite her groin, and make her wriggle on his face as his tongue delved deeply in her. Her heart drummed so hard that she was certain they would hear it. A twig snapped as she moved, but they did not turn. The girl was too intent on the tongue between her legs, and he seemed too ardent to notice the watcher in the wood.

The girl was gasping now, opening and closing her legs while the gardener sucked her nubbin. As he knelt, his veiny phallus stood up stiffly, an angry pink in the light of the setting sun. A pearl of semen rose at its tip and ran down through the valley of its head.

'Beg,' he whispered between the forays of his tongue. 'Implore me.'

The girl was twisting now, her fingers clinging to the branch, her nipples oozing milk. This glazed her breasts and trickled down her belly. From there it ran between her legs.

'All right. All right,' she gasped. 'You've won. Now let me down.'

'I don't hear you begging yet.' He sucked her hard.

'Fuck me, you bastard.'

'That's better, but say it louder. Shout it.'

'Someone might hear if I do.'

'No one will hear. Miss Goody-goody is probably tucked up in bed with a glass of hot milk and a Mills and Boon romance. She's probably got a finger deep in here.'

Gael snorted, then stifled it as he skimmed Sophie between the legs again and licked his finger.

Sophie threw her head back impatiently. 'She's not so innocent as you think.'

'She's pious,' he whispered. 'She's going to use the chapel. She had me clean it up.' He moved to face the housemaid.

Sophie creased her brow. 'You're joking.'

He massaged her nipples, making them weep rich milk. Then he squeezed and licked it off her breasts. 'I'm not joking. She's a prude. She kept her legs shut tight as she eyed my cock this morning.' He stood back and worked his erection. 'I think she wants to feel it but her piety won't let her.'

'Don't kid yourself, Todd Flanders. Not all women are interested in your prick.'

'But you are, aren't you, you horny little minx.' He stood before Sophie, rubbing his sac against her pubis, the tip of his phallus nosing at her navel. 'But if Miss Goody-goody wasn't so religious, why would she want the confessional cleaned up?' He went behind Sophie and fondled her breasts. He put one hand between her legs and worked her vulva thoughtfully.

Sophie moaned. 'I don't know and I don't really care. All I do know is that you're a pig. Now for God's sake do me properly.'

'Are you begging?' He bit her waist.

'Yes – I'm begging. Now fuck me, you bastard. I can't stand this any more. And let me down. You know I only come when I get your cock inside me.'

He put his lips to hers, whispering, 'And what about Miss Melindi's cock? Don't you come with that?'

'She hasn't got a cock.'

'She's got a rubber one. I saw it in a bedroom drawer.'

'You've got no business looking in her drawers. Have you been wearing her knickers again?'

He shrugged. 'I like the feel of my balls against the crotch of a woman's pants, specially when she's been wearing them.'

'She'd fire you if she knew.'

He shook his head. 'She needs me too much to fire me, Sophie, my love.'

'My God, you're a conceited bastard, Flanders.'

He grinned. 'Perhaps.' Then he moved to face her again and parted her legs, placing his shaft between them, letting it nose up to her vulva but not between its lips.

Sophie closed her eyes and took a sharp breath.

He held there, moving her up and down on the stiffness of his shaft, making her feel him without the satisfaction of penetration.

She whispered, 'Fuck me, Todd. Please.'

Now he drove up, hard. Gael flinched at the force of it, but the girl cried out with pleasure.

Again he thrust, the whole of his length coming out of her as she rose on the springing branch, before he was buried deeply once again. The blond mat of his pubis met her tangled ginger hair, nestled in it for a moment and then withdrew shining with her juice.

He pulled her nipples as he bounced her, making the springy branch do all the work, plunging her down on himself then lifting her off again.

She wound her legs around his waist to stop him pulling out. He growled and thrust up harder. His hand came around her bottom and found her secret hole. When he drove his finger deep, it made the redhead gasp.

24

'You brute. You know I can't stand you doing that.'
'Why? Because it makes you come too soon?'
She threw up her head again.
He drove his finger in repeatedly.
Gael had her skirt off now. One finger worked briskly
at her nubbin as she crouched. The other hand eased the
large head of the dildo between her straining labia. She
wanted to join them and feel the real thing. She might
lick the whole length of him as he pulled it out,
surprised to find another woman to vent his passion on.
When he saw that she was naked and ready for his cock,
he might spread her in the grass and take her hard while
Sophie hung there jealously, helpless to prevent him.
Gael killed her fantasies and watched as he let the
housemaid down. Sophie clung to him, his phallus
buried in her. Gael could see his testes swinging beneath
Sophie's bottom, the hairs of his sac quite wet.
He laid her in the grass and pushed her legs right back
so she was open wide to Gael as well as to his cock.
Gael watched his bottom rise and fall. His testes
bounced and swung. She could see the housemaid's
puckered, secret hole, stretched wide as he took her with
such verve that it made Gael's need for him almost too
strong for her to resist.
With his hands on Sophie's shoulders, he pressed her
to the grass and flexed his hips. Her body writhed as his
strokes got fast and urgent. She clawed the muscles of
his back and threw her head from side to side.
Abruptly he withdrew.
He lay back on the grass, his legs splayed wide apart.
His penis tensed. Then a spurt of semen shot right up
his belly.
Gael licked her lips as she watched his phallus pump.
She wanted to put her mouth to it herself and suck it
slowly in, feeling its beat against her tongue, savouring
its taste. She wanted to sit astride him and rub her vulva
on his chest and ride him until she came. But she was

frozen to the spot. Her thighs were tense, her nubbin hard, her vulva swollen with her aching need.

To her surprise, the gardener rose, his penis stiff and beating. Was he one of those rare men who could have a hard-on for hours? Gael closed her eyes at the thought. If Flanders was a stallion like that, could she resist the temptation to . . .? She worked her dildo hard.

'Now lick me, Mrs Sones,' he whispered as he towered over Sophie. 'You know you like to taste my spunk.'

Gael looked back at the scene. Lying with her legs apart, Sophie stared up at his balls as he placed his feet each side of her. A drop of milky fluid landed on her belly. She massaged it into her navel, then took the fingers to her mouth and sucked.

'Lick me,' he hissed as he ran a finger down his shaft.

Obediently, the girl sat up. She put her lips to his scrotum, closing her eyes as she scented him, her tongue darting between his testes. Gael watched them bobble as he flexed his hips and rubbed himself against the red-head's tongue, closing his eyes and stroking at her hair.

'Now open your mouth, my sweet,' he crooned very softly. Gael wondered if he was softening towards the girl. Did he have a romantic side to him after all?

Sophie obeyed again, looking at the rearing shaft before her face. She knelt as he flexed it down and pushed it into her eager mouth.

'Now suck it slowly. You know the way I like it.'

She sucked on him with tenderness and pleasure, closing her eyes and breathing deeply through her nose. She ran her fingers up his belly. Then she held his balls in one palm and massaged the root of his shaft with her thumb.

He held his palms about her ears, pulling her on to himself, easing in and out of her mouth as he had between her legs. He did it very slowly, in the same way as men had pushed into Gael after they had flushed her with their spurt, just feeling her sensual heat around their beating member.

Sophie pulled her mouth away and looked up with pleading eyes. 'When are you going to make me come?' Holding his shaft like a lollipop, she ran her tongue-tip lightly along its groove.

He withdrew from her grasp, stooped and picked up his clothes. 'Some other time, perhaps.'

'Where are you going, Todd Flanders?' Sophie grabbed his shaft again and tried to pull him back, but it was too slick for her to grasp.

'I'm going to bed, Mrs Sones. Where else?'

She sprang to her feet, her hands on her hips, her breasts swinging heavily. 'But what about me, you pig?'

'You had your chance but you were too slow, my sweet.' He touched the tip of her nose lovingly with his finger.

'You're a bastard, Flanders. I hate you. I need to come now – not in the morning.' Sophie raised her fist to strike him but he caught her by the wrist.

'Now don't be a naughty girl,' he hissed. 'I'll have you over the kitchen table as usual in the morning. Wear a skirt and make sure you leave your knickers off. I don't want the bother of taking them down.' He smirked.

'But I need to come now. I want to be fucked. I need your cock between my legs. You know I only come like that.'

'Then you'd better go home and find your husband, sweetheart. Perhaps he'll satisfy you better than I do.'

'You know he won't. Don't go. Please stay and fuck me now. Please.'

He dropped her arm and turned away, his penis jutting upright as he walked. Gael nearly sprang out to stop him, but what could she have done? She might have slapped his face but she couldn't have ordered him to have the girl again even though he was clearly stiff enough to do so.

Sophie shook her fist. 'You lousy bastard. I'll never let you touch me again. Never.'

He gave a cynical laugh. 'Then I'll see what I can do with Miss Goody-goody, for a change. I'm told that the prudish ones are the best, once you get their knickers off.'

3

The Delightful Chamber

Gael fumed as she watched the gardener disappear through the woods. Damn the man. She would teach him a lesson for his arrogance.

She turned back towards Sophie who was angrily picking up her clothes. Gael thought that, far from being shocked at what would go on at parties, this girl might be an asset. Certainly she wouldn't blab scandals around the neighbourhood, as her own actions had been quite scandalous.

A twig snapped under Gael's foot again.

Sophie turned in her direction, her eyes alight. 'You can stop hiding, Flanders. I know you're there.' She dropped her clothes and lay back on the grass, her legs open, her vulva flushed. 'Come on, you brute.' She rubbed its lips and worked her clitoris in small circles. 'I knew you couldn't resist this for long.'

The next few seconds dragged. Gael couldn't sneak away without being seen. Hoping against hope that Sophie would not discover her, Gael dropped the dildo in the grass.

Sophie sat up, scowling. 'For God's sake, Todd, I've had enough of your games. I know you're there.' When she sprang up and rounded the tree, her jaw dropped.

With her blouse open and her skirt around her ankles, Gael felt like a naughty girl caught at the keyhole of her parents' bedroom with her knickers down.

'You? What the hell are you doing here?' Sophie faced her squarely, her pubis pushed out as she set her legs astride and clamped her hands upon her hips.

'I'm sorry,' Gael stammered. 'I came down for a swim. You both took me by surprise.'

'I bet you were surprised.' Sophie scanned Gael up and down, noting her naked pubis and eyeing her breasts. Her own breasts were full and taut from the liaison with the gardener. She threw her head back in that haughty way Gael had seen before. 'But did you learn anything about how a man plays with a woman? Did you enjoy watching him lick my quim before he fucked me?'

Gael's temper rose. 'I'm not so naïve as you seem to think.'

Sophie's nostrils flared derisively.

Gael glowered at her and mimicked her stance. 'I said I was sorry. I didn't mean to pry.'

'Perhaps not. But I asked if you learnt anything.'

Gael was uncertain how she should react. After all, she was the mistress and the girl could easily be replaced if she was going to be obstreperous. But then she relented. The sights and sounds and scents of the man having the girl so ardently had raised her need for sex and left her unfulfilled.

She turned to go but Sophie caught her arm. 'Oh no, you don't get away that easily.'

Gael began to tremble. The sight of the aroused young woman set her pulse racing. Her vaginal muscles tightened.

Sophie sneered. 'Frightened of what I might do to you, are you?'

Gael pulled herself up tall, easily as tall as the housemaid. 'I'm not frightened of you. Let go of my arm.'

Sophie hung on despite Gael's effort to pull away. She stared into Gael's eyes. 'I think you did enjoy watching us.'

Totally naked and unashamed, the girl had an air of self-confidence about her that was surprising. Gael shook her off. 'Yes – if you really want to know – I did enjoy it. I wanted to join in.'

The admission seemed to soften Sophie's demeanour.

Gael lowered her eyes to stop them showing her excitement. Then she raised them. Why should she be subservient to the servant?

'Yes,' Sophie hissed, as she ran a finger through Gael's cleft. 'I can see that you enjoyed it. Do you like being whipped as well?'

Yes, she did like being whipped – just hard enough to feel her skin flush and her sexual energy rise to swell her vulva and her breasts. Whipping had been something which Bunny Grymwell had introduced her to. He had been a master of keeping her on the edge of ecstasy, spanking her as he took her from behind.

Sophie took Gael's chin and pinched. 'I asked you if you like being whipped.'

Gael shook her head. There was no way she was going to let this girl know what she liked or hated. She sensed a sadistic streak in the way the wide mouth curled. She could imagine Sophie always getting what she wanted. She had clearly wanted Flanders to string her from that bough. She had loved the way he'd whipped her with the leafy branch. She'd closed her eyes in ecstasy as he'd raked her body with his nails. Now she was clearly bent upon getting pleasure from Gael in some way – but Gael couldn't work out how.

Sophie backed Gael against the tree, her eyes alight with anger, her breathing short. Her lips came in so close that Gael could feel her breath. She had an urge to kiss that mouth just as she'd wanted to that morning.

Sophie hissed, 'I'm going to whip you for your sneaking. Then we'll see just how much you like it. And if you cry out, I'll whip you harder until you beg for me to stop.' With a slender forefinger, she skimmed Gael's nipple and made a thrill run down between her legs. Then to Gael's surprise, the housemaid put her lips to hers and kissed her tenderly.

Stripped below the waist and with her blouse undone, Gael felt her excitement mount as the girl's bare flesh touched hers. Now Sophie's fingers slipped around the slender waist and down into the crevice of Gael's bottom. She abandoned her resolve not to get involved with the servants. Her lips took Sophie's hungrily. She could feel how warm and moist they were as they pushed out for a moment. The tongue snaked through her lips. Then Sophie pulled away. Her eyes flashed with amusement. 'You don't really think I fancy you, do you?'

Gael struck out. The flat of her hand caught the surprised girl on the cheek. It made her reel.

Sophie glowered. Then she hit back, catching Gael a glancing blow on the shoulder.

Their fingers locked.

They fell.

Then Sophie was on top of Gael, her leg between Gael's legs, her teeth biting at Gael's neck.

The heat of the naked body on her own, the taut breasts touching hers, the belly panting against her sweating skin, raised Gael's excitement. Sophie's legs began to grind, spreading the lips of her opponent's sex, slipping in her moistness. That stimulated Gael more than the gentle kiss had done. When Sophie's mouth came on to hers, Gael began to pant. Her hand found Sophie's bottom and slipped between the buttocks – searching until her finger found the housemaid's anal ring. She plunged the finger in.

'You bitch.' The girl shuddered, squeezed on Gael's finger and bit her shoulder hard.

Gael twisted her finger, making Sophie squirm.

They rolled towards the water, Gael plunging her goading finger ever deeper as Sophie bit her neck. The redhead panted harshly. Her fingers clawed at Gael's breasts.

Gael's leg was slick with nectar as Sophie rubbed her vulva softly against the hardness of Gael's thigh.

Gael raked her back as Sophie bit at her lips, almost stifling her. As she struggled to catch a breath, they rolled into the water, clawing at each other as it closed upon their skin. The coldness was quite stunning for an instant, then brought Gael to her senses. What was she doing? She'd let her senses rule her mind.

She wriggled free but Sophie tripped her and made her sprawl. As she snatched a whippy branch up and thrashed at Gael's bare bottom, her eyes were full of lust and her cheeks brightly flushed.

Gael turned away, pulling her knees up to her breasts. But this exposed her sex lips to the stinging of the branch. As she tried to flee again, the switch whipped through her legs. She gasped and rolled, trying to crawl away. On her knees, her genitals were exposed, the switch catching her labia lips to make them tingle hotly. She flushed and felt her moisture well from deep inside her, the stimulation making her vulva spasm. It always did that when she was just about to come, the walls of her vaginal sleeve clamping and releasing.

Sophie pushed Gael on to her back. With her foot between Gael's breasts, she pinned her mistress down. 'You bitch. You bloody bitch,' she gasped. 'I need you, for Christ's sake. Now suck me off, or I'll whip you till you do.'

Sophie sank to her knees. Astride Gael's shoulders, she thrust her pubis out. Her eyes glared down at Gael hungrily.

'And you can go to hell,' Gael snarled.

Sophie hit her hard across the face and made her gasp. 'You will lick me, you bitch,' she screamed. 'You'll lick me until I come.' She tugged Gael's hair and pulled Gael's face up between her legs. She ground Gael's mouth against her sex and worked her hips.

Water poured from the ginger hair between the housemaid's legs. It ran into Gael's mouth and made her swallow. As Gael's lips met the hot, soft flesh, she began to lick, driving her tongue in deeply.

Seeming to be certain that Gael was mastered now, Sophie squatted widely. Her vulva stretched open, her clitoris protruding from its folds. Now Gael had open access for her tongue. She lapped the housemaid steadily in long, slow strokes from her anus to her nubbin. She took the nub between her lips and sucked, then raked the tightened hollows of the redhead's groin until the girl began to moan.

Sophie came with a gasping cry of pleasure. It made her body shake. As she worked Gael's mouth between her legs, she murmured, 'You bitch. You wonderful bitch.'

When Sophie withdrew she stood up and smiled.

Gael rose to her feet, shaking from the violence of the encounter. Still keyed-up, she needed fast release. Her body throbbed, her skin hot and her mind in a spin.

Sophie's anger seemed to have gone completely now that she'd come. She grinned and put her hand out. 'Truce?'

Still reeling from the passion of the moment, Gael wiped the nectar from her mouth and swallowed hard. Then she put her hand out too and said, 'OK. Truce.'

Sophie's mouth curved up at the edges. 'Good. Now, I'm bloody cold. I need a hot shower, then I want to eat you. I want to see just how much you wriggle on my tongue.' She grinned again. 'I'll fuck you if you like. Melindi's got a strap-on we could use.'

Gael's body was burning with need. She could hardly wait to get back to the house, but she wanted a hot shower as well. She needed to be warm. But most of all she needed to have the housemaid in the way she liked the most. She might have called a truce, but that didn't mean she'd forgiven the tart for the way that she'd behaved.

They walked stark naked, hand in hand, back to the house. It seemed dark and menacing without lights. Nobody would see them except perhaps the gardener if he was still around. Gael couldn't care. She had definite plans for him. She'd show him who was mistress in no uncertain way.

On entering the kitchen, Gael became quite pensive. What was she expected to do now? The nearness and the nakedness of the sexy little redhead was driving her quite crazy.

'Can I use your shower, miss?' Sophie's manner seemed more conciliatory now that she was back in the house.

'Sure. But shouldn't you be getting home?'

'There's nothing to go home for.'

'Don't you have your baby to feed?'

The redhead shrugged. 'The baby's been adopted.' A tear came to her eye.

Gael put her arm around her but Sophie pulled away.

'Don't feel sorry for me. I want to live for a bit, not dwell in the past. I want excitement in my life, I want wild, abandoned sex.'

'What about your husband?'

'I've left him. And if I hadn't found Todd Flanders when Miss Melindi asked me to look after the house, I would have been off looking for another randy man. I need a good hard fucking now and then. Don't you?'

Gael felt sheepish. This girl was a surprise a minute.

Sophie brushed Gael's cheek. 'Sorry if I came on a bit too strong by the lake. He got me so worked up.'

Gael shrugged. 'That's OK.'

Sophie kissed her lightly and whispered, 'You going to let me eat your pussy?' She gave a coy little glance as if she was still not sure of Gael's intentions.

Gael felt her eyes go wide. 'After I've showered, perhaps.'

Sophie grinned confidently. 'Good. I want to see if

you wriggle as much as Miss Melindi. She's a cracker.
And the way she wields her rubber cock puts a lot of
men to shame. Or perhaps you don't know that.' Again
she gave Gael a look of uncertainty. Was she testing to
see just how much Gael knew – or how far Gael might
go?

Saying nothing, Gael took Sophie's hand and led her
up the stairs, wondering where this whole affair was
heading.

The hot shower was delightful. Sophie slipped her
hands under Gael's arms and massaged her breasts
slowly and seductively, lifting them and letting them
drop until they tightened with the stimulation. Gael did
the same to her. She slid her hands over the firm, flat
stomach and into the deep slit between the redhead's
shapely legs. The clitoris was hard again, though it
wasn't as big as Gael's and certainly not enormous like
Melindi's. But it stood up from its hood and wobbled
to Gael's touch as she worked it round and round. Then
Sophie bent, widening her stance and pushed out her
bottom.

'You can spank me if you like, for being so wicked to
you at the lake.'

Gael slapped the proffered bottom with certain satisfaction, her wet hand stinging the glistening skin. It
reddened to each slap. Then she ran her hand between
the redhead's legs and held the swollen vulva in her
palm. She bent her centre finger and rubbed it through
the crevice that she found there. She worked the hollows
of the groin and dug her nails right in to make her
housemaid moan. Then she knelt and buried her mouth
there as Sophie touched her fingers to the floor. Gael
licked between the labia once, from her nubbin to her
anus. Sophie gave a little sound of pleasure as Gael
circled the ring with her tongue-tip then eased her
thumb in deeply. With the lubrication of the soap, it
slipped in easily. And as Gael pushed and twisted it,

36

Sophie wriggled with delight. She took a long, deep breath and sighed, 'I've never had a man that way. Will you do me with Melindi's cock?' She turned to Gael, her green eyes bright. As she kissed Gael fully on the lips she whispered very softly in her ear, 'Will you do my arsehole with that dildo?'

Gael frowned and smoothed her cheek with a fingertip.

Sophie gave a pleading little look.

Gael shrugged. 'It's better with the real thing. But it has to be gentle. Then it's nice.' As she began to dry Sophie's breasts, they bounced heavily to each rub.

Sophie closed her eyes. 'Flanders doesn't know how to be gentle. But he's marvellous when he's horny. He's so impetuous.'

Gael could relate to that. She needed strength and impetuosity from a man at times. At others she needed gentleness and sensuality. She still hadn't found a man who provided her with both. But she was looking. Maybe someone coming to her first party the very next day would be the one.

Sophie took Gael's lips again and kissed her passionately.

Now Gael pulled her tight, hooking her around the neck with one hand, while the other found her breast. She stroked the nipple with her thumb and felt the wetness of its milk.

Sophie gave a little moan. 'Todd never does it as gently as that.'

Gael pulled at the nipple, tugging on it until it was fully stiff. 'Why do you let the brute rule you?'

Sophie shrugged. 'I can't get enough of him. And he knows it. But he only does me when he's really randy. Otherwise he ignores me.'

Gael could relate to that as well. She knew just how it felt to need a man badly and then be toyed with. 'How often does he get as horny as he was tonight?' If the gardener only became so randy at certain times, she wanted to know exactly when those were.

'He doesn't get as horny as that very often.' Sophie stroked Gael's belly with the back of her finger. 'But you got him so hot this morning, he came on strong to me.'

Gael pulled away and looked at her hard. 'I got him hot?'

Sophie nodded. 'Didn't you know? You turned the man into an animal. He hasn't fucked me so hard for weeks.'

Gael was in a whirl. Yes, Flanders was an animal. But she had sworn not to touch him. And was the nineteen-year-old complaining or rejoicing? She wasn't sure.

Sophie eyed Gael with amusement. 'If you didn't notice how horny he was, I think he was right about you being a goody-goody.'

Gael scowled although she knew her eyes were sparkling at the exchange. 'So – you think I'm as naïve as he does.'

Sophie pushed her against the wall. 'I don't know. But I intend to find out.' She knelt and cupped Gael's breasts in both hands and kissed her belly.

Gael trembled as she ran her fingers over Sophie's hair. Hot breath between her legs made her look down. Sophie was sniffing at her, drawing in her perfume, putting her lips to the bristles of her pubis.

Gael set her legs apart. This was crazy, she thought, but she couldn't reject the girl as the hot tongue searched her cleft. Gael held her there, delighting in the sensation which the darting tongue gave her.

Sophie lifted Gael's leg, running kisses up the inside of her thigh until her lips touched the fringes of Gael's sex again.

Gael quivered and gave a little gasp as the redhead ran her tongue through her crevice and made her nectar rise. She whispered, 'Oh yes. That's nice. But I need to feel it harder.'

Sophie's voice was muffled as she spoke between Gael's legs. 'OK – so you're not such a prude, after all.' She lapped the whole of Gael's vulva then pushed her tongue inside it.

Still needing to reach a climax, Gael responded to the touch. But Sophie pulled away again and began to dry between Gael's thighs, tucking the towel deep between them, easing apart the lips of her sex to make sure that she was dry there. But no matter how she rubbed, Gael stayed wet with arousal.

'You should train Flanders better,' she quipped as Sophie dabbed at her breasts then dried her back and rubbed her bottom. She rubbed at the lips of her sex as Gael bent over for her, swinging sensuously from side to side. It made her want Sophie's mouth there again, but she quelled the need. Instead, she took the towel and made the redhead bend over.

'How do you mean – train him?' Sophie asked.

'Play harder to get.' Gael ran her hand over the housemaid's sexual lips, delighting in the way they opened to her touch then closed tightly as her fingers passed.

'He's got too much ego for that,' Sophie sighed as she pushed herself out for more.

'You could tame him if you chose to.' Gael rubbed the tight ring of her shower-mate's anus, then ran her finger around it once again. It always gave her pleasure to touch a lover there.

'Flanders is too stubborn.' Sophie thrust her bottom out for deeper contact with Gael's finger.

'We could tame him together.' Gael knelt and kissed her anus lovingly.

'How?' Sophie stood and rubbed Gael's nipples, making them hot with the friction. They grew hard, the nimbuses proud, although not as proud as Sophie's. Those were dark brown now, large in diameter, her breasts full with milk.

'How would we tame him?' Sophie asked again, whispering in Gael's ear, and flicking at the lobe with her tongue.

'The best way would be to work him up and then deny him until he agreed to whatever we wanted.'

' "We"?'

'Yes – why not? He might be too strong for you but he wouldn't be for both of us.'

Sophie became thoughtful as she sawed the towel between Gael's legs. Gael squatted slightly to accommodate it, feeling the fluffy material chafing on her anus, parting her sex lips, and making her pant. It made her feel so horny – she only needed a few more rubs like that before she came. But Sophie seemed to have other ideas. She seemed to be stringing Gael out. Had she got some plan?

The redhead kissed Gael's mouth and whispered, 'We could lure him to the chamber where Melindi keeps her secret things.'

Gael became alert. 'Do you have the key? It isn't on its hook.'

Now Sophie gave a coy little look. 'I hid it from you. I didn't want you going there. It's such a special place.'

'What's so "special" about it?'

'It's where Melindi and me go when we want to do something really wicked. Sometimes she takes some horny man there.'

The heavy iron door to Melindi's 'chamber of delights' opened silently as Gael and Sophie pushed it. They both stood naked in the entrance, warm from their shower, their bodies glowing from the rubbing of the towels.

The space was dark, but it was not musty like the wine cellar next door. When Sophie switched the lights on, Gael blinked then stared.

The spacious room was carpeted and warm. Mirrors lined one wall. A host of objects stood about which

Gael could only describe as apparatus. Her imagination began to work as she gazed about her.

As Sophie touched a panel of switches, the room became pitch black. Then a pencil-thin beam of light shot down from the ceiling, illuminating a padded bench. Sophie focused the beam so that only a small area was lit, a pool of bright, white light in the blackness of the chamber. Gael could see immediately that if anyone were to lie naked on that bench, only a small part of their body would be visible. To anyone watching in the secrecy of the darkness, this would concentrate all their attention on that part: a woman's breast, a man's erect penis, the twin-lipped vulva of some bending girl.

As Sophie worked the switches, the spotlight dimmed. Then, one by one, each piece of apparatus was highlighted. Pulleys with ropes hanging from the ceiling. A bench with shackles at each end and a winch, which Gael presumed was to stretch a body taut. A silk-lined box, with a glass lid, big enough to take a man lying down. A board with holes for neck and hands, where a female occupant would have to bend with her bottom stuck right out and her legs set wide apart, ready to be whipped or sucked without retaliation. If two men were to fasten a woman in that way, one might feed her with his shaft while the other took her slowly from behind.

Sophie was smiling naughtily when she turned the main lights up. Then she took Gael's hands. 'Come and try my very favourite thing.' She pulled Gael to a rocking horse.

As black as polished ebony, the horse stood in one corner, a saddle on its back. It seemed strange to Gael to have a toy like that in such a sophisticated place. From the centre of its polished saddle rose a dark pink knob. As Sophie made the creature rock, the protrusion thrust up strongly. As curved and stiff as the phallus of a well-developed man, it retracted as the horse rocked back. When Sophie pushed it slowly, the phallus rose and fell.

41

'Get on.' She grinned and made Gael mount, positioning her over the knob. Stretched widely as she straddled it, Gael gasped as it went in her. With her feet placed in the stirrups she could rise and fall with full control.

'Now rock gently,' Sophie whispered. 'You can make it go faster when you've got the hang of it.'

Gael did as she was told. As the horse rocked back and forth, the phallic form pushed up into her sheath, than sank back once again, curving as a cock would, although not as warm, Gael thought. But as she rocked faster, the phallus penetrated her satisfyingly deeply. She built a steady rhythm, clinging to the horse's reins. She stretched herself out wide, delighting in the feelings as the phallus filled her tightly then withdrew.

Sophie mounted up as well, her nipples hard against Gael's back. As Gael rocked the stallion, Sophie cupped her breasts. Then she pulled Gael's nipples gently in rhythm with the rocking, making Gael push out her breasts and thrust down on the cock.

Sophie forced the pace now, making Gael exclaim with the pleasure of the thrusting deep between her stretched-out legs. When Sophie bit her neck, she gasped and kicked the horse to make it serve her faster. Her tension rose as Sophie slapped her buttocks and her thighs. She pressed her belly and her large, tight breasts hard against Gael's back.

Gael began to pant now, whispering, 'Ah. My God. Oh Yes.'

Sophie rocked her faster. She hit her bottom hard, then scored her flanks and clawed at her back.

Gael was at a gallop now, flexing in the stirrups so the cock could enter her and she could take it in just as hard as she liked.

'Oh my God, my God,' she cried as Sophie thrashed her thighs.

'Tally ho,' Sophie laughed as she made the horse go faster still.

'Oh my God,' Gael gasped as a tremendous climax ripped right through her. Her body shuddered with pleasure as she slowed the rocking, her belly swelling each time the phallus pushed inside her.

Sophie sucked her neck. 'And now I'm going to lick your cunt.'

She pulled Gael from the rocking horse and lay her on the spongy leather of a large divan. Lying down beside her, she put her mouth to Gael's breast and worked her hand between her legs. 'Did you like the horse?'

Gael nodded, unable to speak for a second.

'And do you like this?' she whispered and sucked the nipple gently.

'Do I like what? Your mouth on my tit or the way you touch my quim?'

Sophie nipped her breast. 'No, silly. Do you like the room?'

Gael smiled as she looked up at the ceiling. 'I think it'll be marvellous for parties. I'm having a special one tomorrow night.'

Sophie leaned on her elbow and looked down. 'How "special"?'

Gael smirked. 'Just a few carefully selected guests – mostly rich and spoilt.'

'Will there be some horny men?'

'Aren't all rich and powerful men horny?' Gael pulled Sophie's nipple and made the milk ease from its little pores.

'I don't know any rich men. I only seem to meet the poor ones.'

Gael ran her finger around the widely bowed lips. 'We might change that. Would you like to come?'

Now Sophie sat bolt upright. 'You're joking. No – I can see you're not. Christ, do you think I could catch myself a rich stud?'

Gael laughed. 'Rich men are as spoilt as hell. You

have to decide what you want from them and then let them think they're getting what they want from you.'

Sophie worked Gael's nubbin with little, stroking motions. 'Sounds interesting. But what are you going to do for food? I haven't got much in, and I'm not too good at making fancy things. I haven't had a party since I was a kid.'

Gael pulled Sophie down so a hanging breast came to her mouth. She took the nipple and sucked gently at it, rolling her tongue over its hardness. The milk was sweet and satisfying to the tongue.

She took a breath. 'Don't worry about the food. I've arranged it all with caterers. They'll come at five, set everything up and leave as soon as the party starts to swing.'

'Have you fixed the drink as well?' Sophie fed her nipple back into Gael's mouth and squeezed the breast.

Gael nodded as she sucked it. Then she let go reluctantly. 'Don't worry about a thing. Just put something sophisticated on and come. It'll be good for you, and you'll be a help to me.'

Sophie's excitement ebbed. 'I haven't got anything to wear. A clean skirt and blouse are just about as sophisticated as I get.'

Gael suckled again for some seconds before she answered, squeezing at the breast to make it squirt its milk. 'I'm sure Melindi wouldn't mind if you borrowed something from her wardrobe. She's got more clothes than she'll ever wear. You won't get anything more sophisticated than hers.'

Sophie sat astride Gael, dipping her breasts over her, placing first one nipple then the other in Gael's mouth.

Gael had got the knack now of making the milk stream. She even drew away and pressed a breast so that it squirted warmly into her mouth.

They kissed for several minutes, Sophie holding Gael's arms high above her head, her tongue exploring

44

Gael's tongue, her mouth set sideways for the closest possible contact.

Now Sophie spread her legs widely over Gael's hips so that her clitoris worked on Gael's mount. 'That's wicked,' she sighed. 'Your bristles tickle. It makes me really horny. Are you going to shave it or let your curlies grow?'

'I think I'll let it grow.'

Sophie nodded wisely, saying, 'Yes – it's probably a nuisance having to keep it smooth just so a man can see your snatch when he pulls your knickers off.'

Gael smiled at the brashness of the girl.

Sophie smoothed the hairs of her pubis out. 'It'll soon get as hairy as mine if you don't shave it.' She grinned as she knelt, pushing out her bottom to the mirrors.

Gael saw the reflection of two naked, young women. One had her arms above her head, the skin of her breasts and stomach glazed with Sophie's milk. The nineteen-year-old knelt over her, the roundels of her bottom squeezing a bush of ginger hair out from between them. The pink flesh of her secret lips pouted from its curls.

Sophie eased two fingers between Gael's own secret lips, exploring her. Gael clamped tight on Sophie's fingers, making her exclaim. 'How do you make it clamp so hard?'

Gael smirked and clamped again. 'Practice, I suppose. You have to learn how to squeeze.'

'With the lips of your cunt?'

Gael shook her head seriously. 'With your upper muscles, that's all.'

They both looked in the mirror again as Sophie made her vulva open and then close. 'I bet men like it, don't they?'

'Some do.'

'I'll have to squeeze Todd's prick. Perhaps he'll appreciate me more.' She made her vulva open wide and

45

closed it tight again. Then she knelt up over Gael. She squeezed her breasts, spurting warm milk and massaging it on to Gael's own breasts. That sent a wave of excitement flowing through Gael's belly to her vulva. The girl slipped down the bed and pushed Gael's legs back hard. Gael quivered with delight when she felt a warm stream trickle on her mons and down between her legs. As another squirt landed in her cleft she squirmed with the sensation. That felt so much like the hot spurt of a man as he reared over her, his cockshaft pulsing strongly.

When Sophie went down on her and licked her milk from the trembling fringes of Gael's purse, Gael felt a flush of pleasure go through her once again. Her own delightful liquid, which she loved to feel inside her, rose and welled and warmed her vulval lips.

As Sophie sucked her slowly, Gael viewed the chamber and its contents. There was certainly a great deal of potential for experimentation and fulfilment. But she would have to wait to see how her plan developed. Its success would depend upon how many of her guests had fantasies which they wanted to fulfil. She would have to get them to confess their secret needs.

Sophie began to lap at her hard, taking her mind off the problems of the party. It was wonderful to have a warm mouth there – a sensitive and caring mouth that kissed and plucked her secret lips and lapped the hollows of her groin so slowly. There was no urgency as with a man – no need to rake and rasp her into a frenzy of heaving hips so she was wet and open for his cock. No – with Sophie there was just the steady, sensuous motion of a warm, exploring tongue, and it was heavenly.

Gael smiled to herself. She had been right about this girl.

When Sophie turned and knelt astride Gael's shoulders, Gael found herself looking up at those dark pink fringes pulsing with Sophie's heartbeat, and she felt Sophie's searching tongue again.

Gael kissed the swollen labia poised tantalisingly above her. She ran her tongue-tip through their glistening cleft. She bit the tight skin of the inner thigh. Then she ran a finger around the anal ring and made the housemaid squirm and giggle with the pleasure that it gave her. But somehow the spark had gone from the liaison. Her thoughts came back to Flanders. Damn him – he had her mesmerised.

She took the clitoris of the kneeling redhead, pulling it into greater stiffness while her nose pushed between Sophie's labia, forcing them apart. The scent was quite exquisite. It made her temples pulse. But despite Sophie's avid ministrations, Gael could not climax. Not tonight. The sight of Flanders driving between those fleshy lips where now she had her nose, had turned on her heat. It had made her crave for that strength and urgent thrusting that only a man can bring as he loses himself in his need to come inside his conquest.

Despite her anger at Todd Flanders, she wanted him. She wanted him now. But she knew that she could not let him best her like he'd bested Sophie. She would have to work out a way both to have him and to control him. She'd teach the brute a lesson that not every woman would be a pushover and lie down on her back for him and open up her legs.

Sophie had gone when Gael awoke at seven in her own bed.

After she showered and dressed in a skirt and blouse for the heat of the day, she went down to the kitchen. Wearing no knickers, the wafts of cool air coming up the staircase felt pleasant as she glided down the stairs. She was still hot inside from the night before, still needed to orgasm strongly and flush away that heat. Her mind would not let go of the picture of Todd Flanders standing over Sophie with his penis fully hard.

Sophie was busying herself with breakfast. The table was set for two. Fresh croissants, butter and lemon marmalade sat invitingly on the best breakfast china. The smell of freshly ground coffee filled the air.

Sophie smiled as she caught Gael's eyes. 'I thought I might do my job properly, now that we're friends. We are friends, aren't we?'

Gael kissed her on the lips, holding there quite gently while she felt the warm, firm mound of Sophie's breast. She nuzzled up to Sophie's cheek. 'Of course we're friends. But I need a man.'

Sophie shrugged. 'So – a girl needs fucking when a girl needs fucking.'

'You don't mind, do you?'

Sophie stiffened. 'Be my guest. As long as it's not Flanders. He's mine.'

Gael's spirits sank as she saw a jealous look in Sophie's eyes. 'But Flanders is a conceited pig.'

Sophie grinned. 'I know he's a beast, but he turns me to jelly and I love it.'

'Don't you want to pay him back for the way he treated you last night?'

Sophie seemed to think hard. 'I'd like to make him do me the way I want him to.'

'And how do you want him to do you?'

'I just wish he'd strip me naked and stretch me on the bed and fuck me very slowly till I come. That's all. All that tying up and whipping is OK, but I'd like to be done in bed for once, while he kissed me passionately as he pushed inside my cunt. And I wish he'd suck my titties just like you do.'

Raising her T-shirt, Sophie exposed her soft belly to Gael, its navel deep and oval and inviting to Gael's tongue. Then she slipped the T-shirt upward and let her breasts fall out, thrusting one at Gael for her to suckle.

The sight of it aroused Gael quickly. She wasn't sure if the breast was a peace offering or not, but she sat and

pulled Sophie towards her. She sucked one nipple slowly, closing her eyes as she felt the warmness of the milk.
Then she looked up and smiled. 'You eating too?'

'I'll eat you any time you want me to.' Sophie smiled.
'You're OK.' She ran her fingers over Gael's cheek and
whispered, 'I really love your quim.' She pushed her
breast against Gael's mouth. 'It's so beautifully smooth
and firm.'

Gael blushed despite herself. So many people – mostly men – had told her how much they loved that part of
her, and it always made her feel warm inside.

Sophie pulled the nipple away from Gael's lips, saying, 'I wish I had a cunt as big and smooth as yours. It
seems sexier than mine.'

Gael breathed heavily then took the teat again. She
didn't know quite how to reply.

Kneading her hair, the girl gave Gael the other teat
and pushed her hand inside her jeans. It was clear to
Gael what she was doing with her finger as Sophie
trembled.

'When someone sucks your tits,' she asked seriously,
increasing the rubbing between her legs as Gael sucked
her harder. 'When someone sucks your tits, does it send
little tingles of excitement to your clitty?'

Gael closed her eyes and nodded, unwilling to take
her mouth from the elongated teat. Then Sophie pulled
away. She squatted on Gael's lap. She licked Gael's lips
and the corners of her mouth where the milk had
spilled. Then she pushed her tongue between them.

'Mouths are a bit like cunts, aren't they?' she mused,
running a finger over Gael's lips.

'The other way around,' Gael replied. 'At least that's
what men tell me. They'd rather stick their cock down
there than in my mouth.'

'But they do like being sucked off too. I know Todd
Flanders does. He loves it when I drink his spurt.'

Gael's heart was thumping hard as she stroked her

housemaid's breast. It drove her wild to suck a man and make him spurt. And she loved the way his penis throbbed when it gushed inside her mouth. But she wasn't going to tell her secrets to the girl. Not yet. She still wasn't sure of her, even though she had enjoyed sucking her breasts for breakfast.

Sitting opposite her at the table, Sophie kept her T-shirt raised, her breasts resting on the table as she leaned forward for a croissant. She sucked on one end provocatively. Then she clamped it hard between her lips, eyeing Gael mischievously as Gael looked up from her plate. The girl pursed her lips in a little kiss and fluttered her eyelids naughtily, mouthing, 'I want you,' before putting her eyes down coyly.

They munched their croissants and thickly buttered toast; both thoughtful; both intent on each other.

'I loved the way you ran the tip of your tongue round my ring, miss.'

Gael looked up at the remark and studied the green eyes. 'What else do you like?'

Sophie parted a bread roll, making it open and close. She stuck her tongue deeply into the doughy cleft, appearing to be thinking hard about what she liked. Then she closed her teeth on the roll, just as she had the fleshy area of Gael's bottom where it curved inward to meet her anal ring. After some seconds, the girl looked up brightly. 'I suppose what I love the most is being tied up and fucked.'

Gael frowned. 'But you just said that you wanted to be taken slowly.'

'Oh yes. Just once, to see how it felt – that's all.'

Gael shrugged. The girl seemed to be like her. Sometimes she wanted to be taken slowly and with passion. At other times she wanted to have her clothes ripped off and be flung down on her back. She looked back at Sophie. 'So you did like Todd Flanders stringing you up to that tree.'

Sophie smirked. 'Of course. He makes me come so violently at times. Anyway, I can't deny the brute when he's so randy, can I.' She finished off the roll and reached for the coffee just as Gael reached too. As their fingers touched, Gael felt another flush of excitement. She poured Sophie's coffee then her own, trying to stop her hand from shaking.

'I'm supposed to be the servant, miss,' Sophie whispered as she took charge of the pot.

'You can serve me another time.'

'Can I bath you and soap you and massage you with brandy-flavoured oil then lick it off?'

Gael found the tone of the conversation increasingly more stimulating. As she sat, her skirt rode up her thighs, and she could feel the cool draught from the window caress her crotch. She closed her legs. Perhaps she would go and put some panties on. She should concentrate on the business of the day and not give way to her coursing need to have Sophie's mouth or Flanders' cock between her legs. Then she compromised, saying to herself, Wait until the party's over.

'What are we going to do about Flanders?' Gael asked, almost casually between sips of her coffee.

Sophie studied her over her own cup. 'What do you mean, "do" about him, miss?'

'I think he needs a lesson in humility.' Gael fixed Sophie's eyes, intent on seeing if she agreed or not.

A wide smile told her that she did. 'Tie him up and whip him, do you mean? I'd like that. But only if I can have him afterwards.'

'That would only encourage him. He needs depriving for a while. Let him stew.'

'I could touch him up and shut him out for a couple of days,' Sophie said brightly. 'That would get him mad. He's marvellous when he's mad.'

Gael thought seriously. 'You just shut him out. If he comes on strong with you, just slap his face. That should put him off.'

'So he'll come on to you, you mean?' Sophie frowned. 'No way.' She pulled her T-shirt over her breasts and closed her arms across them.

'But don't you want to punish him for last night?'

Sophie frowned again. 'I was a bit slow, that's all. Sometimes I come like a bomb as soon as he slips it in me.'

Gael could see that this was getting her nowhere. She was determined to teach the man a lesson, whether the housemaid approved or not. She got up from the table. 'If you've finished breakfast, you have work to do, Sophie, my dear. I want this house shining like a new pin. The caterers will bring table settings, but I'll cut some flowers and do some general arrangements.'

'Cut the flowers at your peril,' Sophie pouted. 'Todd hates people messing about with his herbaceous borders.'

Gael soon found out that Sophie was right. Soon after she set foot on the border in the sunken garden, secateurs in hand, Flanders appeared through the gateway leading from the stable yard.

'What do you think you're doing, miss?' He closed on her.

She gave him a stony glare. 'I'm cutting flowers for the house.'

He moved nearer, his shirt open to the navel. She could smell him and it made her thrill again. Why did men do this to her? She stiffened her resolve against it and snipped at a blue delphinium spike.

He took her wrist. 'These flowers aren't for cutting, miss. They're for colour in the garden.' His lips came close to hers.

'I'll cut them if I want to.' She tried to pull away. Too conscious of his moist mouth, she began to tremble. His grip on her wrist was hard but she shook it off. 'Now get out of my way or find another job.'

He frowned down at her. With the top buttons of her

52

blouse undone, it gaped wide open to show the cleavage of her breasts. She wore no bra as usual and the dusky pink of her nipples showed plainly through the silk.

He stood back and watched her angrily as she snipped, amassing a great pile of colourful blooms on the short grass at his feet.

'Bring them to the scullery for me, will you,' she snapped as she turned her back on him.

As she strode away, Gael saw him bend and pick up an armful of flowers, his complexion white with anger. She quickly told Sophie to do the upstairs work and had already prepared several vases when he arrived in the scullery. He laid the blooms on the large, pine table and folded his arms. Magnificent now that he was angry, she recalled images of his nakedness and his potency. Angry men had such a stimulating effect on her.

She worked quickly and deftly, well practised in arranging flowers. Flanders made her nervous as he stood close beside her, his arms crossed, the veins of his temple pumping. She wondered what other veins were pumping too. He had sworn to Sophie that he would 'have Miss Goody-goody'. Was he biding his time? Was he waiting for a chance opportunity?

Gael decided that she needed another vase. A terracotta ewer sat on a high shelf. She took a step ladder and climbed. Flanders didn't offer his help so she snapped, 'If you're going to stay and watch, you could at least hold the steps for me.'

He just stepped back and folded his arms, watching every movement as she climbed.

With her bottom above the level of his head, she was conscious that he might be looking up her skirt. When she stretched for the ewer, she thought he might see that she wore no knickers. As she set her legs apart, the ladder wobbled. She tried to steady it but the floor was uneven. When the ewer crashed to the ground, she cried out, 'Help me, Todd.'

53

He darted forward as she toppled, one hand yoking her under the arm, the fingers touching her breast. As she fell towards him his other hand snaked inside her skirt and gripped her thigh. She had no time to tell if the intimate grip was intentional or not. All she knew was that his hand was between her legs, only inches from her cleft, and that she was hot there from the excitement of his presence.

He steadied her, taking the whole of her weight, bracing the ladder with his leg, just holding her and feeling her.

'Now what does Miss want me to do?' he asked cynically.

4

Giving His Mistress a Hand

'Let me down,' Gael snapped, trembling with the sensation of Flanders' hand between her legs as he stopped her falling from the ladder.

He pushed the ladder upright, still supporting her, and his hand slid further up her leg as she leant on him. His fingertips touched the fringes of her sex just fleetingly as he guided her down and set her on her feet.

She turned to him angrily but quenched her rage when she saw that he was genuinely concerned about her. When she began to tremble with the shock, he put his arms around her shoulders and held her closely.

He kissed her head. 'Are you all right, miss?'

Her breasts against his chest felt hot. His heart was beating fast as he yoked her neck and kissed her temple. She pulled away. Damn it, was he trying to seduce her?

Her rebuff seemed to make him angry. 'You might at least say thank you. I could have let you fall.'

She threw her head back haughtily. 'But then you wouldn't have been able to put your hand where it had no business to be, would you.'

He pulled her close again. 'But you liked it. You're moist where a woman only gets moist when she wants a man. Don't pretend you don't want me. I can see it in your eyes, miss.' She felt that he added the 'miss' out of habit, not because he felt subservient to her.

She snapped, 'Firstly, Mr Flanders, a woman might become moist without craving for a pig like you. Secondly, I don't want you, except to do the gardens.'

'But I think you do.' He held her so gently as he whispered the words that she was beginning to soften to him.

She stiffened. 'Then you think wrong. Let go of me.'

As he defied her, she began to feel vulnerable but she was determined not to let him get the better of her.

His breath was hot upon her face as he put his lips to hers. 'Did you enjoy watching me and Sophie last night, miss?'

That took Gael by surprise. 'I don't know what you mean.' She whispered it meekly, realising that she was losing control of the situation as well as her reactions to the man.

'You know full well what I mean. I heard a twig snap and saw you dart behind a tree.'

Gael's solar plexus heaved. So the show had been for her benefit. He had purposely made remarks about having 'Miss Goody-goody' just to goad her. And he had probably put on his display with Sophie in the belief that it would stimulate the watcher.

The veins in his neck pulsed as he looked down at her. 'Did you enjoy watching me fuck her?'

'There's no need to use language like –' She stopped abruptly as he bit her ear.

'But that's what it was. I wasn't making love to her. I was fucking her. That's what she wanted. It's all she ever wants.'

Gael snorted. 'That's what you think she wants.'

He raised an eyebrow. 'And how would you know what the little hell-cat wants or doesn't want from me?'

Gael flicked her hair back angrily. 'Because she told me – that's how!'

Now he came in close again, whispering in her ear, 'And what did she tell you, miss? Did she say how much she likes me to tie her to the bed and lick her armpits, down her flanks and up between her legs while she cries out for my cock?'

Gael didn't answer. He was too close and she was too excited by him for her mind to reason properly.

'Or did she tell you how she likes me to hang her by the ankles in the hay loft with her legs splayed wide apart while I stroke her fanny with a feather duster?'

Gael brought herself up tall. 'No – she did not. And I think you have a very vivid imagination, Mr Flanders.'

He closed on her again. 'Then what did she say she wanted, miss? How does she want me to fuck her in the future?'

'If you must know, she wants to be loved. She wants to be kissed passionately and taken very slowly until she climaxes.'

He stood back, set his head back and laughed loudly, his large hands spread on his hips, his belly pumping. Gael could see that his bulge was swollen inside his shorts but he didn't try to disguise the fact.

She glowered. 'And what's so unusual about a woman wanting to be loved like that?'

He grinned. 'I think young Sophie's been stringing you along, miss. If I know anything about her, all she ever wants is a good whipping before I fuck her.'

Gael was in a spin. She sensed that he was right. And even though he used the F word liberally, it was the only word to use for the way he'd taken the girl. Sophie had clearly loved every second of it.

She tried to move away but he took her chin again and pulled her face towards his own. She trembled as his lips closed upon hers.

He whispered, 'Would you like me to fuck you, miss?'

Gael tried to look away but he raised her chin and kissed her lips again. It was a tender kiss and it made her resolve melt. Perhaps he was romantic after all. Perhaps his hardness with Sophie had only been for show. Or perhaps he'd only been rough with the girl because that had been what she'd wanted.

'Have you ever felt a man, miss?' It was whispered into her mouth as she held her lips apart, breathing deeply to relieve her tension.

She shook her head and swallowed.

He took her hand and ran her fingers down the long bulge in his shorts. As the fingers flexed and rubbed him, a sigh of pleasure passed his lips. Now she knew that he was sure he had her under his spell.

'So – what did you see by the lake, miss?' His gaze was fixed upon her face now, not missing a flicker.

Feeling more confident, she smiled demurely. 'I saw you naked, teasing Sophie.' She palmed his bulge and held it, her fingers curving around his testes. He was so strong inside his shorts. She wanted to bare him and hold his hot flesh in her hand.

'Did you see me lick between her legs?' He whispered it as he pushed his bulge forward.

Gael nodded with her eyes half closed.

'And did watching her being licked there make the place between your own legs moist?' He kissed her lips again.

This time she remained silent.

He took her chin and lifted her face to his. 'And what else did you see me do?'

She turned her head away but he turned it back. 'I think you saw how I spread her on the grass and drove this into her.' He pushed himself into Gael's palm again. 'Do you know how it feels as a man opens you out with the hardness of his cock, then spurts inside you, miss?'

She shook her head again, her eyes cast down. 'I only saw you at a distance. I've never seen . . .' She gulped. 'I've never seen a man in great detail.'

He made her look up into his eyes, a knowing smirk on his face. 'Yes. I thought you were naïve.' He pushed into her hand with little rhythmic motions of his hips, the bulge hard and long now. 'Would you like to feel it in the flesh? There's nothing to be afraid of.'

She lowered her eyes once more, keeping up the pretence of innocence.

Without waiting for her consent, he pulled his zip down and undid his leather belt – the same belt that he'd used to tie Sophie to the bough. Then he peeled his fly apart.

Gael's hand was trembling as she touched the warmness of his penis. It was huge. She wanted it. Here. Now. On the table. On the floor. My God, any way at all. But she knew she must not. She'd sworn to teach him a lesson for the way he'd taken Sophie and the way he assumed he was going to have herself.

As the shaft sprang out, he made her take it, wrapping her fingers tightly about its girth. The musky scent of it made her reel. Her nipples swelled and her solar plexus trembled.

'My God,' she whispered, looking up innocently into his eyes. 'I'm sure that it's too big for . . .'

'For that tight little slit between your legs with its fringe of curly hair?' Then he made her work his foreskin. The glans was engorged, its profile strongly defined. Its scent welled up again.

'You can make it even bigger by stroking it like this.'

He made her stroke the web in the cleft of the glans with the tip of her forefinger. The light touch caused the whole shaft to swell and stiffen.

'Why does it do that?' She gave him a doe-eyed look as she fingered the web gently.

He put his mouth to her ear. 'So that when it pushes up the slippery, hot and pulsing, squirming, yearning slit between your lovely legs, it can fill it fully, miss.' A hiss of a smile accompanied his words.

She pushed him back against the table and drew aside his shirt so she could see him in all his potent glory. Now that she had him horny and exposed she felt elated. So far, so good. But she knew that he could take control of her at any second and have her in any way he liked – he was too strong for her.

'What do I do now?' She looked at him with such innocence that she almost believed it herself.

'Make a tube with your hand like this.' He made her masturbate him slowly, his large hand curling over her fingers. 'Now move it up and down. That's perfect. You've got a natural touch.'

She smiled demurely. 'I suppose I should be flattered. What now?'

He kissed her tenderly on the mouth, and brushed her hair with his fingertips, whispering, 'Suck it. It likes to feel the heat of a woman's mouth.' He kissed her lips again and smiled. 'When she wets it, it slides so easily between the lips of her cunt that it's up to the hilt before she realises it's in.' His tone was so romantic it took the edge off the graphic reality of his words. But the reality set her senses alight all the same. Immediately, her body conjured up the feelings of what it would be like as the whole nine inches slipped inside her.

As she knelt to put her mouth to his glans, she breathed deeply of its musk.

'How should I suck it?' She looked up at him, past the purple head of the rearing penis, over the flat stomach and his swelling pectorals. His eyes were alight with the success he thought that he was having.

'Just put your mouth over it and lick this with your tongue.' He fingered the web. The veins of the shaft pulsed strongly as she kissed it gently. It was magnificent; as huge and strong and curved as any she'd ever had.

Now she opened her mouth, took in the whole helmet of the shaft and traced its sculpted edges with her lips. She tongued the web and made the whole shaft swell. As she drove her mouth down on him, he tugged at her hair, pulling her on to himself. When she glanced up, she saw that his eyes were closed as he felt the sensuous heat and wetness of her mouth.

As she fondled his testicles and slipped one into her mouth, he tensed.

She smiled. It always gave her a great sense of power to do that to a man. She only had to clench her teeth and . . .

He slipped his hands through her hair, kneading at her scalp. Then as she sucked him in, he began to moan and strain between her lips. Holding his scrotum firmly, she pulled him forward. She slid her hands around his hips to run them over the tight, muscular buttocks, and pushed his shorts down. When he stepped out of them she drove her mouth down on to the shaft, stretching his foreskin tightly with her lips, her tongue working at its web.

Then she felt him tense.

Quickly she pulled away, determined that he would not shoot just yet.

When she slipped his shirt off, she delighted in his nakedness. His eyes were tightly closed. With his penis at full hardness, it stood out from his body, her saliva running down its groove, its head shining with a deep, pink lustre from the wetness.

'Lie down,' she whispered. 'Lie on the table.' She pushed him gently back.

In a moment, she had him laid back on the table, his legs apart, his eyes still closed. He raised his hips as she ringed his shaft and began to masturbate him slowly. She sucked his glans and licked his balls. She lifted them aside and ran her tongue between his scrotum and his inner thigh.

Now he rested on his elbows grinning down at her. 'You tease. You've done this before, haven't you?'

She gave him a little smirk and licked his balls. 'So, now do you think I'm so naïve?'

He reached for her breast but she pushed him down.

61

'Lie still. I want to enjoy you more before you have me, Mr Flanders. I want you as big as I can get you before you fill that "tight little slit" between my legs.'

He moaned as she plucked his nipples with her lips. She nuzzled up to him and whispered in his ear, 'I want to sit on top of you.' She took his cock and squeezed. 'And I want to feel this in my quim. But please don't look as I undress.'

'Why not?'

'Because I'm very shy. Close your eyes.'

He pretended to close his eyes but she saw the lids flutter.

She slapped his arm playfully and tied a tea towel around his head and pulled it tight. 'Now lie still and don't you dare move a muscle.' Her lips reached his mouth. She kissed him gently and withdrew, just as he'd done to her.

'Don't be long,' he growled. 'And don't try to run away. I'll chase you and catch you if you do. Then I'll spread you out on this table and tease you until you scream for me to make you come.'

She whispered back as she nipped his earlobe, 'Promises like that will get you nothing, Mr Flanders. Remember, I'm your mistress. You do exactly as I want you to or you find another job.'

He smiled wryly. 'Don't threaten me, you vixen. Now get your clothes off or I'll strip them for you.'

She rubbed his penis slowly and made him sigh, smiling widely as she kissed the tip. She went quickly to the door and beckoned. Sophie was at the sink in the kitchen. Then she put her finger to her lips to tell Sophie not to make a sound as she whispered in her ear, 'Do you want to get your revenge on Todd Flanders for the way he treated you last night?'

Sophie put her head on one side. Then she nodded, clearly puzzled by Gael's behaviour.

Gael drew the girl into the scullery, and put her hand

over the open mouth as Sophie spotted Flanders lying naked on the table, his eyes bound by the tea towel. She looked at Gael with astonishment as Gael raised his penis and sucked slowly on the glans. 'I've taken all my clothes off, Mr Flanders,' she said brightly, 'but you'll have to imagine what I look like naked. Perhaps if you're very good, I'll let you take the blindfold off later.' She licked his testes. 'Now I'm going to sit on top of you. I want to feel you slip inside me very slowly. Lie still.'

He sighed.

Gael slipped Sophie's skirt off quickly, skimming the fair-skinned buttocks with her palm. She wanted to stroke the mons with its mass of ginger hair, but there was no time for that.

The nonplussed maid stood in her T-shirt, naked below the waist, her prominent mons pushed out as she swayed her hips.

Gael signed to her to get up on the table. Sophie caught on quickly to the game. Gael swallowed hard as the girl knelt over the gardener's hips, the swelling vulva plainly visible between her legs. Its lips were already moist, the inner lining of her cleft a dark pink against the paleness of her thighs. Gael wanted to put her mouth to it and run her tongue deep between the lips. But Sophie spread her legs and lowered herself on to the man as she yanked his cock up hard. How Gael wanted to strip herself and press her own purse over that cock. She needed to feel its heat.

Sophie looked down between her legs. She grasped the girth of his shaft in both her hands and stroked it to make it harder. She held it, taut and straining as she lowered herself on to it, her eyes closed, her belly pulled in as she held her breath.

Gael whispered near his ear, 'Feel me, Flanders. Feel me.'

'When are you going to let me lick it?' he whispered back hoarsely.

63

Gael slapped his arm. 'Just be content to have your prick in me, will you. Perhaps I'll let you lick me another time.'

He pushed up into Sophie. She still had her eyes tightly closed as she rode him, pressing her fingertips deep into his belly.

He pushed up again, clearly coming to his climax, which made Sophie open and close herself on him.

Gael trembled as she heard the redhead's moistened parts sucking on Todd Flanders.

Sophie began to pant, making him thrust up even more, his belly going taut as his pelvis surged forward.

Gael thrust her hand between her own legs and began to work it over her clitoris.

Sophie moaned and clawed at Flanders' skin, leaving tracks of pinkness over the sweating belly. He arched his back, lifting her high above him. Sophie gasped as she came, her breasts swelling, their nipples oozing milk.

Gael frigged steadily at herself, her inner thighs trembling as she neared her climax too. She watched with fascination as her housemaid's vulva flooded, glazing the gardener's phallus, his pubis and his sac.

He cried out loudly and drove up one more time, holding his shaft at full extension. Sophie set her head back, thrust out her breasts, and gasped for air as Gael sucked a nipple, running the flat of her hand over the redhead's belly. She could feel the bulge of the man's hard cock, deep inside the body of the girl. She could feel its pulse as it pumped its charge. And then Gael came in a flurry of little contractions which rippled up inside her. Her breasts swelled up, becoming ever more sensitive as they rubbed inside her blouse.

When Flanders relaxed, letting Sophie down, Gael pulled the blindfold off him and sidled to the door. As he opened his eyes it took him some seconds to focus. When he saw Sophie sitting astride him, grinning widely at his cock between her legs, his pleased expression turned to one of anger.

He looked round to see Gael leave the room.

She was busy at the sink when he stormed into the kitchen. He was still completely naked, his penis wagging as he stood with his legs apart, his fists clenched on his hips.

She turned to him slowly and scanned him up and down. He was a really horny brute and she wanted him more than ever. But she fixed his eyes with hers and stared him out.

'Yes. What do you want? And why are you undressed?' She nodded to his penis. 'And do put that thing away. It doesn't impress me in the least.'

He closed on her and glared into her eyes. 'I expect you think you're clever, don't you?'

'Clever?'

'You know what I mean.' His eyes became slits as he scowled. 'You'd better close your windows and lock your bedroom door at night from now on. And I advise you not to walk in the grounds alone, especially in the woods.'

She slitted her own eyes, his anger firing her up again. Why was it that she got so horny when men were angry with her? 'And why should I be careful of walking in the woods?'

He came closer still, the heat of his body reaching her, the scent of his cock mixed with Sophie's musk wafting towards her.

'Because – *miss* – if I find you out alone, I shall catch you and strip your knickers off and have you when you least expect it.'

Gael smirked and held herself up stiffly, even though her legs were trembling. 'But I seldom wear knickers. You found that out when you grabbed me from the ladder.'

'Then I'll have to strip you naked, won't I?'

'But what if I catch you first?' Gael was getting more excited by the second now that the challenge had been made.

A slight smile curved his lips. 'I assure you, you wouldn't find it easy to catch me out again.'

Gael threw her head back. 'But if I did, I could have you any way at all?'

'Any way you want me. But don't think I'll be so foolish as to let you trick me like you did this time.' He kissed her cheek lightly, even lovingly, Gael thought. Had he genuinely been making love to her before? Her body trembled at the exchange. He'd accepted her challenge. Now she must be very careful to keep control. There was no way she was going to let the gardener get the best of her, in or out of bed, even though he had become virtually irresistible. But she knew she must have him soon – and fully – but on her own terms. She couldn't stand this cat-and-mouse affair much longer.

She pulled away from him. 'You're on, Mr Flanders. I'll catch you unawares and have you in whatever way I choose. So – be careful.'

Still stripped below the waist, with her T-shirt up to expose her breasts, Sophie was standing by the scullery door. Her eyes were wide as she listened to the exchange.

Flanders half turned, looked at her and then at Gael. His penis was fully hard again, Gael assumed from the stimulation of her challenge. She saw a fleeting glint of lust in his cold blue eyes.

'Come here,' he growled, pointing to the table.

Sophie came obediently.

'Bend over,' he hissed.

She bent, her breasts against the scrubbed-wood surface as she stretched her arms out.

'Open your legs wide so I can see all of your pussy.' He looked triumphantly at Gael as the housemaid did as he bid. The redhead pushed her feet apart as widely as she could. Now her sexual lips stood out from the stretched membranes of her loins, the opening between them gaping at the triumphant man.

He moved behind her, his eyes still fixed on Gael's. He slapped the redhead's bottom hard then sank his penis into her open cleft.

Gael sprang forward. She tried to pull him off her, but he was too strong and too determined. He simply grinned at her as he buried his cock deep inside Sophie's moist channel.

'What's the matter, miss?' he joked. 'Do you want to take her place?'

Gael slapped him hard across the head but it seemed not to deter him. Then she glowered as Sophie began to moan, 'Oh yes. Oh yes. Do me, Todd. Do me hard.'

Gael stepped back and glared.

Flanders spread the housemaid's labia with his thumbs and pumped himself into her strongly, a wide grin on his face.

'See, miss. She's still my loyal slave.' He slapped Sophie's leg.

Gael glowered as the girl pushed out her vulva and sheathed his whole shaft with a sigh of deep-felt pleasure. As she pushed back at him, his testes jolted between her thighs, and she cried, 'Yes. Oh yes. Fuck me, you bastard – fuck me.'

He took her steadily, making her jolt against the table, her nipples sliding on the wood. At the extremity of his stroke he thrust so deeply into the girl that her buttocks bulged out around his buried member.

Gael turned and strode away just as the girl let out another cry of 'Yes', and shuddered violently as she climaxed for a second time.

Gael couldn't stop herself from turning at the doorway. As she fixed her eyes on Flanders' face, he pulled out of the redhead, aimed his phallus at Gael and spurted into the air. It was a gesture of defiance as well as one of triumph and served to show her just how potent he was.

She slammed the kitchen door and stormed along the

passage. At that moment she knew that she had become jealous of Sophie. She guessed that he knew it too. His brashness and his strength and that subtle hint of romance had caught her off guard. But why was she resisting the temptation? She knew why. He'd taken her for granted and he'd challenged her. To drop her knickers and bend over the table for him to have her like Sophie would only feed his ego, and she would lose face. No – she would make him work hard for what she wanted him to do with her.

'My God,' she whispered to herself as she scampered up the stairs. 'What the hell have I started now?'

5

The Voyeur

The large dining-room looked magnificent. The buffet was set with hired silver and gilded plate. The chandeliers sent their sparkle downward to be reflected in crystal glasses.

The drawing-room was already crowded; couples standing closely while others sat and studied them. Singles scanned for someone they thought might please them or satisfy their needs.

Gael looked out into the sunken garden where several young women paraded, dressed in designer originals, petulant and spoilt. Eyed discreetly by handsome men from the windows of the rambling house, they pretended not to notice. But every one of them was charged-up and expectant.

Melindi and Gael had chosen the first guests very carefully. This first party was an experiment. If it was a wild success, the news would spread. Then everyone would be intrigued. Some would be affronted that they'd not been asked at first, but eventually their curiosity and addiction to sensual pleasures would draw them in.

Now here was the advance battalion who had come to renew old ties with Gael, or to assess Melindi's protégé and the house about which wild rumours had spread. Without the approval of this first group, Gael knew the project would be doomed.

All the bedrooms were open, all the keys in their locks. The uncarpeted back stairs would echo to stiletto heels and the scuff of Gucci leather soles. Everyone would notice but pretend that they hadn't heard.

Dressed in a silken jump-suit of stunning red, a large ruby set in gold filigree hanging in her cleavage, Gael enjoyed making the acquaintance of Melindi's friends. They were all well-heeled and free to indulge themselves in anything they fancied. As long as some of them wanted their fantasies fulfilled, all would be well.

As each arrival handed his or her invitation to the hired butler and took Gael's hand, she knew they were intrigued. They bowed slightly as they took her hand, often a move designed to disguise the scanning of her breasts or the large swell of her mount. She had made sure that her garment was tight about her crotch. She could feel the silk between her vulval lips, unhampered by crotchless knickers or even a scanty thong. Her nipples poked through nicely and took the women's eyes as well. She smiled, a little bit uncertain which of them fancied her more than they fancied the handsome men.

'Hello. I'm Gael. I'm so glad you could come.' It was said a dozen times or more in less than half an hour.

A tall man stood before her now, his dark eyes fixed on hers. His mouth curved slightly as he took her hand and whispered almost conspiratorially, 'Hello. I'm Anthony. Melindi's told me so much about you, but I hope to get to know you better later on.' As he raised her hand, his fingers grazed her nipple, but she pretended not to notice. When he bowed to kiss the hand, she could almost feel his gaze upon her crotch. As his eyes focused on hers again, she could see a look of lust in them. She smiled demurely at the dark brown pools. Good. The party needed horny males, even if she didn't accommodate this one herself. In fact that was not the idea. It was best that she simply put guests together in interesting situations and let them enjoy each other.

As each guest took a glass of pink champagne, passing into the day rooms to start on his or her new quest, Gael read the gold-edged invitation card for about the hundredth time. At the bottom of the usual formalities a line in small print said:

A CONFESSOR WILL BE PRESENT IN THE CHAPEL
FOR THOSE WHO WISH TO UNBURDEN THEMSELVES
OF THEIR FANTASIES.

Most of the guests, Gael thought, would be intrigued but might not dare to see what this was about. But it would only take one or two of the more adventurous ones to try it just for fun, and the news would flash like lightning through the group.

'Gael. Darling. What a surprise.'

Gael spun around and found herself looking into the black eyes of Lady 'Peek-a-boo' Fannshawe. Gael smiled inwardly. 'Boo' was a well-known voyeur. She could be relied upon to gatecrash any party where she might take a peek at couples making out.

Boo pressed her cold cheek to Gael's face. 'When I heard about the party, I didn't know you'd be behind it, Gael darling. What a surprise. Your parties were always pure magic.' She scanned Gael up and down, wrinkling her nose slightly at Gael's garment while fingering the neckline of her St Laurent original, and fiddling with her pearls. 'And, of course, you look scrumptious, as usual,' she added condescendingly.

Gael took a deep breath. 'Hello, Boo.' She kissed the air beside the pale, pink cheek. 'Marvellous that you could come. Did you bring anyone?'

Boo gestured to the tall man, Anthony, who had just touched Gael up. Looking out across the garden, his eyes were fixed intently on a blonde in a see-through top.

'I brought Anthony,' Boo said brightly. 'Isn't he

71

gorgeous? And so horny, my dear. You wouldn't believe how big.'

No, Gael thought to herself, but she was more certain now that she would find out soon just how 'big' he was.

She turned back to Boo. 'What does Anthony do?'

Boo Fannshawe gave her a coy little look. 'For money or with his trousers off?'

Gael shrugged as if either answer would do. She got both.

'He's in the City. Futures or something. Absolutely loaded, darling. And he's an engine in bed. Goes for hours. He wears me out.'

Gael suppressed a smile. 'Wears *you* out, Boo?'

Boo pouted. 'Watching a man doing another woman can be very tiring, you know.'

'And what do you like to watch the most, Boo?'

'Close-ups, of course.'

'Close-ups?'

Boo frowned. 'Not those wretched videos. I mean real-life close-ups, darling.'

'Incognito?'

'Of course.' Boo sighed theatrically. 'But it's so difficult to get really close without the couple knowing. You won't tell a soul, will you?'

Gael smiled inwardly. Everyone on the circuit knew what Boo liked. Some of them enjoyed being watched. Some went out of their way to contrive to have her there. But Boo thought that she was watching them secretly – that was what gave her her kicks.

Gael touched her arm gently. 'I think I can help you, Boo.'

The young millionairess's eyes lit up. 'How?'

Gael put her finger to her lips. 'I'll tell you later. But you'd better watch and see who's going to pair off first.' She grinned and turned away.

Boo caught her arm. 'I think Anthony will move in on that girl in the transparent top. Who is she?'

'That's Francine of Francine de Paris, the international hairdressing chain.'

The next couple of hours sped past. Gael was in the kitchen checking that the caterers had cleared up and gone. The buffet was disappearing fast and people were nicely mellow on champagne. Sophie was enjoying being chatted up as she went around topping up people's glasses. She had poured herself into a sheer, pink body stocking and was causing quite a stir among the men. Gael had caught one or two of the women sizing her up as well. Sophie's breasts seemed larger than before. The nipples stood out proudly as if she were aroused, and the tightness of her garment pulled deeply in her bottom, making the soft cheeks swell out roundly.

A sound from the scullery made Gael turn. She peeked through the ventilation holes in the door. A limited view showed the bottom half of a young woman lying on the table on her back. The woman's dress was up around her hips, and she had her legs spread widely to expose her naked mons. A man spooned trifle from a crystal coupe over her lower belly. The lips of her ample sex were fringed with clotted cream. She giggled as he peeled a large banana and slipped it through the foaming cream. He spread her with two fingers, the pinkness within her sleeve contrasting sharply with the creamy white banana. Her pubic hair was sprinkled with silver balls. Half a glacé cherry bobbled in her navel as she laughed.

The man began to lick her. At first he raised her leg and tongued the inside of her knee.

She sighed and closed her eyes.

He worked slowly up her inner thigh, leaving a trail of moisture from his tongue.

'Higher,' she whispered. 'Lick my quim. I want to feel your tongue there.'

He licked through the hollow of her loin and slowly around the distended lips of her sex.

She gave a little groan and whispered, 'Yes.'

Then he began to chew on the banana, pushing it in and out of her with his teeth to make her moan.

Gael went quickly to find Boo Fannshawe. She drew Boo away from a stunning-looking brunette who was fingering her breast. 'I think there's something you might like to see, Boo,' she whispered.

Boo's eyes lit up. She blew the brunette a kiss and hurried to the kitchen behind Gael. The man had creamed his phallus and topped it with a half a cherry. The woman was on her knees, her tongue working up the centre of his shaft and her eyes tightly closed. Her breasts hung from a low-cut gown, the nipples frosted thickly with fine sugar.

Gael left Boo to watch them and went back to the party. She bumped into Anthony 'Something-in-the-City', just as he was heading for the buffet.

'Hello again,' she said, smiling with her eyes. 'Are you enjoying yourself?'

He studied her closely. 'Yes I am. But I'm going to have a whole lot more fun in a minute. Where's Boo?'

Gael shrugged. 'I think she's powdering her nose. Shall I tell her that you're looking for her?'

His eyes sparkled for a moment. 'Where can I take Francine to talk – privately?'

'You can use a room upstairs. All the rooms are open to my guests. I'll show you in a minute, if you like.'

He smirked and kissed her cheek. 'You're a wonderful hostess, Gael. So attentive to our needs. Tell Boo I might be gone for a little while.'

Gael's eyes returned the sparkle. 'Of course.'

Now he smiled openly. 'And I'd like to fuck you later if I may.'

Gael pretended to be shocked but the statement sent a ripple of excitement running through her. When a man said that so blatantly, she felt so wicked. One of her own fantasies was simply to lie down at such a party

74

and open herself for all to see while a man with a gigantic phallus dropped his trousers and took her without a word.

She threw off the fantasy and made sure the party was going well before she went back to Boo. She sidled up to the door and looked through the vent as well.

The man had the young woman face down over the table edge, just as the gardener had had Sophie. He squirted cream from a pressurised canister, filling the whole deep groove between her buttocks. He ran a foamy ring around her anus and down the fringes of her sex, covering up her whorls of dark, brown hair.

'Oooh,' she giggled. 'That's so cold. I need your hot cock to warm me up now. Please.'

'Slut,' he hissed and slapped her hard, making her buttocks wobble. Then he knelt and put his face between her legs. Inch by slow inch he licked the cream from around the pouting lips until only a strip was left down the centre of her cleft. Extending his tongue, he lapped her from her nubbin to her anus. He licked around the puckered ring until he had the whole of her soft pinkness exposed once more.

She wriggled and pushed herself out at him again. 'Fuck me, Miles. I need you to cream my pussy properly.'

He stood right back, his penis rearing strongly. He reached for a bottle of cooking brandy from the dresser and took a long swig. When he poured it over the distended vulval lips, the woman gasped. Gael knew how that could sting and then go nicely warm.

A hand worked its way between Gael's legs as Boo pressed her face to the vent.

Then the man poured brandy down his penis and closed his eyes as he felt the stinging then the heat. The woman's sex lips were pulsing now. Slick with brandy mixed with her nectar, they began to open and close. This seemed to be too much for him to resist. He opened her widely with his thumbs and put the head of his penis to the tunnel he exposed. Then he poured more brandy, letting it trickle down his shaft and into her widened cleft.

'Oh God,' she moaned. 'That's wonderful. But I need to feel your cock inside my cunt.'

The fingers between Gael's legs began to flex. The forefinger worked deeply through the valley of her sex. She widened her stance to let Boo feel her better, and to get the most sensation that she could. The scene was turning her on, even though she knew she should return to her party guests.

The long shaft sank in deeply. There was a rush of brandy as he buried it right in her. Then there was a whisper from the girl. 'Oh yes. Oh yes. That's nice. Now do me faster.' She began to judder as he took her hard, making the full cheeks of her bottom tremble.

He withdrew and charged again.

She gasped and pushed out more.

The brandy bubbled out of her and trickled down her leg.

He slapped her bottom hard and whispered, 'Slut'.

She beat her fists on the table top crying, 'Fuck me faster, pig.'

He began to spank her buttocks and her thighs.

She wriggled on his phallus as he drove it deeply in, screwing herself about it, closing on its length.

Now he spanked her almost brutally as he drove and then withdrew.

Meanwhile Boo's finger sawed faster through Gael's wide-spread legs.

The woman on the table clenched her fists and closed her eyes. She let out a long, loud moan as she climaxed with a shudder, and her lover drove in his penis to its hilt.

Gael's vulval lips were swollen as she watched the other woman squeezing on the phallus, and gulping it right in.

Then he pulled it out of her. He stood away and worked at his foreskin with two fingers. When it spurted richly it landed on her vulva and trickled slowly down between its lips. The woman moaned as she sensed its heat. He massaged it around her, rubbing at the fringes of her sex, and around the russet muscle of her ring.

She thrust it out at him to rub it harder. Then she turned around and knelt down. She took his beating penis in her mouth and began to suck.

Gael gasped as Boo's finger slowed its motion through her sex. She started as the woman faced her man and hit him hard. His cheek blazed with a five-fingered weal.

He reeled with the shock of it, his penis springing tautly. 'What the hell was that for?' he cried, putting his hand to his burning cheek.

She glared and hit the other cheek just as hard. 'Don't you ever call me a slut again,' she hissed, and pulled her dress down sharply.

Gael and Boo scattered as she came towards the door. She seemed not to notice them as she flounced back to the party. The dishevelled Miles chased after her, his shirt caught in his zip, leaving Gael and Boo staring at his back.

To Gael's surprise, Boo grabbed her behind the neck and hooked her forward. Her large mouth took Gael's lips and kissed her passionately.

Gael gasped for breath and pulled away, but Boo would not be denied. She held Gael by the shoulders and pushed her against a cupboard. Their nipples touched and rubbed together. Then finally, Gael pulled herself away and stood back, dazed.

Boo smiled demurely. 'That was marvellous, darling. And I love you. Will you lick me off? I'm dreadfully horny and I won't come unless someone licks my quim.' She reached out and brushed Gael's cheek with long, red nails.

Gael took the hand and held it. 'No, Boo. Not now. I've got guests to see to. Anyway – I came to tell you that Anthony wants to take the hairdresser somewhere private.'

Boo's eyes lit up. 'How private?'

Gael smiled. 'Not so private that anyone spying through a crack in the door wouldn't be able to see what they were up to.'

Boo beamed. 'You are marvellous, Gael. How can I repay you for your understanding?'

Gael dropped her hand and kissed her lightly on the lips. 'You can tell people what a marvellous party it was and that I'm offering to help those who want to work out their fantasies.'

Boo's eyes went wide. 'Will you help me with my fantasy now?'

Gael took her hand and led her up the stairs. She took her to a bedroom and opened the bathroom door. 'This bathroom serves the room next door as well,' she whispered conspiratorially. 'I'll bring Anthony and his hairdresser into that room.' She went to the opposite door, towing Boo behind her. As she opened it slightly, they could see the double bed just a few feet away.

Gael turned to Boo. 'Now, keep the light off. And keep quiet. If they want to use the bathroom, you'll have to retreat to the other bedroom. Got it?'

Boo smiled naughtily. 'Got it.'

6

A Close Shave

Gael was shaking as she showed Anthony the door to the second bedroom. She retired discreetly as he went to find Francine. The party was in full swing now, people everywhere animatedly engaged in conversation. One couple on a sofa were engrossed in heavy petting with his hand inside her knickers, her finger rubbing his leg. Then she slipped his zip and pulled his penis out. They seemed not to be bothered by the glances from the others, and soon a crowd had gathered around the scene.

The woman knelt and went down on his shaft. Her bottom stuck up in the air. An onlooker casually peeled her dress up her back and another slipped her panties down her legs. She seemed not to have noticed as she sucked on the man, her labia quite swollen as she worked up and down. Then someone took out a silver cigar case from his pocket, dipped it in champagne and eased it into her anus.

The woman gasped and the crowd murmured with anticipation.

The cigar case was like a metal penis, rounded at one end, but open at the other. As he slid it deeply into her smallest hole he wiggled it about.

Still she sucked the man.

Now the man with the cigar case took a lady's fan

and began to smack her lightly on her bottom. As he
struck the case, it slipped in more deeply and made the
woman wriggle on its length. Now he put his finger in
the open end and worked it in small circles. Other
helping hands stroked slowly down her thighs. She
moaned and sucked harder.

'So – how have you been since I saw you last, Gael?'

Gael shook her gaze from the fascinating scene, and
turned to find herself looking at an old acquaintance.

'I'm fine, thanks, Charles.' She threw her hair back
nonchalantly and fixed his gaze. The last time they'd
met, he'd put her over a hay bale in a stable, whipping
her nicely with a rein while she'd pushed her bottom out
to him. But he hadn't taken her or fulfilled her, and that
had made her angry. He'd simply trussed her hands
behind her back and sat down on another bale. He'd
spread her feet with his, and tickled her labia with a
straw, masturbating himself while he'd talked about the
weather and his horses.

'You look radiant, Gael, sweetie.' He bent and kissed
her cheek. 'Have you found someone rich to do you?'

She ignored his 'sweetie' and pulled herself up
straight. 'I'm surprised you came, Charlie. You weren't
invited.' She stared him coldly in the eyes.

He smirked. 'I came with Penny.' He nodded to the
brunette who had been fingering Boo. 'She mentioned
that you were going to be here. I just had to see what
little game you're playing.'

'So that you can go running back to tell Bunny
Grymwell?'

He shrugged the question away, but she knew that was
what he'd do. Good. The sooner that bastard Grymwell
knew that she'd made good, the better she'd like it. But
now she had to have recruits for her fantasies game.

She changed her demeanour, fingering the lapel of his
tuxedo. 'Have you come to confess your sins, and reveal
your deepest secrets, Charlie?'

He frowned theatrically. 'No way. But I know a man who has.'

'Oh? And who might that be?'

He smiled. 'Tell me where to send him, and you'll find out.'

Gael ignored the question as she ran the back of her finger up the inside of his leg, and over the bulge of his genitals before she turned away. Then she went upstairs and into the bathroom where Boo was kneeling on the floor.

Boo nodded to the slightly open door, putting her finger to her lips.

Anthony was already stripped bare on the bed. The naked Francine knelt astride him, facing his feet. Her clothes were scattered on the floor, except for long, black stockings which reached up to her crotch, cutting into the hollows of her loins.

She rubbed her vulva on his lower belly as she brushed his scrotum gently with a silver-backed hair brush. Then she ran a comb through his pubic hair, holding the curly strands between two fingers just as she might when combing out a client.

'How do you like it, sir?' she quipped over her shoulder.

'Any way I can get it, miss.'

'Any way at all, sir?' Francine reached for her bag lying at the bottom of the bed, showing Boo and Gael a flash of her cleft as she knelt and stretched. She took out a battery shaver. Then, pulling up the most enormous cock Gael had seen for years, she took the head of it between her thumb and forefinger and began to stroke it with the side of the shaver, making it vibrate. He trembled as the shaft between her fingers swelled.

Now she began to shave his scrotum, all the time rubbing the wide-stretched mouth of her sex upon his hairy belly. It seemed that she needed to feel his heat as she worked him deftly. Soon she had his sac smooth and hairless. Gael watched as she stroked his balls, making them retract. Then she set to and ran the shaver over his pubis, shearing him expertly. All the time he moaned and pushed up through her fingers, trying to make her work his foreskin.

Gael was reluctant to leave. She knew that the most exciting scenes were yet to come. But she had her guests to think of and she had a more important job to do.

Downstairs, she checked with Sophie that there was enough food and drink. The couple on the sofa were lying panting, his trousers around his ankles, her dress around her hips. She worked his limp penis idly while her other hand worked her nub, her eyes closed, her mouth in a constant smile. Their audience had returned to little huddles, and everything seemed all right.

Gael decided that it was time for her to start the theatrical performance she had planned. She ran up the stairs to get dressed. But just as she was about to turn towards her room, she felt impelled to return to the bathroom and see how Boo was getting on. What was a few minutes more delay? The night was still young.

Boo had her nose to the barely open door. As Gael stood behind her, she could see a slice of the action in the bedroom beyond. Anthony was still on his back, Francine still astride him as she worked his penis slowly with long fingers. He clawed her back and buttocks with his nails, sighing, 'Make it as hard as iron, darling. Then I'll shag you harder than you've ever been shagged before.'

Francine's eyes lit up as she gazed at the shaft between her legs. It reared up strongly, the pubis naked, the form of his testes clear within their smoothly shaven sac.

She worked herself backward until her crotch was above his face, then bent down and took his cock into her mouth. As she pushed her mouth down its curving length, he put his face into her crotch and drew deeply of her scent. Then as she bore down on him, he pushed up into her mouth. At the same time he took the leaves of her sex between his lips.

She licked his shaft from deep between his balls up to the head.

He lapped from her nubbin to her perineum, making her slick with his saliva.

She wriggled on his tongue and sucked him harder.

Now he ate at her. He buried his nose in the valley of her sex and sucked her nubbin until she cried out, 'No, don't. That's too nice. I want to feel your cock inside me first.'

Gael put her finger in her cleft and felt how slippery she was. She needed that length of flesh between her legs. Lifting Boo's skirt, she laid it along her back. Boo was naked underneath, her bottom pushed out as she knelt.

Quickly Gael went to a cabinet and took out a double-ended dildo. It slipped into her sex so easily she hardly felt it. The testicles at the junction of two supple rubber shafts nestled between her thighs as she knelt astride Boo's legs. Parting Boo's sexual lips with her thumbs, she slipped the dildo in.

Boo let out a breath of surprise but kept her face to the crack in the door. Gael pushed as hard as she could, needing to feel the pressure of the rubber hilt against her nub.

Boo clamped down as Gael pulled it out, holding the rubber in herself. That enabled Gael to withdraw from it and feel the solid head ripple down the tunnel of her sex. But she could not come.

Her vaginal muscles closed around the cock. Driving the other half into the kneeling voyeur, she hung on the intruding member, working herself gently on its stiffness, trying to break the dam of her tension. Then she withdrew and looked down at Boo, her bottom still bared. Her knees were wide apart. One shaft of the dildo protruded from the lips of her pulsing sexual purse. Gael knelt and worked it gently with her hand as they watched the bedroom scene.

Francine sat astride her man, facing him now, his baby-smooth scrotum hard against her pubis. For the first time, Gael could see that she was shaven too. Her mount was bare, the swell of it prominent against a taut, flat belly. Her breasts hung heavily as she worked herself against the man, the nipples as large as Sophie's, the nimbuses dark brown.

Anthony lay with his eyes closed, clearly enjoying feeling the slippery, hot vulva of the woman as she began to slide it down his cock. Holding it against the lips, she enclosed it between them, running it through her cleft, painting it with her moisture. As the plummy head nudged against her clitoris, she sighed, clearly savouring the sensation.

Then she got to work again. She took the shaver to his belly and his chest and swept away the whorls of fine, brown hair.

He reached out for her breasts and cupped them in large hands.

Gael wanted her breasts clutched too. And she needed that huge strength of the man between her legs. As she bent to the crack in the door she was becoming much more needy by the minute. Now she knew that she was anybody's if she wasn't careful. She slipped right out of her skin-tight suit which had become wet at the crotch from her excitement. She revelled in being naked once again. Her finger found her crevice and began to work it. Her nubbin was proud – as proud as it had ever been under the ministering tongue of Melindi Mocambo.

The insides of her legs began to tremble as she fixed her attention back on the couple on the bed.

Francine had finished her shaving. Now she was spreading musky oil on to the man's chest and belly. As the scent of it reached Gael's nostrils it shot straight to the centre of her forehead and made it throb. This seemed to make her breasts go tight and made her nubbin throb. She strummed it more.

Francine was working the oil into his cock now. She pushed his legs back and knelt between them. She bared his balls and his anal ring. Then she began to work him with her oily fingers, her long forefinger slipping deep into his anus.

He moaned and wriggled on it. His penis curved up stiffly. The head of it was glazed with oil, its profile sharp, its eye wide open. He closed his eyes and sighed.

While his eyes were closed, Francine delved into her bag and brought out some slender ropes with nooses at the ends. She slid them over his wrists, disguising the manoeuvre with her beguiling hands. Slipping the ropes around the brass bed head, she left them slack. Then she did the same to his ankles, massaging them and his calfs, making him sigh and smile.

When she spread his legs and pulled the ropes through the brass rails at the foot of the bed, he didn't notice. But, when she spread his arms above his head and pulled the ropes tight, he came to with a start. He tried to escape but Francine already had him fast.

'What are you doing, vixen?' he gasped as she stood on his chest. The note of alarm in his voice told Gael that this was not what he had planned. He probably had been humouring her by letting her shave him and thought he could turn her and spread her out then have her without any thought for what she wanted.

Gael smiled wryly.

Francine's eyes flashed as she looked down on him haughtily. 'I'm going to do you, mister. Now just lie still.'

He struggled but her weight on his chest held him down and made him gasp.

Then she stepped back. She stood between his legs and put one foot on his shaft, pressing it deep into his belly, her heel on his sac.

85

Gael trembled. She had to go back to the party, but found she could not move. She knelt behind Boo, looking over her shoulder, her knees astride the other woman's legs. And then she eased the dildo into her sleeve again and began to work it between herself and Boo.

'What's she going to do with him?' Boo whispered over her shoulder.

Gael shook her head. 'I don't know. But for Christ's sake be quiet or they'll hear us.'

They focused on the scene again. Francine had taken another cord. With her bottom to the man's face, she tied a noose and slipped it around his balls. He gasped as she pulled it tight, making his testicles bulge in their supple sac.

'Now,' Francine hissed over her shoulder. 'You're going to lick me off. Bite me and I'll tug your balls. Understand?'

'You bitch,' he barked and strained at the ropes.

She tugged the cord and made him wince. Then she eased herself backward until she was squatting over his face. Gael could see him looking up into her crotch. Gael's legs began to tremble more and her labia throbbed. She could feel the little veins in them pulsing as she closed them on the dildo. Her hands slipped under Boo's arms and took her breasts. Firm and round in her palms, they felt so warm. The nipples poked strongly. The little rings of bumps around the nimbuses were plain to Gael's light touch.

Boo pressed her bottom back against the double header and sighed, but did not take her eyes off the bedroom scene.

'Lick me,' Francine whispered. 'Lick me very slowly. If you don't please me, I'll tug your balls.'

She lowered herself on to him, sliding her knees apart. Gael watched with awe. She could imagine how it felt to have her vulva stretched so widely. The tension on the woman's inner thighs must have been so sensitising, the least touch might set her off.

The long tongue of the man came out. It ran slowly through the open lips between the woman's legs. She made a little sound of appreciation, and he licked again.

She wriggled to get closer contact, her knees spread wider apart, her hands on his chest, buttressing herself with her arms.

Gael's hands massaged Boo's tight breasts.

Boo began to saw herself backward on the dildo, pushing deeply into Gael as it came to the limit of her vaginal sleeve.

On the bed, Francine was working her vulva in small, tight circles on the tongue of the man. Her hands clawed at his chest, leaving white marks. His cock was as big as ever despite the noose around his testes. As Francine bore down on him, she picked up her panties from the bed and began to swipe at his penis. The panties were so flimsy they could not hurt him, but the soft whipping seemed to make the veins pulse strongly and the shaft rise up even more tautly from his belly.

Now she whipped between his legs, making him writhe. This seemed to have the right effect for Francine as she growled with pleasure to see him writhe. The woman moved position. 'Now – lick my arse, you conceited male,' she hissed. 'Lick me until I say you can stop.'

She closed her eyes as she felt his tongue.

Gael closed hers too. She worked harder on the dildo. She pulled on Boo's nipples and made her gasp.

Francine worked her bottom hard against the obedient tongue.

Gael clawed Boo's flank as Boo jabbed the dildo deeply into her cleft. Gael wriggled on it tightly, desperate now to make it push against that most wonderful of places just inside her sleeve.

Francine moaned and clawed at the heaving chest.

Then she turned and straddled Anthony again. She pulled his penis up and sank down on it slowly. In a second it was in her, her labia pressing on his pubis as she spread her legs.

'Slut,' he whispered, clearly liking every minute of her treatment now.

'Prick,' she gasped. 'Fuck me.'

'Why should I?'

'Because I'll screw your balls off if you don't.' She gave a demure little smile.

'Untie me and I'll do you properly.'

'And let you pin me to the bed while you fill me with your prick. Oh no. I'm not so naïve as that.'

'But you want it – don't you?'

'I want it the way I want it, not the way you do.' She drew herself off him and took a ribbed condom from her bag. She quickly rolled it down him then wiped it through the moisture in her sex. He tried to push back into her but she held him down. Then she repositioned herself, pushing the head of his penis against her anus.

'Not there,' he gasped but could not pull away.

'Yes,' she whispered as she held him stiffly upright and sank down on him. 'Ah, yes. My God, that's nice.'

Boo shuddered as she watched the man's erection disappear deep into the woman. The shudder transmitted itself to Gael through the rubber cock.

Gael could not stop herself from groaning, recalling how it felt to have a length of male flesh in her bottom. But she had not had a man like that for a long time. She closed her eyes and pushed down on the dildo. Trembling, Boo and she hung together, neither of them wanting to cease their watching so that they could bring each other to a climax. Gael knew that she would have to go in a few minutes. She prayed that the hairdresser would finish soon. But then he might start again once she let him free.

Francine was riding her stud now. Her hands cupped

her breasts, her fingers rubbing at the nipples as she rose and fell.

'Buck,' she hissed. 'I want to feel you, buck.'

'Like hell,' he groaned. 'I can't stand this any longer.'

'You'll stand it as long as I want you to.'

'But your arse is so tight I'm going to come.' He smiled grimly as if coming would spite her.

'Shoot and I'll wring your balls.' She threw her knickers in his face.

He inhaled deeply and smiled as if it pleased him to have her knickers there. 'Do your worst, you bitch.'

She took his belt from his trousers and began to whip his flanks. Recoiling from each blow made him judder. This seemed to goad her more. She whipped him faster, bringing red welts to his smooth, brown skin. His belly heaved and his shaven pubis ground against her nub. She bore down on his shaft, clearly trying to get more contact for her nubbin and the empty, stretched-out mouth of her sex.

Gael rode on the dildo between Boo and herself. She leant on Boo, rubbing her breasts on the sleek back. And as she rubbed she massaged Boo's breasts, pulling at the nipples to make them stand. It always gave her pleasure to do that to a woman, and made her own teats rise.

Now Francine leant right forward, her breasts hanging over the man. She lay on him, rubbing them against his chest. And still she rode him, the long shaft in her anus plunging deep as she pushed back.

Gael pulled the nipples of her kneeling partner as Boo worked her vulva on the cock. Gael pushed down on its stiff, hard rubber, wanting even more inside her sleeve. The whole scene made her feel so dirty; being penetrated in that way while watching Francine plunging on the man. 'My God,' Gael whispered to herself, 'I need a real one in me.'

Francine bit her slave's neck.

He winced then hissed. 'Stop that, you witch. Wait till I get free. I'll show you who's the boss.'

Francine smirked and ground her bottom on his shaft. 'Promises will get you nothing, Anthony, my dear. Now shaft me or I swear I'll squeeze your balls.'

'And then I won't be able to do you, you tart,' he hissed again.

She took his mouth passionately, riding on him hard. Gael sensed Francine was becoming frantic for her climax. His refusal to do just as she wanted was making her passion mount. Perhaps it was planned. Or perhaps he was just being stubbornly chauvinistic.

Francine stopped. Tears ran down her cheeks as she lay panting, her breasts squashed hard on his.

'Bastard,' she whispered between gasps for air. 'Why are men such bastards, Boo?'

Gael stopped kneading Boo's breasts, and Boo's vulva stopped its motion on the slick shaft of the dildo.

Francine looked towards the door. 'You can come out, Boo. I know you're there.'

7

Trussed and Betrayed

Gael shrank back from the bathroom door, worried that Francine had spotted her as well. She pulled the double-headed dildo from the lips of Boo's slick sex, leaving the other half deep inside herself. As she glanced down she saw what a man would see – a huge and slick phallus erupting from her crotch.

Boo stood slowly but didn't go into the bedroom where Francine sat astride Anthony, his penis still buried in her bottom.

'For Christ's sake, Boo,' he snarled. 'Come out. We know you're there.' His voice broke with his anger. 'Come out and untie me. I'm going to give this bitch something she'll remember for a long time. Then I'll have you too, you sneak. I'm sure that's what you want – isn't it?'

Francine struck him hard across the cheek. Then she put her hands behind herself and gripped his testes. 'One more peep out of you and you'll be singing alto.' She sliced a finger across her throat to reinforce the sentiment. 'And for hell's sake, Boo – come out. This useless prick can't make me come. I need a woman's tongue.'

Gael pushed Boo gently in the back. She didn't want Francine to come in and find her there as well. Boo went meekly. The bathroom door swung almost shut behind her. After a minute, Gael dared to look again.

Boo stood demurely before the double bed. Francine had stripped her naked. Boo seemed not to know quite what to do.

Francine pushed her down. 'Kneel.'

Boo knelt – cowed before the fired-up Francine; her sapphire eyes were alight with lust, her breasts swinging as she moved.

Francine turned and leant upon the bed. She spread her legs and pushed her vulva out at Boo.

Boo needed no more orders. She put her mouth to the swollen lips and licked them tenderly, closing her eyes as if the succulent flesh was the essence of a gourmet meal.

Francine sighed then growled at the man as he watched them from the bed. 'Why couldn't you lick me out like this? Why did you have to eat me and chew me instead of savouring me like she does?'

Boo sucked Francine with great finesse, pulling her elongated clitoris between her lips. Her nose pushed deep into the proffered cleft as Francine spread her feet and pushed back more. Then she began to wriggle on Boo's mouth. She moved her bottom in small circles.

Boo thrust her nose between the pulsing labia, rubbing it up and down as she worked the nubbin with her mouth.

Francine began to moan. She stripped the condom off the man and pulled his penis up. Then, taking it like a lollipop, she sucked in unison with the working of Boo's mouth between her legs.

The man began to move his hips. He thrust into her mouth. Boo's fingers scored her down the legs with long, red nails.

Gael was on her knees now, her hand on the rubber phallus stuck in her vagina. She worked it like a man would do as he pulled himself to climax, each pull rubbing at her clitoris, each thrust driving the other half inside her.

Francine's breathing shortened as Anthony thrust up hard, into her mouth. Boo took long, deep licks from the nubbin to the ring, dragging her tongue as deeply as she could through the spread lips of the vulva. It opened and closed as Francine worked the muscles of her thighs.

Anthony writhed and ground his cock into the woman's mouth, and Francine shuddered deeply as she pushed back hard on Boo. Boo clawed her inner thighs and bit her thigh where the inner surface met the soft flesh of her vulva.

Gael worked the dildo in frantic, shortened strokes, gripping it about the glans, widening her stance. She came with a little tremor which started in the hollows of her loins and spread up to her womb. But she didn't climax fully. She needed more. She needed that real, hot cock that Francine had thrusting into her mouth.

Anthony tried to bring himself to climax but the hairdresser withdrew. Then she put her tongue to his shaft and began to lick it slowly underneath the glans. When he tensed his belly she stopped. She was judging him to a T, preventing him from spurting while she derived her pleasure from the act.

The women licked and sucked and rasped at the flesh before them. Then Francine came. Gael watched her thighs as they quivered, the open cleft clamping hard then opening once again to Boo's probing.

Now Boo sprang up. She pushed Francine aside, then straddled the man's hips and drove herself on his shaft. She plucked at her nipples and thrust out her breasts, putting back her head and giving a long, deep cry.

Francine lay on the rug, her eyes shut tight. She worked her nubbin in small, circular motions, her legs spread widely so Gael could see the deep gash of her cleft. Beyond the black of her stocking tops, the hollows of her loins were pale. The fair hair of her pubis was gold against the sheerness of the stockings. Her furrow

93

chafed against the hardness of the man, pulsing steadily now that she had come.

Boo squeezed herself on to the phallus pushing up inside her, as Anthony pushed on to his own climax. She clawed at his belly and his chest. When he tensed and pushed his hips up, she slapped him down. Then just as quickly as she had mounted him, she pulled herself up. She let his cock lie flat against his belly, rubbed herself over it once and stood.

Gael sank to the floor, the rubber cock clamped hard inside her tight sleeve. She needed to come again. She was as horny as a bitch on heat.

Francine rose. She looked at Boo and smirked. 'I think we've wrung the most out of him, don't you?'

Boo kissed her lightly on the lips. 'I think we have. But what do we do about him?'

Francine gave Anthony a cursory glance. 'I think we'll leave him for someone else. I know one or two that might like a ride on this.'

He spat at her as she worked his foreskin seductively. 'Let me go, you tart, I'm not lying here while any of your cronies have their lascivious way with me.'

Francine shrugged. 'You've got no choice. And if you're so particular about who you screw, I think we'll have to blindfold you. Just concentrate on how they feel as they suck your prick between their legs or rub their quims along it. I'm sure you'll like it, even though you might protest.' Without more ado, she stripped her black stockings off and wound them tightly around his head, making certain that he couldn't see. She threw Boo her dress and pulled on her own. Then she took Boo by the hand and led her out.

Gael knelt by the bathroom door. She hardly dared to breathe. She knew that she should leave as well. The guests would be wondering where she was. And if she was to put the next part of the plan into action, she mustn't wait too long. It was already nearly ten o'clock.

Then she thought, what the hell, as she looked at the naked man tied up on the bed. His penis was up hard, his belly pumping from exertion. Perhaps the excitement of being tied and blindfolded was keeping him stimulated. Perhaps he was thinking about another woman coming to enjoy him and hoping she would bring him off.

Gael tried to leave, but the pull of that great, long cock was too great for her to resist. Her need to climax was growing stronger by the second.

She slipped into the bedroom, went to the door and locked it from the inside. Why should she not be one of the women who might come to play with Anthony? She brought a bowl of hot water, a flannel and some soap.

'Who's there?' His voice was anxious.

She wrapped his cock in the hot flannel and made him start. He tried to break his bonds.

'Shhh,' she whispered in his ear. 'It's only me.'

'Who's me?'

She laughed. 'A woman with a deep-seated need for a long cock like yours.'

'Then you can go to hell.'

She lathered it liberally, washed off the suds and dabbed it dry. As she kissed under the glans of his penis, it rose from his belly and curved. 'This seems to want me,' she whispered as she licked his sac, smooth from being shaved.

He thrashed his head. 'Oh no. I don't think I can stand this.'

'Would you like me to make you come with my tongue? Or shall I rub my quim on this?' She stroked him from his glans down to his scrotum.

'I'd rather fuck you properly. Just untie me and I'll show you what this can do.' He pumped his phallus up and made the veins stand out.

'Thanks a lot, but what do you mean by "properly"?'

'With your legs pushed back and my cock inside your hole, you tart. You know that's what you want.'

She laughed and pulled his foreskin down and licked the groove of his glans, delighting in the way it swelled and the whole erection twitched. 'Perhaps I'm a lesbian,' she whispered. 'Perhaps all I want is for you to lick my pussy.'

He groaned. 'Not another dyke. I don't think I can stand this. Why don't you just lie back and let me do you? I'm sure you'd get to like it once you tried it.'

'We can't have everything we want in life, you know.' She put her mouth over his glans and sucked it gently.

'It's not much to ask, is it?' There was a note of humour in his voice now. 'At one time that was all a woman wanted.'

She licked his scrotum and up along the shaft until she reached the web. 'But we women are more independent now, you know. We don't just want to lie there with our legs apart being screwed by some mindless brute.' She took the whole shaft deep into her mouth.

'OK. So I'll fuck you gently.'

'As I said, it's very kind of you to offer.' She laughed. 'But I think I'd rather have this my own way.' She plunged her mouth down on him until his glans touched the back of her throat.

'I could do you from behind.'

'Like an animal, you mean?'

'A lot of women like it that way. They like the feel of it ramming against their bottoms.'

'And a lot of women would rather ride it and take it at their own pace instead of being pounded into the bed springs.' She sat astride him and pulled his penis up. The head glistened with her saliva. It was beautifully swollen. The veins pumped strongly and she thought she felt it pulse. Quickly, she rose to her knees and placed the head against her vulva. She worked it through her crevice until it was fully lubricated with her nectar. 'Yes,' she whispered to herself, 'that's so, so nice.'

'Tart,' he hissed.

She slapped his belly. 'Prick. Lie still.' She lowered herself on to it just as slowly as the other women had. She felt the large head opening her out. She felt it ripple deep into the sleeve of her vagina. Now it was at her extremity. Her vulval lips were spread about its base. She moved to get better contact for her nubbin. Now she worked the muscles of her loins. She squeezed him tightly. That was so nice – it was so hard and so strong. She could feel the veins pumping inside herself. She could feel the head of it in her belly as she pushed down with her fingers.

She rose and sank back on it to make the head push hard against the roof of her vagina. It found the spot which sent ripples of delight right up through her belly.

She began to ride him faster as he began to heave his hips. He bucked high under her, trying to come inside her. She was glad she'd kept in her contraceptive coil in case he did.

But she could not come. Perhaps the small orgasm earlier had taken the edge off her need. She still had that ache but without the explosive tension which went with it.

She sank down on to his torso, her legs spread along his thighs, her breasts against his chest.

'Let me go and I'll do you nicely,' he whispered as she rested, pleasure from his penetration coursing through her body.

'How "nicely"?' she whispered back.

'Whatever way you want it. What makes you come the best?'

'It depends on my mood.' She listened to his heartbeat speed.

'What mood are you in now?'

'I don't really know. I like the feel of your cock, and I want to come – but there's something missing.'

'We could experiment. I'll shaft you very slowly if you like.'

She sighed at the thought as she imagined it. 'I don't think I want it slowly.'

'Would you like me to fuck you brutally and fast?'

'I'm not sure I want it "brutally" tonight. And anyway, I must go in a minute. I can't lie here with your prick in me. I've got guests to see to.'

He laughed aloud. 'You're Gael, aren't you?'

She cursed herself. But it didn't really matter.

He pushed in hard. 'As my hostess, aren't you supposed to be pleasing me?'

'I'm not here for guests to screw.'

'What are you here for then?'

'I'm here to see that people have a good time, whatever that might mean.'

'But I've been having a lousy time. It's not my idea of fun being tied to a bed while a whole procession of lustful women have their wicked way with me.'

'I'm sorry. But it wasn't me who tied you up.'

'If you're sorry, make amends. Let me fuck you.'

'Perhaps another time. I really must go now.' She rose to squat astride him again, savouring the sensation of having a penis buried in her. It seemed so long since she'd had a large, thick one like this. Of course she could have had Flanders', but she was reserving that. She still intended to have it when and where she wanted it and in the way she wanted it.

He ground his pubis against her nub. 'Are you going to untie me before you leave?'

She crossed her arms over his chest and looked down at him, her finger running circles around his nipple. He really was a handsome brute. And with his shaft still pulsing and making little pushing motions inside her, she was very reluctant to go. But she doubted she would come now, even if she rode him hard.

'I'll let you go if you promise to behave.'

'What do you mean by "behave"?'

'Lie still until I've gone. Then you can dress and come down.'

'All right.'

'Promise? On your honour?'

'On my honour.'

She pushed herself up and splayed her legs widely, feeling his length again before she pulled herself off it. As she removed the blindfold he grinned.

'I fancied you from the moment I saw you.'

'Well, you can *unfancy* me. You promised on your honour to behave.'

'Don't you trust me?'

'I never trust a man when his cock's up like a pole.' Slowly she undid the ropes at his ankles. He brought his legs up and spread his knees. She thought that he was only doing it to show her his balls as his cock lay along his belly, the head of it at his navel. It was a real brute of a thing and she began to think that she was mad to leave it just lying there. So – she tried to ignore him. But seeing a man display his genitals always turned her on.

Now she eased herself along his belly, loving its warmth between her legs.

He lay still as she released one wrist. Then she made a mistake. Instead of getting off him and going round to the other side of the bed, she leant over him. He reached up and took a nipple in his lips.

She pulled back and glared. 'I told you to behave.'

He smirked. 'I am behaving – like a man wanting a woman. Anyway, if you will hang your tit in my face, you should expect it to get sucked.'

She slapped his arm playfully, energy coursing through her. This was getting dangerous. Was that what she really wanted? Was that what she was doing it for?

The final knot was tight and it took some time to free it. All the time, Gael was conscious of her breasts swinging just above his lips and the moistness of her vulva rubbing on his chest.

She sighed with relief as the rope went loose at last. Then things happened so fast, they were a blur.

He grabbed her and pulled her down beside himself. She twisted to get free. But now he flipped her on her front, his whole weight on her back to hold her down. He pinned her arms to her sides and bit her neck.

She tried to wriggle, but he was too heavy for her. 'Let go of me, you pig,' she gasped. 'You gave your word of honour.'

'But I'm not a very honourable man. And anyway, you said you never trusted a man whose cock was like a pole. You were right, my sweet. Now you're going to feel it where you like it most of all.'

As he held Gael down, his whole weight on her back, she wriggled harder but he was too strong for her to escape.

He bit her shoulder. She yelped but could not move.

Then he pushed her legs apart with his ankles. She felt the heat and the hardness of his phallus in the crevice of her bottom. She felt it nose between the twin swells of her sex, then gasped as he drove it in hard. In one thrust he had it in her. She was so slippery from the accumulated stimulation of the evening that its whole length went to her limits.

He withdrew and thrust again, this time with more vigour, letting out a howl of pleasure as she clamped down on him hard in an effort to stop him penetrating her. She loved the way they pushed when she did that.

She wriggled to make him think that she wanted to escape, but really to feel him better.

He stretched her legs out wider and pushed again, feeling her compliance as she relaxed her muscles and let him slide right in.

'Bastard,' she croaked into the pillow.

'Slut,' he whispered as he drove in again, the hardness of his pubic bone jarring on her anus.

'My God,' she whispered to herself, 'that's nice.'

'It's very nice,' he whispered back. 'You've got a gorgeous cunt. Squeeze me with it again.'

100

'Shut up talking about it, will you. Just do it, for God's sake. Fuck it hard. I need to come, blast you.'

Now he held her strongly, bringing her wrists up to the centre of her back so that her breasts were thrust hard into the bed. He bore down on her, pivoting on his arms, flexing his hips so he could drive into her repeatedly with power. Each jab took her breath away. Each withdrawal left her wanting more.

'Feel that,' he gasped with every thrust.

'Yes,' she rasped, 'I can. But fuck me harder, you brute. I need to come. *Jeees*, I need to come.'

He took her at her word. He became almost bestial, seeming to lose all restraint. But it was what she wanted. It was what she had needed ever since she'd watched the gardener with her housemaid at the lake.

The sensation between Gael's legs was exquisite. It was a mixture of pain and intense pleasure. But still she could not climax.

When he withdrew from her, her labia seemed cold without his heat. Then she felt the strong shaft nosing at her anus. She pushed her bottom up to it. The whole of her body trembled as the head popped through her ring. The muscle of her anus shrieked with the pleasure-pain that brought.

He took her steadily and strong, she grunting out her tension as he pushed her into the mattress.

She came in a flood of nectar and muscular contractions. The whole of her body racked on him, the muscle of her anal ring closing on him tightly.

'My God, that's so, so beautiful,' she gasped.

'You wanted that all the time, didn't you, you vixen?' He entered her again, working his shaft in circles as her muscles clamped and opened, making her judder with escaping tension. The whole of her body went stiff then she relaxed.

When he pulled out of her, he drove himself up between the cheeks of her bottom. The loose skin of his scrotum rubbed her anus nicely, keeping her sensations going. As he parted the cheeks with his thumbs to stretch her anal ring, she pushed up, pressing it against him, wanting him inside it once again.

He turned her, eased her legs back to spread her wide and looked down with pleasure at the engorged purse of her sex. As he aimed his penis at it, working the foreskin, she peered down through the valley of her breasts.

Then he spurted against the hot lips of her sex and she felt the semen trickle down her furrow. The second spurt reached her ring. As he changed his aim, the third one shot over her belly and landed between her breasts. She licked it off her skin, the salty tang sending more ripples of excitement through her throbbing nub. A man's come always had that effect on her.

He straddled her belly, his penis lying between her breasts. She pushed them together, squeezing the last drops of his come from the eye.

'Bastard,' she grinned.

He put his head back and laughed. 'Aren't all men bastards?'

She pulled his penis hard. 'Not as big a bastard as you. I haven't been fucked so beautifully for months.'

8

Secret Confessions

The babble of small-talk ceased instantly as a figure, dressed in a hooded robe, passed through the party throng. The face was hidden by a cowl, the hands clasped inside the sleeves. Silently, the figure went through the open French windows and across the sunken garden. The watchers could see its progress through the gateway in the garden wall. They focused on the tall, black form until it melted into the shadow of the doorway of the little chapel on the far edge of the lawns. Then a riot of chattering voices broke the silence.

All pretended not to notice as, a short while later, a tall, athletically built man followed in the footsteps of the black-clad figure. But all attention was glued to his back until he too disappeared through the doorway of the chapel. Again the house was filled with babble and a riot of speculation.

With her heart pounding, Gael sat in the darkness of the confessional box, wondering if anyone would be curious enough to come. They had been told of her reputation for holding exciting parties, and she guessed they would assume that this one would have a unique twist to it.

As the chapel door squeaked open, she felt a draught waft through the curtains of the box. Gael stiffened.

When the seat next door to her creaked and she heard

103

harsh breathing, her pulse began to pound. She pulled herself together and spoke in a voice that she had practised – as deep as she could make it.

'And what might I do for you, my child?' She knew that the supplicants would know that it was her, but it was important to keep up the theatricality of the occasion.

'Forgive me, Father, for I have sinned.' The reply was soft, but the voice was deep. She judged that the man was in his late twenties. Who could that be? Quickly she recalled the guest list. But there were too many men of that description to choose one on such a slight clue.

'And how have you sinned, my son?'

'I keep looking at women, Father.'

'Looking at them?'

'Yes. In the health club I own.'

'And how is that a sin?'

'I watch them stripping themselves after swimming, their skins all glistening with water, the hair between their legs dripping as they rub their pussies dry.'

'And do they object to you looking at them while they're naked?'

'They don't know that I watch them. As they bend and dry their feet, they don't realise that I can see every little fold of their quims and every little hair around the fringes.'

Gael took a deep breath. 'Then how do you watch them in such detail without them knowing?' She quelled a note of interest in her voice.

'I have one-way mirrors in the changing rooms. And I use powerful binoculars. I know it's a sin but I just can't keep myself from watching.'

'And is that the whole of your sin?'

'No, Father. I have a fantasy.'

'What is your fantasy, my son?'

'I want the women in my club to be naked as they exercise. I want to see them lying on the benches with

104

their legs apart as they use the apparatus. I want to see their breasts bouncing freely as they jog on the treadmills. I want to see the lips between their legs open and close with the tension as they bend with the hand weights and touch the floor.'

'And if you were able to do this, would you be cured of your fantasy?'

There was a pause. 'If I was able to do that, I'm sure I would be cured, Father.'

'And what are you willing to do in return for such a boon?'

'I would give generously to a charity of your choosing.'

Gael smiled. 'Then perhaps the good Lord will provide for your salvation. But should you not give up your desire once it has been fulfilled, you may be punished severely.'

There was a sigh from the other side. 'That is another of my sins, Father. I enjoy being chastised. I have a fantasy to be tied hand and foot and to have my bottom whipped by the women when they find me watching them exercising without their clothes.'

'Then I think you will be punished hard, my son. Is that all you have to confess?'

There was another pause. Gael could hear him breathing deeply through the brass grille of the box.

'I have another problem, Father.'

'And what is that?' Gael's voice was trembling.

'I have a tail between my legs which keeps on swelling.'

'When does it do that?'

'When I watch the women. The sight of their hairy cracks make it swell up. It goes very stiff.'

'How large does it swell?'

'May I show you?'

There was a small wooden door in the partition of the box. Gael presumed it was there to allow the votive offerings to be passed to the priest. It opened, and, in the dim light, something long and pale appeared.

'See how it grows, Father.'

Yes – she could see. It was very slim and curved, the glans much larger than most she had seen.

'The only way to stop it swelling is by rubbing it,' he said wistfully.

'I see.' She did see. The shaft was hardening by the second.

'Would you heal it to stop it swelling, Father? Please. I would give anything if you would do so. Put a blessing on it so it may be cured.'

Gael touched the web under the glans with the tip of her finger. The shaft did a little spring and swelled further. Now she began to work the foreskin slowly, excitement from the act making her own erectile tissues rise. Her nipples hardened and she felt the leaves of her sex first warm then swell.

Working the organ until it strained, she heard its owner panting. Now she cupped his testes, weighing them carefully, and rubbed her wrist up and down his shaft. She drove her finger deeply into the loose skin of the scrotum so that it pulled the foreskin taut.

'Oh, Father, that makes it swell even more. Kindly anoint it with your holy oil.'

Gael thought for a moment and then smiled. She took a small hip flask of brandy liqueur she had carried beneath her habit for Dutch courage, and wetted the tip of the phallus rearing beside her.

There was a gasp from next door. She knew that the liqueur would sting him.

'Oh, Father, I must be wicked. That's the heat of the devil. Please cool it with a soothing balm.'

She knelt and slipped her lips over the shaft, savouring the brandy which made her mouth warm nicely. It was such a stimulating taste that she began to suck on it steadily, licking up the drops of brandy which had run

106

down to his scrotum. She rubbed more in, sure that this would bring such stinging heat to the wrinkled skin that he would beg for her to cool it.

'Ah – I have been wicked and this is my penance,' he moaned. 'Kindly cool the devil's heat and make this tail go limp.'

She knelt and licked between his balls, tonguing him with long strokes. Now she was exhilarated, both with the brandy and the act of pleasuring the man in such a secret way. She didn't even know who he was.

She closed his foreskin over the glans and held it, knowing that the brandy would warm it. As she held it she licked his sac, sucking on his balls. But when she felt him tense and shudder, she slipped both her hands over the spouting head and enclosed it so that it filled her palms with a copious gush. He let out a sigh of relief. As she held him, bathing him in his own fluid, the shaft went limp.

'That's a miracle,' he sighed. 'You've cured me of my affliction, Father. How may I repay you?'

'You may leave your offering on the plate, my son. I shall make certain it reaches those who need it.'

'And may I come again?'

'Come?'

'May I confess my sins to you again?'

'You may.' She opened her habit and anointed her breasts with the thick cream from his spurt, making the nipples rise. 'But first you have to overcome your fantasy.'

'And how might I do that?'

'Leave your card with the hostess of the party. She'll give you a time and date when your fantasy may be fulfilled and you may be rid of it for ever. But, be warned, you will be chastised soundly by the naked women should they catch you. So take great care.'

'Forgive me, Father, for I have sinned.'

Gael took a deep breath. Some time had passed since

107

the first confessant had left. She had sat in the box wondering whether anyone else would come. Twice she had thought that she heard someone in the chapel. But when she had peeked out of the box, the place had been empty, the door closed tight.

Now the slight Scottish brogue of a woman on the other side of the box was quite plain to her. Lady Jannine Wellington-Moncrief was quite a catch. She had a reputation for prudishness. Now, Gael thought, she would perhaps find out just what made Lady Jannine tick.

'And what is your sin, my child?' Gael said, again in as masculine a voice as she could manage.

'I have a fantasy that I cannot rid myself of, Father. What shall I do?'

'What is your fantasy, my child?'

'I'm fascinated by the . . .'

'By the what?'

'By what hangs between a man's legs.'

'And where is the sin in that?'

'I have lustful impulses.' There was a little sigh which told Gael that the supplicant was indulging herself in picturing her fantasy.

'And what are the lustful impulses which bother you?'

'I desire to experience a man.'

'Many women have that same desire, my child. The Lord has enjoined that desire in us in order to . . .'

'Yes, I know, Father. But I don't want the man. I only want his . . .'

'His?'

'His thing. I want to toy with it and make it rise up stiff and put it between my legs and feel it as it spurts. I want to put my mouth over it and suck on it. I want to lick the eggs that hang in the bag beneath it. But I don't want him. Just his thing.'

Gael frowned to herself. This was a tall order. Of course Lady Jannine might use the same kind of rubber

108

replica she and Boo had used. She might do whatever she liked with that kind of toy. But Gael knew that was not what the lady needed. Sometimes she had had thoughts herself about having those attributes of a man to her heart's desire without his ego or his impetuousness to take control over her. She thought about how she might meet the lady's wishes and her own.

'Can you help me, Father? I'm desperate to live my fantasy out and feel what I need to feel.'

'I'm sure that can be arranged, my child. And now that you have confessed your desire, I'm sure that the Lord will provide a solution to your problem. What penance are you prepared to do to have your sin absolved?'

'I'll give anything, Father, if only I can rid myself of these desires.'

'Then contact the hostess of the party in the morning and I'm sure she will be able to guide you towards your salvation.'

As Lady Jannine left the box, Gael began to form a plan. Only ten minutes passed before the door creaked again. The idea of confessions seemed to be catching on. Gael wondered how many more there might be before the party ended.

'Forgive me, Father, for I have sinned.' The voice was cultured and mellow. Gael thought of two possible identities.

'And what is your sin, my son?'

'I have recurring dreams.'

'And why is that a sin?'

'The dreams are of carnal lust. I wake up sweating in the night with my cock as hard as iron.'

'And why is that a problem?'

'It won't spurt when I rub it.'

'Do you ever have a woman in your bed?'

'Oh yes – sometimes a different one each night. But it won't spurt when I fuck them, either.'

'Why's that?'

'Because of the dream.'

'What happens in the dream?'

There was a pause. Gael could hear him breathing heavily.

'In the dream I meet a wise old man dressed in white. He tells me that if I want to spurt I must take six women at once.'

'That's quite a lot.' Immediately, Gael started thinking of six women who might want to play this game.

The breathing on the other side of the screen became more laboured. 'The old man leads me into a room where six women sit around. I'm naked and they're dressed in short skirts and tight tops. I can almost see the hairs of their quims through their flimsy panties as their skirts ride up about their thighs. And their nipples poke out hard through the material of their tops.'

He stopped.

'What happens next in your dream?'

'The old man says I must show what a man I am by fucking each one in a different way. Only when I get to the sixth will I spurt. Then I must make her suck me as I pump into her mouth.'

Gael took a long, deep breath.

'The problem is the women take no notice of me when I walk into that room. They carry on talking and sipping tea as if I were not there.'

'So what do you do?'

'I wrestle them one at a time while the others continue to talk and eat cucumber sandwiches. I strip their knickers off and take each one in a different way.'

Gael could imagine the scene quite vividly. But who would want to play his game?

'Go on, my son,' she prompted.

'After I've done the fifth one, I'm so horny it's almost painful. But when I turn to take the sixth one, I find she's gone. I chase after her but she always evades me.

110

The old man says that if I can catch her and rip her knickers off, I will be able to fuck her properly and then come. But I don't ever catch her. Then I wake up sweating. What should I do, Father?'

Gael thought carefully before she spoke. 'So your problem would be solved once you'd caught and had the sixth woman?'

'The old man says it would.'

'And there must be six?'

'It wouldn't work with less.'

'And if your fantasy is resolved, what are you prepared to do for penance?'

'Anything you say, Father. I'm a man of considerable wealth. If only I could find six women who would serve my need, I would be eternally grateful.'

When the last confessant had left, Gael decided to take a break. She needed to see how things were going at the party. She stretched and took a long, deep breath.

She closed the black curtains and was about to leave when there was a sound behind her. She tried to turn but was not quick enough. Someone took her from behind and encircled her in strong arms.

'Get off me,' she rasped as the arms tightened across her chest, stopping her from breathing. She struggled, but could not free herself. Her hands groped behind her and felt something loose and soft. The material of a tracksuit?

A wide mouth bit her neck. 'I've come to confess, *Father*,' a deep voice growled.

She threw her head back. 'You're too late, whoever you are. Confession's over.'

'But I have a fantasy.' He whispered the words so she couldn't recognise his voice.

She tried to turn but could not. 'I said you're too late. You should've come when the others came.'

'I did come.'

111

Now she drove her elbows into his ribs and managed to get free. But the light was very dim and all she could see was a black silhouette against the greyness of a window.

'Then if you did come, I've heard your confession already. Who are you?'

He placed his hands on his hips and stood with his legs apart. 'I didn't come into the box.'

'What do you mean?'

'I was here before you came, sitting on the floor behind the confessional all the time.'

'You were waiting in here before I arrived?'

'I wanted to see why you needed the confessional cleaned.' He pulled her to himself and bit her neck.

She pushed him off. 'Get off me, Flanders, you sneak. You can consider yourself fired.'

He thrust her back against the confessional box and took her mouth so she couldn't protest. Then he opened her robe and pushed it aside to bare her breasts to the cool night air.

'What do you think you're doing?' she protested even though she knew perfectly well.

He laughed. 'I'm getting in the habit.'

'My God, that's so corny. Now, let me go.'

'Not until you've heard my confession.'

'Go to hell.'

'I probably shall unless you let me confess, *Father*.'

'That was a game to amuse my guests.'

'You're fond of games, aren't you, miss? Well – I'm going to play a game with you.'

'Do your worst.' She threw back her head defiantly.

'Hear my confession, and then I'll do my worst. Or perhaps you might think it's my best.'

'Get off me.'

'Hear my confession for I have sinned.' He bit her neck again and pressed himself hard against her pubis.

'You'll burn in hell for this.'

'I shall if I continue to have fantasies about a certain woman. Let me confess my wildest dreams so I might be absolved.'

'What woman do you mean?'

'A sensual creature who pretends she doesn't want me, but who flaunts herself around me and leads me on. A witch who teases me then shuts me out.'

'Then you deserve everything she gives you, you jerk.'

'But it doesn't serve my needs. I have thoughts about her that I can't get out of my head.'

'I can imagine the kind of thoughts you have.'

His hand was around her naked bottom now, the long fingers slipping through its crevice. He pulled her to himself so that her pubis was hard against his erection.

'I have wicked thoughts. I want to take her to the stable loft and hang her by her ankles, her legs open, her quim level with my mouth.'

'Pervert.'

'And I want to lick her as she wriggles and struggles against my tongue and pleads with me to make her come.'

'Don't kid yourself that I'd plead with you for anything.'

'And she might swear that she wouldn't plead. But I'd run a feather up and down the inside of her thighs, and stroke her quim so nicely that she'd be driven to distraction. And when she finally pleaded with me to bring her off, I'd pluck at her nipples and bite her in the hollows of her groin.'

Gael was trembling and she knew that he would feel her.

'And when she'd almost come, I'd cut her down and leave her lying in the hay, begging me to fuck her.'

'Bastard.' It was whispered as Gael found her anger melting. She was softening in his arms with the sensations he was instilling in her. The thought of being hung up by the ankles and sucked between the legs was making her excited beyond all reason.

She sighed before she could stop herself. Then she hardened her manner. 'And now, if you've finished, you can let me go.'

'But I've got two other fantasies to confess.'

'Keep them to yourself.'

He whispered them in her ear and sent his tongue in after the words. The graphic descriptions which he gave made her tremble.

He sucked her earlobe. 'But now I'm going to teach that woman a lesson. I'm going to finish what she started in the scullery.'

Gael began to struggle but he held her by the wrists. When he wrestled her to the stone floor, only her robe kept her from yelping from its coldness.

She felt him immediately, strong between her legs. He must have slipped his tracksuit down sometime during the banter and bared himself so he was ready to have her at the slightest chance.

His shaft was hot against the coldness of the air. He held her arms above her head and eased slowly into her so that she felt the heat of it, a millimetre at a time. It seemed ages until she sensed the prickliness of his scrotum between the hollows of her inner thighs and instinctively widened her legs so that he could fill her fully.

Then he drew out, just as slowly, holding her down hard, the whole of his weight squashing her breasts, his belly rasping against hers.

'Is that slow enough for you, miss?' He pushed against her clitoris with the root of his erection. Then he withdrew just as slowly and tantalisingly.

'It makes no difference how slow or fast you do it. You won't make me like it.'

But he did. He kept the slow, long strokes going steadily, pressing briefly on her clitoris each time, until she wanted to scream at him to take her hard and fast. But she would not scream like Sophie had. She would not give him that satisfaction.

His mouth came down on hers.

She tried to turn away but he matched her movement and kissed her tenderly. Again she felt her anger melting. Despite his brashness, he seemed to know how to take a woman with passion.

'And I have this fantasy,' he whispered, 'to have a woman underneath me, with my cock deep in her cunt, while she writhes and screams at me repeatedly to fuck her hard.'

'You can forget anything like that, you pig. I'd never beg a brute like you.'

He bit her neck playfully and whispered, 'Assuage my need, *Father*, and I'll reward you well.' He continued his slow motions between her legs, occasionally biting at her neck, and landing little kisses on her lips.

Now she wanted to come. She needed release again. The whole of her body was alight from the stimulation of hearing other people's fantasies. And she was trembling from the strength and audacity of this man as he worked on her without a pause.

At last she could stand it no longer. 'All right. You win. Fuck me, Flanders.' She said it to herself, more than to him. It was barely audible, but he heard it.

'Ah, so she prays and repents. Say it louder, my child, and your prayers will be answered.'

'I've said it once. You've won. I hope it does your damned ego good. Screw me and let me go.'

He took her strongly, each stroke driving deeply into her so that her breasts bounced as he lifted himself on his hands. She felt the curve of his penis as he arched his back and thrust. She felt his testicles knocking against the softness of her bottom. Now she wound her legs around his hips so she was stretched widely for him to push down into her.

She came as he wanted her to, wriggling on him and gasping, 'Fuck me. Oh God, that feels so good.' But still she did not come as fully as she had when Anthony had taken her from behind.

Then she felt the heat of Flanders' ejaculation on her belly before he rubbed his scrotum up and down her, using the lubrication of his semen and her nectar to slide in. He slipped over her, rubbing his scrotum on her pubis, over her navel and then between her breasts. The tip of his penis pushed under her chin, its wetness leaving a trail of his living fluid on her skin. The scent of it drove her to need him again already. She needed a longer, more explosive orgasm. Now she bent her neck and captured his cock in her mouth, sucking on it lightly.

He pulled it away from her, rubbed his sac over her face and let her kiss it. But then he rose and looked down on her smugly as he forced her legs apart with his feet, her body glistening with his seed, her sex lips still moving with her orgasm.

'You two-faced little minx,' he whispered, pushing his toe between the lips of her sex, opening it out as he rubbed her nub.

'You're fired,' she hissed, and closed her legs on his toe as he continued to wiggle it.

He shrugged as he stood back from her, the moonlight highlighting his shaft. It was standing just as stiff as it had when he'd abandoned Sophie by the lake. So he was one of those men who could keep it up for ages.

He turned to leave, his penis jogging as he moved. 'Good night, miss. Leave your donation for the service on the plate. I'll see you in the morning.'

9

A Change of Gear

Gael wrapped the habit tightly around herself. She skirted the woods and entered the stable yard so as not to be seen approaching the house. She wanted to shower and wash away Todd Flanders' semen. She wanted to put on some decent clothes. The charade of the confessional was over, for that night, at least. But she felt that the game which she and Flanders were playing had hardly begun.

A red Ferrari stood in the shadows by the coach-house. Bentleys and Jaguars hemmed it in. Its hood was down and the engine was running. As Gael watched, it rocked. She approached it from behind, curious to see what was making it move.

The occupants were quite unaware of her, they were so engrossed in their game. The seats were angled almost flat. A blond-haired man reclined behind the wheel, dabbing the accelerator pedal occasionally to make the car vibrate. His penis reared powerfully from his trousers. Gael could see in the rear-view mirror that his eyes were closed.

His companion was one of the girls who had come in see-through tops. She knelt in the centre of the car, facing to the rear, a knee on each black leather seat. With her skirt up around her head, she had bared her lower body. Even if she looked up she would not have seen Gael standing in the shadow in her robe, the cowl obscuring her face.

'Brrm, brrm,' he whispered and dabbed the throttle as the girl gripped his penis. 'First gear now.'

She pulled his shaft as if she were changing gear.

'Brrm, brrm. Change it into second, darling, and drive me into ecstasy. You do it so very well.'

As she worked it to and fro, her bottom bobbed, the cheeks almost brushing the polished dash.

Now Gael realised what they were doing. The girl was crouched over the gear stick. She seemed to have it deep between her legs. And as he revved the engine, Gael could imagine how it vibrated in the tunnel of her sex.

'Faster,' she whispered.

He revved the engine and let it die.

'Oh my God, that feels so nice.' She changed gear with his cock, making him raise his hips and strain it upward. Then she plunged down on the gear stick and gave a gasp.

The man spurted high into the air.

The girl shuddered and took his penis in her mouth.

Gael turned away, unable to stand the stimulation. She wanted to mouth that cock just as she had loved to mouth any man after he'd spurted and left her needing more of it. But Flanders had pulled it away from her. She had nearly chased after him and made him take her again. She hated the way he made her feel.

She entered the house, trembling at the knees, not knowing how much longer she could stand the torture of not coming properly. The downstairs rooms were sparsely populated. She guessed that the bedrooms would be busier. She checked with people to see that they had as much coffee as they wanted and that there was still food on the buffet.

As she ran up the staircase to her room, the sound of laughter coming through the door stopped her in mid-stride. She eased the door ajar. Two naked men knelt on

118

her bed beside a reclining young woman. She was reaching up, a phallus in each hand, shrieking with laughter as one of them ran a feather duster on a stick up and down the insides of her legs.

'Now, which one of you will I do?' she said, working each penis slowly. 'I only want the biggest.'

Each man thrust through her fingers pumping up his shaft.

The girl sat up and studied them, seeming to be trying to decide. She pulled them together and measured one against the other. Then she pouted. 'I think they're the same. Oh dear. I'll have to try them both.'

Gael was tired. All she wanted was to get to her shower and dress in something decent. She pushed open the door and went in. They all looked up and smiled. 'Cracking good party, Gael,' one man said. 'When can we come again?'

'I haven't come at all yet,' the girl shrieked as one man slipped his hand between her legs and worked at her firmly. She wriggled on the hand and plucked at her nipples.

'Don't mind me,' Gael said with a careless wave. 'I'm going to freshen up.' She slipped into her bathroom and flung the habit down. She turned on the shower and stepped in. The heat was delicious as it trickled down her body. The rivulets of water crept in between her legs. She raised her arms and ran her fingers through her hair. My God, what a day and night it had been. She stood in the streaming water for some minutes. Then hands around her breasts made her freeze. Another pair running down the inside of her thighs made her sigh. Then a third pair, more gentle and with a lighter touch, slipped between her legs. She didn't turn as they lathered her. The heat of the water and the illicit touching of the hands was already bringing her body back to life.

She moaned and closed her eyes.

10

A Swinging Foursome

As the edge of a slim hand sawed through the warm, wet place between her legs, Gael set her feet apart. She closed her eyes and waited. It was so long since she'd made love in a group. Perhaps it would be better than with a single man. It must be less fraught than with Todd Flanders.

One man, standing behind her in the steaming shower, lifted her breasts, kneaded them lovingly and touched the nipples lightly.

The other man was on his knees beside her, one hand running over the hollow of her back, the other up and down her front. He paused at her pubis, stroked it gently and then eased his finger into her, toying with her nubbin. Here it met the fingers of the girl, her thumb already deep inside the fleshy purse Gael had opened up by widening her stance. The fingertips of man and woman met. 'Get out, Matt,' she protested, 'she's mine.' Their fingers fenced between Gael's legs, trying playfully to take possession of her.

Gael didn't really care who won the contest. All she wanted for the moment was to be touched there, tenderly.

The man at her breasts kissed her neck and whispered in her ear, 'I'm going to fuck you, hostess.' His whisper was only just audible above the hissing of the shower.

She recalled him well when he'd arrived, his black hair parted in the centre, slicked back, 1930s style. He had worn a black tuxedo, a white scarf flung nonchalantly around his neck. But what had caught her eye the most was the way a prominent bulge in his trousers had shown that he had already been aroused.

'I want to suck your quim,' he whispered, as he ran his fingers round her teats.

She took a deep breath as he flicked them gently.

The girl looked up across Gael's steaming belly. 'I want to suck her too, James. You shan't have her to yourself, you randy dog.' The other man had pushed her fingers out of Gael's purse and her probing finger had migrated to Gael's anus.

Gael wanted to bend to give her better access, but the finger of the kneeling man demanded that she give him all of her attention.

'So – you *are* a dyke, Fiona, darling,' he laughed, pushing the girl aside.

'I like a bit of soft now and again,' she said petulantly. 'Hard cock isn't everything, you know.'

'But you love it, Fi,' the other man retorted. 'You were practically begging for it a minute ago.'

'That was before I had the choice,' Fiona said defensively.

'You had the choice between mine or James's, you fickle creature.' Matt grinned. 'But you couldn't make up your mind.'

Fiona slapped him playfully across the head.

'Stop arguing, you two,' James laughed, pushing them both aside. 'Which of you wants Gael?'

With that he turned Gael around. He bent and hoisted her over his shoulder.

Gael yelped and slapped his back with the palms of her wet hands, but could not free herself. Now her bottom was exposed to two pairs of eager eyes. Hot water rained over her anus and through her swollen cleft, feeling wonderful as it pattered at her skin.

121

As James pulled her legs apart, exposing her more, she felt the heat of the water enter her. Or was it a hot tongue? Then, as it wriggled, she knew it was a tongue. But whose? The man's or the girl's?

Fingers massaged round her anal ring as a mouth took her nub and sucked it gently in. Hot water trickled down her thighs making them tingle. The mouth became more determined now. Surely it was Fiona's; it nibbled her so delicately. A finger wriggled deep into her anus.

Now the mouth moved down the fringes of her sex. It bit the insides of her thighs and the hollows of her loins. The finger now withdrew and a tongue-tip took its place. She shuddered as she felt it ranging around the muscle of her ring.

She began to quiver nicely.

'She's coming,' her captor whispered. 'You'd better stop your licking, Fi.'

'No – please,' Gael protested. 'Don't stop now. It's far too nice.'

'But we have better ways of making you come.' He laughed and took her to the bedroom. He set her, dripping wet and shaking, on her feet.

Fiona and Matt flung themselves before her on the bed. Matt lay on his back. He grabbed the girl and pulled her to himself, her wet back to his chest, his hands around her ample breasts.

'Stop it, Matt,' she giggled. 'I want to play with Gael.' Wet and slippery, she wriggled and pretended to resist him. Then she shrieked as his slender penis entered her with one, skilful jab. As he spread Fiona's legs with his ankles, Gael saw it go right in. His testes bulged out roundly as it sank up to its hilt, the whole eight inches swallowed by the large lips of a very hairy vulva.

Gael trembled as she watched them work together, Fiona enclosing him tightly, he massaging her breasts.

'And now, my sexy hostess,' James whispered in her ear, pulling at Gael's nipples as he ran a line of kisses

122

down her neck. 'This is a rare occasion when you can have a horny man and a ready woman both together.' He picked her up and swung her around, one hand pushed through her crotch, the other around her waist. With her bottom to their faces, he placed her astride the others. As she looked down, Fiona's crotch was immediately below her. Matt's testicles bobbed freely as he thrust. Immediately Gael knew what she was supposed to do.

She lowered her mouth and licked his balls. He moaned and thrust up harder into Fi. Gael then licked Fiona's nubbin, delighting in the sensation of the man's large shaft sliding past her tongue.

He withdrew almost completely now, baring his glans to Gael. She stretched her tongue to lick that too. She lapped his penis slowly, tickling at the nubbin of the girl as he slid the cockshaft into her again. She lapped them both together, making Fiona moan. The penis in Fiona's vulva pulsed to every lick. Then Gael felt the bedsprings sag. As James knelt above the couple's faces, Gael felt his swollen cock and gasped as he prized her sex apart and pushed it in.

Then the other man pushed Fiona up. He made her lick at James, just as Gael was licking at his cock. James withdrew his penis just enough to expose the head. Then Gael felt Fiona's tongue lapping at her nubbin. She felt it migrate to James's cock and back. Now she resumed her own work, her tongue making a long foray down Matt's penis to lick his balls before returning to the other woman's nub.

'*Jeees*,' she whispered. 'This is really wicked.'

'But isn't it nice.' James slapped her bottom hard, still wet from the shower, the soapsuds tingling as they burst. 'Hussy,' he growled. 'What lengths will a woman go to to get a shot.'

'A shot?'

'Of adrenalin, my dear. And then a shot of jism.' He laughed aloud and drove deeply into Gael, holding his shaft at full extension.

Gael could feel Fiona licking at his balls. She wriggled to get her contact with the tongue. Then she lapped the balls and clitoris below her.

Now James began to thrust in hard. Fiona licked them both in a frenzy of rising passion. Gael rasped around the edges of the other woman's cleft as it sucked at the thrusting penis of the man.

James began to slap Gael hard. This only made her lap at Fiona with almost manic zeal.

And then they all came.

Gael felt James pump inside her, the firm root of his cock pressing hard against her nub as Fiona lapped it fast. Gael's tongue sensed the vibration of Matt's penis as it pumped inside the girl. She felt Fiona's spasms as her muscles clamped down hard on to his cock.

When Matt withdrew his shaft, Gael took it in her mouth. She sucked on it slowly, lapping at its head. Meanwhile, the long slick shaft of James was pushing at her anus. He rubbed her with the glans, slippery from his ejaculation. Eventually they fell apart.

One by one they kissed. The men kissed Gael between her legs and Gael bit playfully at Fiona's crotch. They all took turns in sucking Fiona's swollen breasts, and the half-hard organs of each man.

James sucked Matt's cock while Fiona licked at James's, and Gael sucked gently on Matt's hanging balls. It was so excitingly strange to lick a man like that while James sucked on Matt's cock, taking it deeply into his mouth just as she would do to any man she wanted. When Gael's mouth met James's, they paused and then resumed their work.

Eventually Gael lay on her back and smiled, a man's mouth in between her pulled-back legs, while the others sucked her breasts. It had been so undemanding. It had been totally lascivious, wicked, but so very nice. It had been so different from the way she had been dominated by Flanders.

11

A Soft Touch

The grandfather clock in the drawing-room struck four as Gael surveyed the wreckage of the party. Dressed in a silk kimono, she sank into a large armchair and groaned. It would be light in an hour and time to get up soon after.

Sophie stood before her, her pubis bulging in the skin-tight body stocking. She looked almost naked.

'Did you get many people confessing their fantasies and sins?' Sophie asked as she looked down on Gael.

Gael smiled wanly. 'After the first one they came in droves. I've got enough fantasies to be fulfilled to last me quite a while.'

'It was a good do.' Sophie smirked as she slumped full-length on the Chesterfield. She ran a finger through the crevice of her sex, moulding the pink material to its form. 'I had a nice time. I went for a ride with someone from the Palace.'

'A ride?' Gael lay back, hardly able to take any notice.

'He took me out in his Ferrari.'

'A red Ferrari with a soft top?'

Sophie frowned. 'That's right.'

'And?'

'And we smooched a bit.'

'Then he made you suck his prick while you squatted over the gear stick.'

Sophie frowned deeper. 'How did you know that? Have you been spying on me?'

'Brrrm, brrrm,' she said mischievously.

The girl slitted her eyes. 'He's had you too, hasn't he?'

Gael shrugged. 'He has anyone he can get that way, my sweet.'

'But he said he loved me.'

'He says that to all the girls he has in his Ferrari. You're too much of a soft touch, Sophie my love. Now – I really must go to bed.'

'Alone?'

'Alone.'

'Can't I come too?'

'Shouldn't you go home?'

'It's too late now. Anyway, I told Mum I would be staying here for the night.'

Gael was too weary to argue. They switched the lights out and went up, arm in arm.

Sophie eased away Gael's kimono and stood studying her. In the mirror, Gael could see that her skin was flushed. Her cheeks were rosy, her breasts tight, the nipples a dusky shade of pink. Her orgasms had warmed her through and through.

Sophie took a nipple gently between her lips. 'How many have you had tonight? This little stud looks positively rampant.'

'Don't ask,' Gael yawned. 'It's been a hell of a night.'

'And I hope there'll be more like it,' Sophie grinned. She slipped the front zip of her suit down, baring the deep cleavage of her breasts. Gael watched as the elongated navel was exposed and then the pubis. She closed her eyes for a second, not sure if she could stand having another naked woman in her bed.

But as the curvaceous hips and the long, sleek thighs were bared before her eyes, she found her body waking even though her mind was tired. She didn't know what it was about nudity which roused her so –

126

particularly the nudity of a man or woman clearly ready to mate.

She stripped back the covers of the bed, still damp from the shower party. Then she lay back on the pillows watching Sophie pose as she strutted before the dressing mirror, pushing out her breasts. She pulled her belly in to make a flat, smooth plane from which the prominent pubis swelled, its ginger hair shining in the light of the bedside lamp. Sophie smoothed over it with a long-fingered hand and gave Gael a sultry look. Then she pirouetted, showing the full roundels of her bottom swelling from her hips. When she bent to pick up her garment, the purse of her sex was plain to see. Gael knew that she was meant to notice how moist it was.

Sophie stretched, pushed up her hair in the manner of Bardot, and pouted mischievously at Gael's reflection in the mirror. Her breasts hung heavily as she raised her arms above her head, the nipples quite huge. She had not yet stopped lactating and Gael suspected that the glands were full of rich, warm milk.

Sophie dropped her hair again and sidled to the bed. She laid her slinky length beside Gael's naked form and rested on one hand. Then she dangled one breast against Gael's lips, and sighed as she felt Gael's mouth.

Gael closed her eyes and sucked for a while.

'Did he fuck you?'

Gael stopped sucking and looked up into the girl's large eyes. 'Did who fuck me?'

'Todd. Did he screw you?'

'What makes you think that?'

'I saw him leaving the chapel in the moonlight. Did you arrange to meet him there?'

Gael shook her head. 'He crept in and listened to the confessions. He grabbed me just as I was about to leave.'

'And did he fuck you then?'

Gael stiffened as she focused on the eyes of the girl.

127

The look was hard. Gael felt as if her answer might make the difference between anger and relief.

'He tried to.' It was a lie and she hoped it wouldn't show.

'But you fought him off?'

Gael nodded, unwilling to add further to her deceit.

There was the look of relief on Sophie's face as she whispered, 'He's a bastard but I love him.'

Gael's spirits sank. It was the first time she'd heard Sophie confess that there was more to the relationship than lust. She stroked the girl's soft cheek.

'Why do you love him if you think he's such a bastard?'

'Because I can't get enough of him.'

'But that's not love. It's infatuation.'

Sophie shrugged. 'OK – but I love the way he teases me before he fucks me.' Sophie played idly with Gael's nipple, twisting it gently between her fingers.

'Isn't that just because it's exciting?'

'Maybe it is. But when he's not around I hanker after him.'

'But does he – does he *care* for you?' Gael couldn't bring herself to say the word 'love' in the context of Flanders and the girl.

The redhead shook her head. 'He only cares about getting his end away. I'm sure he'd screw anyone available if she lay down with her legs apart, her fanny winking at him in the moonlight.'

Gael thought that didn't say much for herself. She had thought that Flanders had really fancied her. Even though she had played hard to get, he had still come after her strongly. But perhaps that was just sheer bloody-mindedness on his part – his unwillingness to be bested by a woman. Perhaps now that he had had her in the chapel, he would lay off. Perhaps his threats to carry out his fantasies about her were just bravado. Gael felt disappointment at the thought. Was it because she wanted him? Was it because she was not willing to be bested by him, and was determined to have him on her own terms? She wanted to have him in a way that would satisfy her and make him angry. Anger in a man seemed always to turn her on so much more than soft, gentle treatment. She liked soft treatment from a woman – just as Sophie was toying with her breast. She liked the softness of a woman's vulva against the lips of her mouth. She loved the elastic tension of breasts about her face. But in a man she needed hardness – the hardness of a fully rigid cock. The hardness of his thighs as he wrenched her legs apart. The hardness of his hips and belly and chest as he squashed her beneath himself and filled her with his length.

'Todd fucked my arse yesterday.' Sophie bent and sucked Gael's nipple.

Gael was taken aback for a second. Then she asked matter-of-factly, 'Did you like it?'

Sophie ran her finger over the soft curves of one breast. Then she looked up from the wet, hard stud of Gael's teat. 'I loved it. The man's an animal. He got me over a hay bale and pried my bum apart.'

Gael closed her eyes. She knew how that would have felt. There was something about anal penetration which turned an ordinary orgasm into an avalanche of exquisite sensations. Would Flanders try to take her that way too? But if she let him, that would be capitulation, unless he tied her helplessly first. She couldn't just kneel over a bale of hay and present her bottom to him. No – that wasn't true. She could do that – but she wouldn't.

'Do you like your arse fucked, miss?' Sophie ran the flat of her hand down Gael's belly and stroked her mons.

'If I'm in the mood for it.'

Sophie kissed her lips. 'I'd like to lick your arse. It's really wicked the way it winks. Can I lick it now?'

Gael stopped stroking Sophie's breast. Would she like

that? She had liked it when James had hoisted her over his shoulder and presented her bottom and her genitals to the other two. She had wriggled as someone had run their tongue around her anal ring. But did she want that from Sophie now?

'Perhaps some other time. I think we ought to sleep, don't you?'

Sophie turned. She put her face between Gael's legs and breathed hotly on her vulva.

Gael found the pouting sex lips of the girl presented to her mouth. She put her head between the warm, firm legs and kissed the swollen lips.

Sophie moaned and sucked Gael's nub.

Gael responded dreamily. She took the firm little stud of Sophie's clitoris and licked it once or twice.

And then they slept for just two hours before the alarm clock shocked them into a busy day.

12

Helping Hands

As the clock struck eleven, Gael was sitting in the study over her third cup of black coffee.

Three of her guests had rung to ask if she could put on a party for them. Money, to them, was no object, so she was smiling to herself when Todd Flanders entered. She looked up and frowned.

'What do you want?'

'I've come for my money.'

Now she scowled. 'Surely you weren't serious when you told me to put money on the offering plate.' She looked him up and down, his shirt open as usual to show his chest, his shorts bulging.

'No – I didn't expect you to pay for what you had last night.'

'What money do you want, then? I gave you your wages a few days ago.'

'You told me to find another job. I want paying for the last three days.'

Recalling how she'd told him he was fired, she thought quickly. 'Look – I was a bit hasty. I was tired. And I was angry.'

'Angry at my cock?'

'Leave your *cock* out of this.'

'That's not what you wanted last night.' he smirked.

She scowled again. 'Why can't you talk about something else but your prick?'

'But you liked my *prick* when it was angry.'

'All right, all right. So I liked your prick. Now let's drop it and be serious.'

'I am serious about fucking you again.'

She stood up angrily. 'For Christ's sake will you shut up! I don't want that from you. Do I make myself clear?'

He shrugged. 'Your mind might not want it but your pussy does.' He nodded to the crotch of her jeans.

She was wet. She had began to moisten the minute she had seen him. And the argument with him about his penis had made her belly tremble. She did want him. She wanted him here and now. She wanted to rip his shorts down and take that wicked cock in her mouth and bring it to such hardness that she'd feel every millimetre of it as she eased herself down on it. She cursed herself – she was fantasising about the fellow yet again.

He fixed her eyes with his gaze. 'So – do I keep the job or not?'

She pretended to think for a while. 'All right. You can keep the gardening job, on two conditions.'

He smirked. 'That I pleasure you twice a day?'

She ignored the quip. 'You can stay if you don't have tantrums every time I want to cut flowers for the house.'

'And?' He raised one eyebrow.

'And if you help me with a special project in the house occasionally.'

'What kind of "project"?'

She shrugged. 'Doing what you're good at.'

'I can't plant flowers in the house. And I'm not polishing or dusting.'

'I didn't mean that kind of thing.'

He moved in closer. 'What kind of "thing" did you mean, then?' He took her hand and put the palm to his bulge.

Now she hesitated, stopping herself from closing her

132

eyes as she felt his heat. 'I might need a man for something else.'

He dropped her hand now that he had fazed her. His face showed more interest but he kept his manner stony. 'What else, exactly?'

Now she lost her nerve. 'Fixing furniture and general maintenance.'

'All right. I don't mind a bit of screwing and banging now and then.'

'Do you ever talk about anything but sex?'

He shrugged. 'Will that be all, miss?'

'Yes, it will. Now – you'd better get back to your work. The boundary hedge needs cutting.'

'I'll cut it when I'm ready.' He looked at her haughtily.

She confronted him closely. 'You'll do what I want you to.'

'And what do you want me to do right now, miss? Take your knickers down and kiss your quim?'

Gael felt a flush go to her cheeks. Her knees were weak, her belly churning.

He took her chin between his fingers and made her look into his eyes. His breath was hot upon her mouth, and as he closed his lips to hers, she held herself taut.

'You might think you can rule me, miss,' he whispered. 'But I can't be ruled.'

He slipped the buttons of her blouse and ran a finger over a nipple. It stood hard immediately, confirming that she liked him doing that.

He put his lips to hers again and whispered softly, 'And if I want to fuck you, I will – in whatever way I like. Wherever I like and whenever I like. As long as you understand that, I'll stay. If you don't like it, you can find another gardener to plough your furrow.'

He turned and left.

Gael screwed up a piece of writing paper and threw it at his back. Damn the man. He had her hooked. But he

133

was so arrogant. She should have stuck to her resolve and kept him at arm's length.

Melindi arrived unannounced on her way from New York to Paris. Gael was excited to see her and Sophie was clearly delighted. But when Gael saw knowing glances pass between them, she felt left out.

'I heard the party went like a bomb.' Melindi smiled as she sat in the drawing-room sipping a dry Martini.

'How did you hear that?' Gael was on the edge of her seat. She knew that news travelled fast around the circuit but not that fast, surely.

'That Francine of Francine de Paris told me when I went into her Knightsbridge salon to get my hair fixed.'

Gael gave her a sideways glance. Melindi didn't have the kind of hair that needed 'fixing'. She'd been on a fishing expedition.

'So?'

'So,' Melindi said, her eyes twinkling naughtily, 'I hear she did a little bit of cutting and setting last night.'

Gael raised her nose. 'And what if she did?'

Melindi grinned, seemingly amused at disconcerting Gael. 'You ought to have been a hairdresser, Pinky. You wouldn't have needed that old confessional. Just a basin and a chair. But I think it was inspirational of you to think that one up. They loved it. Are some of them going to get their fantasies worked out?'

Gael sat back and pretended to be nonchalant. 'Perhaps.'

'Don't "perhaps" me, Pinky. You know damn well they are. Can I join in?'

'That depends on how long you're going to stay.'

Melindi screwed up her face. 'Got to get back the day after tomorrow. Jean-Paul's show on Wednesday, Mashimoto's in Tokyo at the weekend.' She sighed and wiped her brow theatrically.

'Don't give me that bull. You love it.'

'I love the loot they pay.' Melindi grinned that face-wide, piano-key grin Gael had come to love so much. It lit her up.

Sophie came in with a tray of coffee and biscuits. Gael thought that she looked even more provocative than ever. Her jeans were so tight Gael could see the form of her vulval lips, and the tight pink T-shirt she wore made her look quite naked above the waist.

She handed Gael yet another coffee, set the tray down on a finely veneered table and stood by Melindi's chair, swinging her hips.

Melindi caressed her bottom with a long hand. 'And has my little slave been behaving herself while I've been away?' It was said both to Gael and the girl.

Sophie gave Melindi a coy little smile and tossed her hair. 'Of course I've been behaving.'

'Fibber.' Gael frowned at her.

Melindi smacked the tight, round bottom hard. 'Have you been bothering the gardener again? I'll whip you if you have.' She spanked Sophie again, playfully.

Sophie pouted. 'Is it my fault if he won't leave me alone?'

'I'm not surprised he won't let you alone. The way you flash your tits and push your mount out at him, the man would have to be made of stone if he didn't make a move on you.'

Sophie smirked. 'Why, Miss Melindi, I do believe you're jealous.'

Melindi put her head back and laughed. 'Jealous of you and Flanders? You're so naïve, my pet.' She began to saw a hand between Sophie's legs, rubbing at her sex lips. 'I've just been screwed almost into the bedsprings by two of the horniest and the richest men in New York. The gardener doesn't really interest me.'

By the look on Melindi's face, Gael knew that wasn't true. Melindi certainly didn't keep Todd Flanders there just so that her housemaid could have someone to play with. By the way Melindi's eyes lit up each time his name was mentioned, Gael was sure that there had been something quite deep between the gardener and the owner of the house.

Melindi pulled down the zip of Sophie's fly and said quite casually as she drove a finger deep between the girl's legs, 'And how many men did you contrive to accommodate in here last night?'

Sophie wriggled her jeans down to her thighs and widened her stance. 'I went for a ride in a very expensive car. That's all.'

Melindi smirked as she sawed the finger through the lips of Sophie's sex. 'How nice for you. Now – let me guess. It wasn't a red Ferrari with a soft top, by any chance?'

Sophie pouted again.

Melindi hooked the finger up into the housemaid's vulva, as if examining her. 'Yes, I can see that you've had a gear stick in here, you wicked creature. And I suppose he made you change gear with his prick.'

Sophie frowned petulantly as Melindi withdrew the finger and zipped her up. Then she slapped the girl's bottom and whispered, 'I'll play with you later, darling. Now, who are we going to amuse ourselves with today?'

Gael looked at them both. 'Do you girls want to work out tonight?'

Melindi slitted her eyes. 'What kind of "work-out" do you have in mind, my little pink marshmallow?'

'Just a few exercises in a gym. Then a sauna, a jacuzzi, and a massage.'

Now Melindi studied her hard. 'And what's the ulterior motive, pink pussy lips?'

Gael got up to leave. 'You'll see. I think you'll enjoy yourselves.' She turned in the doorway. 'Oh – while I remember – bring a whip and some handcuffs, will you?'

13

Three Nymphs Working Out

Maximillians was plush. It was not the kind of place Gael would think of as a gym. It was more like a palace with exercise equipment placed among antique furniture.

In the marble-pillared changing rooms, Gael spotted the one-way glass she'd had described to her. A long telephone conversation with Maximillian had worked out all the details that morning.

Maximillian was more attractive than she'd remembered him to be. Bronzed and muscular, his Italianate complexion and upright stance seemed to fit him with the marble facings and the Roman-style baths. They exchanged cursory greetings as Gael led the girls into the changing rooms.

Now they were alone, Melindi looked at Sophie then at Gael. She grinned as she produced a short-handled whip with long, thin thongs of leather. She whacked the whip stock in her hand.

'So what's the job, Pinky?'

Gael shrugged. 'We just work out on the equipment in the gym next door.'

Sophie was clearly puzzled. 'Is that all?'

'Of course. Except . . .'

Melindi closed on Gael and fixed her with those searching eyes which made Gael melt every time they scanned her; particularly when she was naked.

'Except what, my little pink morsel?' She flicked Gael's thigh with the whip and made her jump.

'Except we do it nude.'

'And?' Melindi raised an eyebrow.

'And the guy watches us,' she whispered, gesturing to the mirror. 'So let's put on a good show, shall we?'

Melindi scowled playfully. 'Is that all? I have men eyeing me naked all the time in the dressing rooms at shows.'

'So it won't be a problem for you then.'

'It doesn't sound very exciting, that's all. What else does your boyfriend do apart from gawping at us naked?'

'*He* doesn't do anything. *We* chastise him for being a very naughty boy.'

Melindi grinned and whacked the whip again. 'Oh, good. That sounds like more fun. When do we start?'

Gael undressed Melindi slowly, making sure she was facing the mirrored wall. She lifted the hem of a white T-shirt, exposing the deep navel then the breasts she loved to touch. With Melindi's arms above her head, her breasts were taut, their nipples already long. Gael fingered them from behind to make them stick out at the mirror. Then, standing behind Melindi, she slipped her hands into the waistband of the model's slacks and slowly pulled them down. She watched in the mirror as the prominent pubis came to view, covered in little black curls. When Melindi stepped elegantly out of her slacks and cast them aside with her foot, she was magnificent. Tall and slim and graceful, she looked the part of a Nubian princess. Gael wanted to kiss her satiny skin all over.

Then they turned to Sophie who had stood aside, pretending to be shocked.

Melindi hooked her finger. 'Come on, my pet, take your clothes off. We want to see your ginger pussy.'

Sophie cowered away. 'Don't touch me. I'm not stripping in front of you.'

138

'You'll do as you're told, you naughty girl,' Melindi smirked, thwacking the whip stock into her hand.

As they moved in on the girl, she tried to flee, but Gael had locked the door. Sophie lashed out at them. Now they dragged her as she fought them and pushed her to the floor before the mirrors.

Sophie struck out so hard it took Gael by surprise. She grabbed the housemaid's wrists and pinned them to the floor above her head. Then she knelt on the arms, stretching the large breasts inside the flimsy, cotton blouse.

Melindi held the redhead's legs as she tried to struggle free.

Gael took the edges of the blouse and ripped it open, baring the breasts and belly which were heaving from exertion. In the soft lights of the room, the breasts looked flushed, the large-rimmed nipples dark. Gael could not resist squeezing them to bring milk to the pores and to smear it over the rounds to make them glisten. She imagined that Maximillian would have his fly undone by now and be strumming at his cock. In one hand he would probably have his binoculars focused on the wet nipples of the maid; or perhaps he was gazing at her crotch, anticipating seeing how it strained as she had her jeans pulled down.

On cue, Melindi knelt with her bottom to the mirror. Gael could see her labia pouting out between her tense legs as she unzipped Sophie's jeans and dragged them off. Flinging them aside, this left the girl naked but for a lacy thong, the little, copper hairs of her pubis peeking from its sides. Melindi pushed the knees apart. She slipped her black hand between the pale pink legs and caressed the thong.

Sophie struggled more, almost too hard for Gael to hold. 'Get off me, you sluts,' she cried. 'I hate you.'

'Lie still, you wanton creature,' Melindi laughed as she drew the thong down to reveal the pubic mount. 'Lie

139

still, I want to see your quim.' She ripped the frail material with strong fingers, then turned to Gael, her eyes alight as the ginger-haired crevice of the girl appeared through the slit she'd made.

Gael could see it clearly in the mirror. Melindi widened the slit to show the whole of Sophie's dark pink purse, pushing through the rent in the pure white of the thong. Melindi then ripped the strings off and pulled the thong away to show the opened cleft. She ran her fingers around the hairy lips and made the redhead squirm.

Now Sophie began to quieten as Melindi caressed her thighs. She lay with her legs forced back, her green eyes closed as Melindi slid a long thumb through her crevice and made her breathe in deeply as she thrust it in her sleeve.

Melindi worked the long thumb slowly, her fingers rubbing at the anal ring as Sophie began to moan, pushing her vulva out to meet each thrust.

Melindi slapped her inner thigh and stood up. 'Right, that's enough. I think you're enjoying this too much, you harlot.'

When Gael released her arms, Sophie sat up straight and grinned as well. 'My God, that was wicked. You can strip me again like that any time.'

Now it was Gael's turn. She turned her back to the mirror. She slipped off her blouse, knowing that her breasts were reflected in a mirror opposite. She dropped her slacks and showed her crotchless knickers as she bent to pick her slacks up. When she looked through her legs she glimpsed how wet she was, and how much her swelling labia poked out through the lacy hole.

Wiggling out of the knickers provocatively she let them fall around her ankles. Then she closed her legs as she bent again to pick them up, watching the reflection of her sex tucked tight between her buttocks.

In the equipment room next door, Melindi lay on a padded bench. She spread her legs out widely and began

140

to lift a bar above her head. With each exertion, her long thighs tensed and the lips of her sex parted.

Sophie stood with her back to the mirrors with her legs wide apart, and touched the floor with the tips of her slender fingers. Her breasts hung heavily, and the copper curls which fringed her sex bushed out towards the man. Then she worked her muscles to make her vulva open.

Gael lay on her back working overhead pedals with her feet. This wound a set of weights up towards the ceiling. When they got to the top, she pedalled to let them down. As she lay with her bottom to the mirror, she could feel the lips of her sex rubbing together, getting warm, becoming very moist. She knew that he would see this close up in his glasses, and it made her even moister. She knew he would see her anus too as she tensed and flexed her thighs.

After a while, they changed around, presenting the man with different views of different-coloured skins and differently developed female parts.

Gael sat down on a rowing machine placed close to the mirror. As she leant forward, she felt her vulva gape and saw in the mirror just what Maximillian would see. On each and every stroke, it gaped a little more. She could plainly see her nubbin, fully erect from the stimulation which came from being watched.

They took a rest, wet with perspiration. It trickled down their breasts and beaded on their bellies. Melindi's skin was shining. Her thighs were taut, her breasts welling as she stood with her hands on her hips, pushing them out. Gael knelt and put her arms around Melindi's waist, resting her cheek against the panting belly while she caught her own breath. Then she reached up and took a nipple between her lips, surprised at how salty it tasted as she tugged at it.

She made Melindi lie down on a mat and sat astride her, her hands massaging the black skin, cupping the large breasts and running her palms up the neck. The insides of Gael's thighs were slick with perspiration, and as she rocked on Melindi's pubic bone, her skin slid along with the lubrication.

Sophie stood at the mirror, so close that she almost touched it with her nipples. She set her legs apart and worked at her breasts, rubbing them on the glass. Then she slipped a hand between her legs and rubbed herself in small circles, her eyes closed as her legs began to quiver.

'You wicked, wicked girl,' Melindi snapped, getting up. 'Stop frigging yourself this instant.' The whip cracked on the redhead's thigh and made her yelp.

They made her turn and bend to touch her toes, and Melindi lay the whip across her buttocks hard enough to bring colour to the pale pink skin, but not too hard to hurt her.

The reflection in the mirror showed a female with her legs apart, her sex lips pulsing from the whipping.

Gael trembled at the sight, recalling how Flanders had whipped her at the lakeside. She sank to her knees and put her lips to Sophie's vulva, sensing its warmth with her tongue, drawing the scent of it deep into her lungs. Then she turned to the mirror and peered at it hard. She pretended to see something in the glass. Rising, she went quickly from the room. Following directions she'd been given, she found the office quickly. Inside it was quite dark, but one wall glowed with light from the exercise room next door. Silhouetted before the one-way glass, Maximillian stood, his tracksuit bottoms down, his penis in one hand. Silhouetted against the light, it gave Gael quite a thrill. She wanted it already.

Gael crept in and slipped her hand around his waist. He tensed, clearly having heard her come. Her fingers touched his penis. They slid right up its length until they reached the glans and stroked the web. He sighed.

142

Through the one-way mirror, Gael watched Melindi do a cartwheel, her breasts fluid and mobile. She tumbled like an acrobat, her belly tightening as she came over and stopped before the mirror. Her legs were widely spread now, her feet flat on the floor and her thighs straining tightly. Her belly and her breasts were stretched with tension, their nipples pointing at the ceiling.

Sophie knelt between her legs. She ran her tongue up the straining thighs to the sinews of her groin and tickled Melindi's clitoris with the tip of her wet tongue.

The penis in Gael's hand surged as the voyeur thrust it towards Melindi.

Gael pulled his tracksuit up and, pulling him by the ear, dragged him into the other room.

'Look, girls. Look who I found watching us work out. He was gawping through this one-way glass. What shall we do with him?'

'Take his trousers down and spank him hard,' Sophie said, parading haughtily around the crestfallen man.

'Take his trousers down and whip him,' growled Melindi.

He rolled his eyes. 'No, please. Please, ladies, don't whip me. I'm sorry if I . . .'

Melindi gagged him deftly with a silken scarf to cut his protest.

'And woe betide him if he swells,' Gael added, recalling vividly how she had 'cured' the swelling of the man the night before. He shook his head and Gael could feel him trembling, but she saw how much he was aroused.

Melindi touched between his legs with the hard stock of the whip. 'Let's see what you've got in there, mister. I hope it's big enough to be worthwhile.'

His eyes were wide, glancing from Gael to Melindi and back again.

Sophie put her hand inside his trousers. 'I don't think you'll be disappointed, Mel. It feels worthwhile to me.'

143

She slipped his tracksuit down his thighs and pulled his penis out.

He dragged his trousers up again and held them tightly.

Melindi stripped them down again. Maximillian was naked a few seconds after that. Gael was surprised at how big he was. She'd only seen him in the darkness of the confessional. His rigid penis erupted from a mass of silky hair. His balls were tight up in his scrotum. Her hands twitched as she recalled how she had cupped them as he'd spurted, and now she wanted to hold them once again. But that wasn't the game.

'Bend over this bench, you wicked boy,' she hissed. 'I want to see your bottom.'

It was a tight, trim bottom, tanned as darkly as the rest of him, that nutty brown bestowed by a tropical sun. She ran her hand over it slowly, feeling the smooth contours, trailing her fingertips up and down the insides of his thighs. Delving between his legs she cupped his balls. They were larger than she recalled, even larger than the gardener's. They contracted as she stroked them and parted them with a finger.

Melindi pushed Gael aside and lay a couple of lashes on the buttocks. 'Don't play with him, Gael. You'll give him pleasure. He needs a good hiding for his sins.' He moaned, Gael thought, with pleasure.

Melindi lashed him harder.

He moaned again.

She sent the tails of the whip flicking through his legs, more to tickle than to sting him. It had the right effect. His penis curved up stiffer.

The chastisement went on for some minutes, each girl taking a turn, delighting in the way the man trembled with the lashes. They tried to make him stiffer still, each one of them knowing how much better a really rigid cock felt.

They turned him and lay him on a padded bench, his

arms tied above his head by Gael while Sophie sat astride his chest facing his feet and pulled his legs right back. With his knees beside her breasts, his inner thighs were taut, his genitals exposed to Melindi's gaze. The penis curved towards Sophie, standing stiffly from his body, his testicles tight as Melindi brushed them with the whip tails. She stood with her legs apart, her dark eyes flashing with excitement.

He shuddered as he felt the leather thongs.

She brushed again, a feather-light touch which made him writhe, but Sophie held him down. She held him open to Melindi's ministrations, riding on his heaving chest, her vulva moist and sucking on his skin.

Gael stood astride him, her knees against his armpits as she looked down on him. All he could see as he looked up was her sex as she worked her finger on her clitoris and made it hard.

Now Melindi lay some lashes on his anus, just hard enough to make it contract but not enough to hurt him. She whipped the taut thighs a good bit harder. Then she took the whip stock and eased it into him. He groaned and twisted but they had him fast, each one of them delighting in her conquest of the man.

Melindi knelt then worked the whip stock very slowly in his ring. She licked a long finger and drew it from his cherry to his balls. Lightly, she drew it again and again, stretching the foreskin tight, making the glans swell even larger. With every teasing stroke she pushed the whip stock deeper, as if she had a phallus embedded in the man. She began to work her body slowly back and forth. And as she worked, Sophie stroked his web.

Gael stood astride his face and watched herself in a mirror. Slowly, she spread her feet so that her open sex came closer to his mouth. She slid the gag aside and made a gesture to him to keep quiet. Then she lowered herself just a little bit more so that when he put his tongue out, he could run it lightly through her gaping furrow.

She trembled as he licked her and rocked slowly over him to increase her pleasure. Now she came down on his nose, rubbing herself against it as his tongue delved deeper, his breath upon her anus.

She came in little waves of delight which seemed to run up and down her spine. And while her contractions lasted, she rested on him gently, allowing him to suck upon her nub.

Now she had had her pleasure, she changed places with Sophie, and took up the task of further stimulation. She stroked the insides of his thighs with the very tips of her fingers, and worked his foreskin very slowly, back and forth.

Melindi worked him slowly with the whip stock, clearly delighting in the way the leather rubbed her vulva.

He spurted without warning.

His penis stiffened and rose so that it shot the first spurt over Gael's belly to run into her navel. The second flush was caught by Melindi's pink-palmed hands. She took it to her breasts, giving them a shine as deep as polished ebony.

Sophie, watching as he pumped and spilled his seed, caressed the underside of his shaft, keeping the contractions going for some seconds.

All the time, he moaned and moved his head.

Then they tied him to the bench and left him while they went to the jacuzzi. They sipped at pink champagne and ate black grapes. Gael sat opposite the other girls, grinning as she sipped her drink, one foot between each of their legs. She flexed her toes, delighting in the mobile softness of their labia in the warmness of the water, while their feet massaged her breasts, plucking her nipples between their toes.

When they were rested from their exertions in chastising the man, they dried with fluffy towels and stood over their host and loosed his arms. With Sophie and Melindi

146

at his sides he massaged between their legs, while Gael fed him grapes. They giggled from the champagne and from his fondling as he worked their vulvas with his thumbs and curled his fingers in their anal rings. They poured champagne into his navel and supped it out. They washed his cock with it and licked its head until it stood erect.

Gael straddled him and pulled his penis up. She eased herself down on to it, closing her eyes as she felt its heat buried deeply in her body. Flexing her toes she sprang, making him take her at the pace that she dictated, feeling the head of his champagne-wetted shaft rippling in her tunnel.

As his fingers worked, Melindi came with little whimpers of delight.

Sophie came next, her breasts pushed out as she lowered herself on his probing thumb.

Both of them squatted and rose upon his thumbs to prolong their orgasmic throes.

Gael had a little tremor and closed herself tightly on his cock. But, when he flexed his hips and drove up strongly, she slipped off him and masturbated him slowly with the very tips of her fingers while she rubbed her vulva on his hairy scrotum.

He fountained strongly once again.

They massaged his thick emission into his sac and penis. Each rubbed her vulva over it to smear herself with its slipperiness. Then each girl glazed his torso as she stretched herself over it to glide her open vulva on his skin. They ran his arms between their legs, to leave him slick and scented with their nectar. Then they left him in the darkness and quietly shut the door.

14

Fully Stretched

The next few days went quickly. Gael was working at full stretch, planning two more parties. One was to take place at Melindi's house with a list of special guests. The other was to be at the castle of an earl.

The afternoon was balmy as she walked the leafy gardens, searching for Todd Flanders. He had not bothered her since the morning after the party, and she wondered if he had forgotten his intention to have her whenever and however he wanted. Of course, she would not let him. He was an arrogant pig and there was no way she would allow him to think she was excited by his threat.

She called out in the stable yard, hoping that he was somewhere within earshot. 'Todd? Todd, where the hell are you?'

'I'm here.' The voice came from the hay-loft door, just above her head.

'Come down here. I want to talk to you.' She looked up against the light.

He leaned out and stared down on her. 'Have you come to fulfil my fantasy, miss?' he grinned.

'No, I have not. Now come down here at once. I'm not going to shout up to you.'

He shrugged and turned to go. 'Either come up or leave me to my work in peace.'

'I said come down, or find another job.'

'Don't threaten me with that old line,' he smirked and went back in.

She stormed up the ladder, her loose skirt billowing behind her. This time she was going to dismiss him. She would not stand such insolence from a servant.

As her head emerged through the trapdoor, she didn't see Flanders standing behind her with a horse rein. She was not quick enough to stop him slipping it over her head and shoulders to pull it tight. He kicked the trapdoor shut and pulled her to himself. Breathing over her shoulder, he whispered, 'Have you come to apologise for leading me on?' He kissed her neck and made her tremble.

As she spun around to face him, her eyes glared, but her stomach fluttered wildly. When his mouth came down on hers, she went to pieces. Her lips began to work his lips. Her tongue-tip met his as he thrust it into her mouth. Helpless in the tightened rein, she began to pant.

He pressed his shaft against her mount as he kissed her. 'So, you have come to fulfil my fantasy.'

She pulled away. 'No – I have not. Now, untie me. I'm not playing your stupid games.'

He sat on a bale of hay and smirked at her, holding the rein firmly. 'But when you let your guests confess their sins and fantasies, miss, you promised they'd be fulfilled.'

'You were not invited to that party. Go and fetch your things. You're fired.'

'I'm what, miss?'

'I said you're dismissed.'

He shrugged. 'Then I'd better have my fun with you first, hadn't I?'

'Touch me and I'll ...' She stopped as he rose. Taking a step backward she tripped over a coil of rope and fell into a pile of hay. Looking up at him towering over her, her body began to tremble. She closed her eyes. When she opened them he had slung a rope over a beam and was making a loop at one end.

Now she was alarmed. 'What the hell are you doing that for?'

'I'm fulfilling the fantasy I confessed, miss. I told you I would.'

She scanned her memory frantically but could not recall a thing. Her excitement when he had held her tightly in the chapel had taken precedence over all else.

'Surely you remember how I told you how I would like to string you up by the ankles and lick between your legs.'

She did recall that now. And she remembered how it had sent the strangest kind of thrill racing through her. Part of her had always liked to feel helpless as a man had played with her. The excitement must have shown in her eyes as he smiled widely.

'There you are, I knew you remembered.' He quickly slipped the loop over her ankle and pulled the rope. To Gael's alarm her leg rose in the air. A second loop was tied as she made a token struggle, quite unable to escape from the first one.

'Let me down, you bastard. I'll have you arrested!' Her heart was thumping hard as he grinned at her and shook his head.

'You won't make a fuss unless you want a scandal in the neighbourhood, miss.'

She glowered. 'You wouldn't dare. 'I'll have you –'

He put his finger to his lips and smirked. 'Don't say anything you'll regret, miss. Just say sorry to me for the way you tricked me into fucking Sophie when I thought it was you I was doing.'

'I'll burn in hell before I ever say sorry to you.'

He hoisted her higher so that her skirt fell back. She wore no panties, and as her legs parted, he could look right down into her most secret parts. She wriggled

150

again but it only served to make her labia open and close, a sight she knew he would take great delight in. She was right. He knelt in the hay and examined her, her bottom level with his crotch.

Resting with her neck and shoulders in the hay, she could do nothing but hang there.

He ran a finger through her groove, exclaiming, 'Now, that's nice. Very nice indeed. I didn't see it properly in the darkness of the chapel. Shall I lick it or would you rather have it rubbed?'

She tried to shut her legs but could not. He'd set the ropes too far apart.

He smoothed her pubis with the flat of his hand, then ran it down the inside of her thigh. 'And you've got lovely legs, miss. Do you like them kissed?' He ran a line of kisses from her knee into her crotch.

'Stop it. Stop it this instant.' She wriggled but it only gave her more stimulation.

He grinned. 'Say sorry for what you did to me.'

'Get lost.'

'OK. I'll go home and leave you strung up here.'

'You wouldn't dare.' She glared up at him.

Now he grinned boyishly. 'I will unless you say how terribly sorry you are for leading a poor innocent fellow on.'

' "Innocent",' she snorted. 'My God, you should have seen yourself at the lakeside with Sophie.'

'She likes being tied up.'

'Well, I don't. Let me down.' Gael struggled to no avail and it simply made him smile.

He ran his finger through her furrow.

She was wet with excitement and anticipation, and could do nothing to hide the fact. He raised his finger to his nose and scented it.

'So you're not turned on by being tied up?'

'I said, get lost, you pig. You might think you can do what you like with me, but don't kid yourself I'll enjoy it.'

He put his mouth to her vulva and kissed. His lips were hot on the flesh of the inner lips, his breath warm on her anus. It made her tremble violently. Her clitoris rose as he licked it and made it stand. He ran his tongue repeatedly through the hollows of her groin and bit the taut skin.

She shuddered and took a deep breath.

He parted her labia gently with his fingertips and pushed his tongue between them, wriggling it around so that it gave her such a pleasurable feeling she could not suppress a moan.

'Bastard,' she hissed through clenched teeth.

'But you like it, don't you? Your clitty's standing up asking for more. And you're so slippery inside I'm surprised you're not begging for my cock.'

'Your imagination's running away with you, Flanders.'

He ran his tongue-tip through her furrow and made her moan again. 'Then why are you making do-it-some-more noises?'

'Chauvinist.'

'And you're nothing but a temptress.' He bit her loin.

'What the hell is that supposed to mean?'

He licked her deeply, from the taut bridge between her anus and her vulva, and slowly up to her clitoris. The flat of his tongue pushed the lips of her sex widely aside as it ploughed through them.

'I asked you what you meant by calling me a temptress.' She tried to shut her legs but could not.

'I meant that if you hadn't made eyes at me since the first minute you entered my gardens, and hadn't played with my cock in the scullery I wouldn't be playing with your pussy now.' He ran his hands over her flanks and scored her with his nails. It made her gasp.

'I'll get my revenge, Flanders,' she gasped as he bit her playfully in the groin.

'Good. I'll look forward to that.' He reached down

and drew aside her blouse, pulled at her nipples and made her breasts go taut. His neck rested on the hot flesh of her vulva as he peered down at her.

'It might be sooner than you think, Flanders.' She wriggled against him, feeling the hard knot of his adam's apple working on her clitoris.

'Good,' he said wistfully as he withdrew and sucked on her clitoris to make it swell. 'Good. I like a challenge from a woman.'

'I'll tie you up and see how you like it, you conceited pig.'

He grinned from between her legs, his mouth wet with her nectar, his eyes alight. 'I don't think you've got the strength to tie me up, miss. But, if you do manage to, you can do anything you want with me.'

Gael's pulse raced. The plan she had in mind required that he be tied up. But how could she do it against his strength?

The working of his lips on her sex lips and the sucking of her nub began to take its toll on her resolve not to respond to his domination of her. She began to work her hips to make the movement of his mouth upon her sex much more pronounced.

He dropped his shorts and knelt again between her legs, his penis stiff, clearly aroused from the way that she was trussed and quite helpless. Now his penis rested in her groove, his testicles tickling her skin. He ran his hands up and down her thighs, pulling her on to himself, making her rub him as she swung against him.

This made the underside of his shaft wet. She felt herself slipping on it as he pushed it through her groove. She began to writhe, her climax close, her need to get relief fast becoming too great to withhold. She threw away her resolve to resist him.

He stood up, naked before her, looking down into her crotch, his penis rearing above it. Then he moved around her, straddled her, his bottom to her face, his ankles against her shoulders.

She looked up through his legs, just managing to see his balls between his tight thighs. And then he laid his penis in between her legs and began to rub her gently.

Had her hands not been tied, she would have raked the brown skin of his back with her nails. She would have slipped a hand through his legs and taken his balls and pulled his foreskin tight as the tempo of his delightful rubbing sped up.

His thumbs parted her widely, pressing into the hollows of her loins. Then she felt a finger in her anus and tightened it reflexively.

He rubbed and probed together.

She writhed, partly on his phallus, but mostly on his finger.

He drove his thumbnails deep into her groin and made her gasp.

'Say you're sorry that you led me on,' he hissed over his shoulder as he worked, making her labia hot with the friction.

'I told you, I shall never say sorry to you.'

He slapped her bottom hard. 'Then I'll leave you to the rats.' He stepped away and stood back, the huge shaft of his cock wet with her juice.

Her heart sank. 'You wouldn't dare leave me here.'

He grinned and moved towards the trapdoor. 'Say that you're sorry for the trick you played on me.'

'You loved every second of it. You could have got away any time you'd wanted to.'

He shrugged again and raised the trap to leave, still naked, his penis springing with each step. As he descended the ladder, he stopped, his cockshaft just visible, jutting up above the floor.

Gael realised that he did intend to leave her. She thought quickly. She could shout and hope that Sophie would hear her. But then the girl would be angry when she saw her mistress hanging from the beam, her vulva bared, her breasts hanging out. The maid would know that Flanders had done it, but she would conclude that Gael had wanted him to. And she couldn't do with Sophie being petulant again.

'All right,' she called out to Flanders as his face dipped below the trapdoor. 'I'm sorry I tricked you. Now cut me down, you bastard.'

He came back slowly, standing over her, horny and magnificent. 'Not good enough, miss. Say it as if you really mean it.' He put a bare foot on one breast and worked it in small circles. Then he took a harness strap and lashed her belly. As she heaved, the sole of his foot rubbed hard against one breast. Her other breast bounced.

She swallowed her pride. 'I'm very sorry. There, I've said it. Now let me go.'

'Say you're sorry that you took my shorts down and sucked my cock to make me think you wanted me to fuck you.'

She shook her head hard.

He pushed his foot down on her breast and nipped the nipple between his toes.

She gasped as he pulled at it but kept her mouth shut tightly.

'Say it.' He tugged again. 'Then perhaps I'll untie you.'

She took a deep breath. She needed to be freed. Then she could lie back in the hay and let him have her properly. She couldn't stand the tension any longer. As he looked down between her legs, her vulval lips were trembling.

'All right. I'm sorry I made you think . . .'

'To think what?'

'To think I wanted you to . . .'

'Wanted me to what?'

'To fuck me, you pig. To fuck me. Now, let me down or I'll scream for help.'

He knelt and kissed up and down her legs ending with

his lips on her pubis. Then he let her down, unlooped the reins and massaged her ankles gently.

She propped herself up on her elbows and scowled at him.

He smiled. 'Do you want me to fuck you now?'

She said nothing but pulled her legs back and gave him a coy little look which she immediately regretted.

He pushed her legs back hard, stretching her widely. He knelt forward and put the head of his cock to her opening. She felt its heat and lay back waiting for his thrust. She needed it after all his titillation. She couldn't wait another moment more.

Then he let her go.

Looking at his watch, he shook his head. 'Sorry, miss. You'll have to wait. I've got a darts match at the Red Lion tonight and I need to practise.'

15

Take Six

Three days passed painfully for Gael. She fumed to herself about letting Flanders best her again, leaving her unfulfilled. Melindi's assignment in Paris had been postponed and so she had stayed. But, much to Gael's hurt, the supermodel almost ignored her. She seemed to be preoccupied with Sophie. Whenever they met Gael together there seemed to be some kind of conspiracy between them. Sophie no longer took orders from Gael. Whenever she asked the housemaid to do even the simplest thing, the girl simply pouted. Gael didn't ask what was going on between them. She would not let them know that she was hurt.

Flanders was no better. After their conflict of wills in the hay-loft, he kept well out of her way. Gael had seen him talking to Melindi in the stable yard one morning and he seemed to be quite animated. He seemed not to be able to take his eyes off the beautiful woman.

For the first time since she had met Melindi Mocambo, Gael felt angry with her. She felt jealous. But one good thing came out of Melindi's presence. She made up the numbers Gael needed for the six-woman tea party one of her confessants had asked for. Gael had had quite a hard time finding enough people to play the game of fulfilling that particular fantasy.

Now it was time for him to arrive. Fiona from the

shower party, Boo Fannshawe, Melindi and Sophie all sat around a coffee table in the sitting-room, chatting animatedly. A girl called Anastasia made up the five, with Gael to join them as soon as the man arrived. They were all dressed sexily, some in skirts, some in jeans or ski pants, and blouses which showed their breasts. Melindi looked stunning as usual in jeans and a blouse of shimmering pink. Gael could see that she was naked beneath it, the satiny texture of her skin, the deep cleavage of her breasts, that wonderfully undulating belly only the flick of a few buttons away from a lover's touch.

Sophie looked quite nervous. Gael wondered if she should have included her. Was she still hankering after Flanders? Had she got a crush on Melindi?

The other four looked refined, elegant and animated. Each one seemed supremely confident in her sexuality.

'All right, ladies. Pay attention.' Gael clapped her hands to stop the chatter. They all looked up.

Anastasia, a stunning young brunette who had been at the first party, raised her Minton tea cup and sipped, crooking her little finger exaggeratedly.

Gael was stern. This was serious business, even though she didn't want them to take it too seriously. 'OK. Remember, you must ignore him. Whatever he does with any one of you, the others carry on as if nothing at all was happening. I'm sure you'll all get your kicks in turn, so don't be too eager.'

'Can't we play with him?' Fiona piped up, her black eyes wide with excitement.

'Only if he wants you to respond that way, Fi. Remember, it's his fantasy, not yours.'

But what do we get – apart from the prospect of a good rogering?' Anastasia asked, sucking provocatively on a long chocolate éclair.

'You get your own fantasies fulfilled in due course. That was the deal when you agreed to come and help him out.'

Fiona grinned. 'I haven't told you my dream yet.'

Gael fixed her gaze and held it, pleasant warmth coursing to her labia. Just talking about other women's fantasies turned her on. Arranging and executing them made the whole of her body tingle.

'I'm sure I can satisfy your need, whatever that might be, Fiona.'

Fiona licked a chocolate finger and smirked. 'I've always wanted three horny men at once, one in each hole and one in my mouth, pumping me full of their hot, hard flesh.'

Gael kept her eyes on Fiona's eyes and said softly, 'I'm sure that won't be a problem, Fi. We'll talk about timing later.' She started racking her brains to think of three horny men who might like to have Fiona all at once.

'Don't forget mine,' Anastasia crooned in a deep, almost masculine voice. 'I'm going in the Maiden.'

'What's the Maiden?' Fiona piped up.

The brunette smiled sideways at Melindi before she focused on Fiona's wide eyes and tapped the side of her nose with her finger. 'The Maiden is a fiendish device of Melindi's to drive a woman absolutely wild, darling. I just can't wait to try it.' Her hair bobbed about her shoulders as she threw her head back excitedly.

'Your wish is easy to fulfil, Anastasia,' Gael said, looking at her watch. 'The Maiden is ready and waiting. Just say when you want to use her.'

Anastasia threw her hair again. 'I'll have to be in the mood. Wait until I'm really horny. Perhaps I will be when your friend has done his stuff on me this afternoon.'

'You'll soon be horny the moment you enter the Maiden, darling,' Melindi whispered in her sexiest voice. 'Why don't you let me take you down to the chamber later?'

Anastasia's eyes brightened. Then she fluttered her eyelids as she sipped her tea again.

The doorbell rang at last.

As Gael swung the great oak door back, her eyes met a tall, dark, thirty-something man, silhouetted against bright sunlight. She hadn't been able to put a face to him when she had taken his confession in the chapel. Now she recalled him arriving for the party with a rather brassy young woman on his arm. Arriving in his Aston Martin, she certainly hadn't been in his class. Gael had had the impression that she might even have been a hired escort.

She pushed the thoughts aside and held out her hand.

'Hilton Markwell,' he said, taking her hand warmly.

'Hello, Hilton. It's nice to see you again.'

'Thanks.' He looked at his shoes. 'Thanks – I . . .'

Seeing that he was nervous, she towed him in and closed the door.

He pulled his hand away from hers. 'I nearly didn't come.'

'But you're here now.'

He fumbled with something in the pocket of his slacks.

She led him through to the salon off the foyer and closed the door. 'So – now that you are here, tell me what happens first in your recurring dream?'

He wiped his forehead with the back of his hand. 'I'm starkers when the dream starts. My prick is as big as a barber's pole and I rush into a room where six attractive young women are sitting having tea.'

She looked down at his crotch, to see how aroused he might be. There was nothing showing there that she could see.

'But – in your dream – how do you get naked and horny?'

He shrugged. 'Don't know. I just am. And I want to screw like mad. But the old man who appears in white robes says I've got to have them all before I'll come.'

Gael pushed her hair back thoughtfully. 'OK. Let's

160

do it like that and see what happens. Now – I must get back to my guests. I've got five women friends having tea and cakes.' She smirked and turned to go, but he grabbed her arm.

'Will you strip me first?'

'Is that part of the dream?'

'No.'

She put her hand on his. 'Don't you think we should stick to the dream?'

'We can't stick to it exactly. There's no old man telling me I must shag them all before I'll come.'

She sighed. 'All right. Can't you pretend he's already said his piece?'

Markwell's face brightened. 'Brilliant. But remember – in the dream, the last woman runs out just as I'm going to shag her.'

'And what do you do?'

'I run after her. But . . .'

'But what?'

'But the dream usually ends just as I'm chasing her up some stairs.'

'Does it always end like that?'

'Usually. But I did catch her once. She fought like hell and I had to drag her to a bedroom.'

'And what did you have to do then?'

'I pinned her to the floor with one hand and ripped her clothes off with the other. And then the dream ended. That's why I'm here. I need to end the dream.'

She kissed his cheek. 'OK. Let's end the dream.'

He held her shoulders as she tried to withdraw. 'But will you strip me, anyway? I don't think I can get it up on my own.'

Her hands trembled as she parted the buttons of his pristine shirt. He had nothing underneath it and his sun-browned skin felt silky to her touch. His belly tightened as she slipped the shirt off and ran her hand down it. Then she went behind him, slid her fingers over

161

his back and traced the bulging muscles of his shoulders. He certainly would have the strength to hold a woman down while he stripped her.

She knelt and ran her hands down the outsides of his thighs. He set his legs apart. She slid a hand between them, turned it and cupped his crotch. He stirred as he felt the heat.

Now she slipped her hands up over his hips and undid his belt. Then she circled around him, kissed each nipple in turn and slipped his trouser zip slowly down.

He closed his eyes and put his head back, his large hands on his hips as she bared them.

The trousers fell away easily. He kicked them and his shoes and socks off. Now he stood only in a pair of posing briefs. She trembled more as she ran her finger-tips over the twin-lobed bulge contained tightly within the pouch. He was magnificent and she wanted him already.

She knelt before him. She put her lips to his bulge and kissed. The warmth of his penis came to her lips immediately. She felt it stir. She kissed again – and again. Each time she put her lips to it it grew up more. Then with trembling fingers she pulled the briefs away.

The head of a half-hard penis rose from inside the elastic. She kissed it, revelling in the sensuality of the smoothness of the glans against her lips.

She breathed his scent, strong and musky as it flooded her nostrils. Her tongue-tip came out and ran through the groove of the glans. It swelled and erupted quickly. Now she pulled the pouch slowly down, baring his balls. They swung loosely, the hairless sac taut and unwrinkled. She loved a man with a smooth and hairless scrotum. It was so sensuous to lick.

His penis reared above her.

She made him step out of the briefs. Now she had him completely naked, his belly shaking as she ran her tongue up the inside of his leg untill it touched his sac.

162

He widened his stance and pushed his pelvis out to make his cock go rigid. When she licked it from the scrotum to the web, he shuddered.

'I want to screw you,' he whispered as he pulled her head into his crotch, making her put her mouth to his sac.

She looked up over his taut belly and into his eyes. The shyness had gone. There was a glint there now. This was the man from the dream, not the shy one who'd just arrived.

She licked his glans again. 'That's not in the dream, is it?'

He grinned wickedly. 'I don't know what happens before I go into the room with the six women. For all I know, I might screw one of you first.'

Gael sat back on her haunches. 'I think we'd better stick to the plot, don't you? Let's take it from where you go into the room stark naked with this rearing between your legs.' She put her mouth over the head of his penis and sucked on it slowly. It always felt so good to suck a man that way. It gave her a sense of power when they stood and let her do it. There was no contest. No rivalry. They were getting what they wanted most – a hot and mobile mouth to spurt into. Some said it was better than the feel of woman's vulva. More responsive. More tantalising. Sometimes they said it was so satisfying as the woman sucked him in. When he spurted and she milked him with the suction of her mouth, he'd usually beat for several minutes, moaning as he lay there.

Gael stopped herself fantasising and tickled the web of the cock with the tip of her tongue.

Between her legs, she could feel her moistness. The kimono she'd chosen was loose and she wore the flimsiest of panties. It would be so easy to lay back on the rug, pull aside the gown and have him rip her knickers off.

She resisted the temptation and rose.

'I'm going in.' She kissed him lightly on the lips. 'It's your show now, Hilton Markwell. Enjoy it. I hope it ends like you want it to.'

Before he could grab her again, Gael slipped out. But she was only halfway down the corridor when he came after her, his penis wagging as he ran. He'd been transformed, his eyes alight, his mouth set in a determined grin.

She slipped into the sitting-room and closed the door quickly. The other women looked up with surprise. 'There's a horny man coming down the passage,' she panted. 'He tried to grab me but I managed to escape. I need some tea.'

Gael had just sat down on the Chesterfield next to Anastasia when the door was flung violently open. The man stood naked, his phallus huge, his testes swinging to his laboured breathing.

They all looked away and continued their chat. Sophie poured tea. As she handed a cup to Gael, it rattled in the saucer. It continued to rattle in Gael's hand.

They took no notice as he entered the room, although Gael saw Sophie's eyes flick in his direction before she picked up a plate of cakes and handed them around. 'Have some cake, ladies,' she said in a falsely bright voice. 'My mum made it this morning.'

Anastasia took a bite and closed her eyes. 'Scrumptious, my dear. Really scrumptious. I love homemade goodies.'

As Markwell closed in, Fiona was the closest. He stood behind her armchair looking down.

Ignoring him completely, Anastasia munched her cake. 'Remind me to get the recipe before I go, Sophie. I'll give it to my cook.'

'And mine,' Boo joined in.

Without warning, Markwell took hold of the back of

164

Fiona's chair. She squealed as he tipped it. He had it on its back in a second, Fiona's legs in the air. Now she lay looking up between his legs. He knelt on the head of the chair, his testicles swinging just above her face.

Fiona's skirt fell about her hips, her pink, lacy panties coming to view. The black hair of her pubis poked clearly through the lace as a beam of sunlight struck the scene.

'Have you seen Martin Frobisher lately, Anastasia?' It was Melindi, scowling hard at Anastasia who was staring at the man drawing off Fiona's knickers to bare the upturned furrow of her sex.

Anastasia shook herself and looked at the enquirer. 'No – I think he's in Barbados for the summer. I. . .'

Fiona squealed as the man spread her legs, opening her up to his gaze. And as she lay looking up at his ridged penis, he put his lips to the mouth of her sex and sucked it.

Gael tore her attention away from the scene and fixed her gaze on Sophie. The maid was staring at the man mouthing the whole of Fiona's sex, making her wriggle with the sensation and evoking little moans of pleasure from deep down in her throat.

'Sophie! Pass the biscuits, please.' Gael nudged the maid. 'And is there any more tea in the pot?'

Sophie shook the pot and then her head.

'Then go and make a fresh one, will you?' Gael prompted, trying to divert the girl's attention from the way Hilton Markwell was stretching Fiona out to lick her deeply.

Sophie pouted and looked at Melindi for support. She clearly didn't want to leave. Markwell was now running his mouth up and down the inside of Fiona's leg. Then he started taking lip bites at the widely stretched hollow between her vulva and the tight skin of her thigh. The frilly inner lips of her sexual purse were pulsing pinkly. And the clitoris, which Gael had sucked on during that mad time of the shower party, was standing proudly from its hood.

'Do as you're told, girl,' Melindi snapped at Sophie. 'There's nothing to interest you here.' Then Melindi turned to Boo. 'How's your mother keeping these days, Boo? Is her arthritis any better?'

Sophie picked up the Georgian silver teapot and moved towards the door. But Markwell abandoned his first catch and tackled her to the floor. The teapot rolled away. With Markwell hugging her legs, Sophie was flattened under him, her ski pants dragged down her thighs. She landed stomach first over a padded footstool, her bottom bare, the lips of her vulva showing between her legs. Gael saw she was moist and felt her own nectar welling between her legs.

As Sophie tried to rise, Markwell bit her bottom. She wriggled hard, but Gael thought that it was mostly for show and not because she didn't want to be taken strongly by this animal of a man.

'I saw Olga, Lady Swaningham in Harrods on Tuesday,' Anastasia piped up brightly, taking another éclair.

Melindi turned to her. 'And who's the cow screwing at the moment? Last time I saw her, it was some Italian millionaire.'

Anastasia shrugged, trying not to stare at Sophie and the man. Gael could hardly take her eyes off them either. As he pushed her over the footstool, his penis was poised to plunge.

'Do you know Olga, Gael?' Anastasia clearly asked to divert Gael's attention, but she would not be diverted. With Markwell's bottom to them, his balls bobbing between his legs, he wouldn't know that they were all anticipating his thrust and imagining how it would feel in them.

Sophie gasped as the phallus drove in hard. She moaned as she felt its length. He withdrew and charged again, so ardent in acting out his dream that he was clearly oblivious to the five pairs of eyes watching each swing of his testicles, and every dynamic thrust of his straining cock.

With his hands in the hollows of Sophie's back, he braced his weight on his arms. Now he began to flex his hips as he drove into her.

His motion became rhythmic.

He began to pant.

Five fingers slipped between the folds of five, wet, swollen furrows.

Gael was sure that he was coming. The excitement of the scene and the wriggling, clamping pressure of Sophie's purse seemed to be bringing him off. She sighed, half glad that the charade seemed to be played out, half saddened by the fact that she probably wouldn't experience him. But she might take him aside alone before he left. She might tow him up the stairs to her bedroom. She was still frustrated at the way Flanders had stoked up her passion before he had abandoned her. The cold-shouldering that she had had from Sophie and Melindi had made her need warm, naked flesh against her own, now even more than ever.

Sophie was pushing back at him as he charged. His anus seemed to wink as he pulled and thrust. Sophie was panting harshly now, partly because her belly was pressed so hard against the stool, and partly, Gael judged, because of her rising need.

'Fuck me, you brute,' she gasped as he slid eight inches of curving flesh between her sucking labia again. 'Yes. Oh God, yes.'

Gael remembered her role. 'Did anyone see who took Francine home after the party?' she said brightly.

'She went off with some creature who Nicky Sanders dragged along, I think,' Boo said as she watched intently as Markwell increased his stroke.

'Did you see Mandy on the stairs with those four blokes?' Fiona chipped in.

Markwell was thrusting into Sophie so hard that her buttocks swelled and bounced to every thrust. Gael was sure he would come very soon.

'I saw one man standing over Mandy with his prick in her mouth, while she pulled two others off and had the fourth licking at her pussy,' Anastasia said dreamily, her dress up around her thighs, her hand between her legs. The other hand massaged one large breast through the thin material of her blouse.

Fiona had recovered from the licking. She had righted her chair and was kneeling in it, her bottom still bare, her knickers in shreds on the floor. Her labia were slick from the licking as she thrust them out, her eyes fixed on the man plunging into Sophie.

Suddenly he put his head back and closed his eyes. His back was bowed, his penis thrust as deeply as it could be inside the panting girl. Then he let out a groan.

At first, Gael thought that he had climaxed. Then she realised that it was a cry of frustration. She knew how it felt not to be able to come despite an aching need and the pounding of her sex upon the phallus of a man. Surely, she thought, he must be feeling the same as his foreskin strained when he thrust to the fullest extension of his cock.

'Have you ever had a gear stick up your cunt?' Anastasia volunteered, trying not to notice as Markwell withdrew his penis from its hairy, thick-lipped prize. His eyes were ablaze with energy. Glazed with the moisture of Sophie's excitement, his penis steamed in the heat from her body and the temperature of the sunny room.

Gael turned to Anastasia. 'You weren't caught by that guy in the Ferrari, were you?'

She grinned then turned as Sophie turned and grabbed Markwell's penis hard. 'What the hell are you doing? I need you, you bastard. Don't stop now.' As she tried to grip his penis, all she succeeded in doing was to pull the foreskin over the glans before her fingers slipped off. The foreskin slid back slowly to expose the swollen head again.

Without any heed for Sophie's plight, Markwell rose and took a couple of strides to where Anastasia sat munching on another éclair.

He thrust her back into the settee and pushed her dress up to her thighs. He dragged her panties off her with such force they tore. Then he hooked her under the knees and pushed her legs back to her breasts.

'I understand that the Van Hagens are having a do at Bramwell Castle on Saturday. Anyone going?' Anastasia asked. Then she sucked on the éclair as Markwell forced her legs back, showing a mass of reddish-brown hair. It formed a beard which ran down the edges of long and prominent sex lips, and finished in a whorl about her anus.

With hardly a pause Hilton Markwell aimed the head of his penis into the beard and pushed. Gael watched with fascination as the shaft was engulfed. It was as if some hungry animal hiding in the thicket had been lying in wait. Now as it gobbled, the eager shaft was gone.

Gael looked at Melindi and whispered, 'Christ – did you see how she swallowed it?'

Melindi grinned. 'She's the most voracious woman I know, darling. And she looks so innocent too. Many a man has been quite surprised at the way she sucks him in and devours him whole.'

Anastasia wound her legs tightly around Markwell's hips. She clawed at his flanks, pulling him on to herself. The éclair stuck out of her mouth like some chocolate phallus, its cream spread out around her lips.

He tried to pull away from her, but she had him fast. He struggled and pushed at her hard, drawing out of her at last. Pushing her legs down roughly, he sat astride her belly and ripped her blouse apart. Then he took each breast in his hands and began to knead.

Now it was she who struggled to be free of him as her

nipples swelled from between his wide-spread fingers. But he pushed her down uncompromisingly. Now he snatched the éclair from her mouth. He slid it over his cock like a chocolate-coloured condom. Then he rose and drove the éclair against her mouth.

She took it in and began to suck on it. Encompassing his penis, it seemed to give great pleasure. Gael watched as the brunette widened her legs again. The lips of her vulva began to tremble. As she stretched her legs as widely as she could, it gaped. Then it closed tightly with the spasms of her orgasm. As it closed, the lips were engulfed by the hairy mass, only to reappear as it opened up once more.

Now the éclair had gone. All that was left of it was a chocolate coating on Markwell's penis. Anastasia gobbled at this as greedily as the mouth between her legs had done on his cock. She licked it hard, trying to scour every smear of chocolate from its length.

He pulled her head to make her take him in.

Sophie stood at the end of the settee, scowling.

Gael was fascinated by the whole affair. Never in her wildest imaginings had she thought that this charade would turn out quite like this. She had not noticed Melindi for some seconds. Only when the supermodel rose and stripped herself naked before them all did she see the light of lust in the jet black eyes.

Melindi was magnificent as she stood before them looking down on Anastasia gobbling at the man. Her wonderful breasts were caught in a beam of sunlight, the nipples highlighted strongly, the undercurves perfectly spherical. Melindi thrust her pubis out. She always did so when she was aroused. It was as if she was pushing forward for contact rather like a man would flex his hips to thrust his cock inside her quim.

Melindi picked up a short whip from under her chair. Gael hadn't noticed it there. What she did notice now as Melindi bent, were the purple lips of the girl's sexual

170

purse. Melindi had the largest and most luscious vulva Gael had ever seen. She had often wondered how the model had walked the catwalks so elegantly with such a purse of flesh between her legs. But Melindi had told her that was her greatest asset. She could feel herself at every stride. She could feel the leaves of supple flesh working together, slipping over each other in the rich lubrication in which the sensuous sexual mouth seemed always to be bathed. She said that it made her sexy and alluring. That allure transmitted itself to the men in the audience, and it was they who bought the clothes, thinking that their wives would look as sexy as the supermodel did.

The whole of Gael's body trembled as Melindi straightened, raised the whip above her head, her breasts tightening. They hung silhouetted against the light. Then Melindi struck.

The lash landed across the thighs of the recumbent Anastasia, making her raise her hips.

Now Melindi lashed at the back of the man. This only made him take the mouth of the brunette more ardently. Then suddenly he pulled his penis away. He turned and caught the whip as the lash came down. He pulled it hard, taking Melindi off guard. He reached out and toppled her, sending her sprawling on the carpet. In a fraction of a second he stood astride her, his legs apart, the veins in his penis even more prominent than before. From Gael's position low down on a sofa, the profile of the man's erection was classical. It erupted from his scrotum in a long, hard curve, the tip of it almost rising to his navel. As he lifted the whip, his phallus strained. Then he brought the lash down across Melindi's belly.

She yelped and tried to rise, but he pushed her down with his foot, placing it hard on her pubis. Then he lashed again, making the thongs land in the valley of her breasts.

Melindi's nostrils flared. She made a valiant effort to rise.

171

He moved his foot to her mons and pushed her down. When she looked up at his rearing phallus, her legs were open and her belly panted with exertion. Or was it with excitement, Gael wondered. Why had the woman taken the whip to him? Had it been because she had wanted his attention? Or was it because she liked dominating men and wouldn't sit there meekly, waiting to be taken at his whim? But he had turned the tables. He was dominating her. With his large foot on her pubis, much of his weight bearing down on her, the man was her master. What would he do with her now?

The moment was taken over by Sophie. With a howl she leapt at him. She sprang on to his back and tried to pull him off Melindi.

He simply threw her into the Chesterfield. Then, before she could overcome her surprise, he flattened himself on top of Melindi. He forced her arms back hard above her head. Pushing at her ankles with his feet, he widened her legs. Then he was in her, thrusting strongly, his eyes staring into Melindi's eyes, his lips only an inch from hers.

Boo stroked his buttock as it rose. She glanced at Gael and smiled demurely, whispering, 'Do you think he'll try to fuck me too?'

Gael grinned and whispered back, 'He might if you play your cards right, Boo.'

Sophie sprang again. She tried to pull him off. She sat astride his back and beat him with her fists.

'Get off her, you brute. Get off,' she cried as she hammered at his shoulders. Tears streamed down her face, her breasts bouncing as she pummelled him. He rose and fell as he took Melindi hard. His back became slick with the nectar from the redhead's sex. Her tears streamed down her breasts. But the man was in full spate, his animalistic energy at its height. He would not be moved by the slip of a girl. Instead he drove his shaft deep into the receptive cavern of his conquest. He was dominating her totally, pounding her into submission.

172

At first Gael was alarmed. This was not going according to the 'dream' unless, of course, he had been making that up from the start. Then Gael smiled with relief as she saw Melindi grin. She seemed to be loving every second of it. Even as Sophie pounded jealously at the man, this seemed to make the union more sensational for both him and Melindi.

Sophie gave up her attack and sat cross-legged on the floor, staring at the man's buttocks as they rose and fell, watching his shaft curving into the hot, slick sleeve between Melindi's legs.

Boo stroked his balls through his open legs.

Melindi began to moan and throw her head from side to side. She raised her hips, gaining strength from her approaching climax. This made her nipples chafe against his chest. Their bellies rode and slipped with perspiration. Melindi's brow, her shoulders and her thighs were beading so profusely, it made her skin shine. Anastasia and Fiona raised her legs and pulled them back. They made her as open as she could be. Like this they presented her to him to drive down into. Wide and expectant, she seemed to need faster, harder treatment.

Boo rubbed his anus with one finger, pressing it in as he rose, withdrawing as he fell.

As he plunged it made Melindi's body shudder. It made her gasp for breath, as she panted, 'Yes – you bastard, yes.'

When she came, she let her tension go in a raucous cry and shuddered deeply from her vulva to her breasts.

Gael had seen that shudder many times. Melindi Mocambo had the most volcanic orgasms of anyone she'd known. She'd seen those breasts quiver and the nipples push right out until they stood like studs in their swollen rings of pimpled flesh. She'd seen that enormous vulva sucking on a cock, the bristly little hairs around its edges rasping at the shaft to make its owner moan with the sensation.

173

As Gael watched she saw the purple labia open, grip the paler cockshaft, then begin to spasm slowly. Like a large and succulent oyster, it contracted around his manhood. And Gael knew that with her legs wound around his hips, Melindi Mocambo would not release that cock until her pulses died.

Gael was right. He moaned as the woman squeezed him with the powerful muscles of her vaginal walls. And she knew what it must feel like to have that shaft inside them. She wanted it deep between her own.

The liaison ended as suddenly as it had started.

Melindi pushed him off. She stood over his hips, placed a bare foot on his cock and ground it into the tight flesh of his lower belly. She worked the scrotum slowly with her heel, holding the foreskin between her toes, masturbating it, making him push up against her sole for harder contact still.

As he writhed under the dominating foot, she had a look of triumph on her face. He worked himself against her frantically, trying to bring himself to climax. But he could not.

Anastasia sipped her tea.

Fiona took a chocolate finger and sucked on it thoughtfully as Melindi rubbed him with the sole of her foot.

Boo said dreamily as she opened an éclair and licked the cream inside it, 'Do you think he'd come in my mouth if I sucked him very slowly?'

Six pairs of eyes watched Markwell closely, twisting and turning, opening and closing his legs. They watched his hips rise and his cock thrust, just as if it were thrusting into one of them. Gael wished that it was her.

Then he stopped the gyrations of his hips. He looked up at Melindi's crotch, over her undulating belly, between her breasts and at her face-wide smile. Now he seemed to realise that she had had him in the way she'd wanted him, making him think that he'd had her.

174

Gael smiled too. The Nubian princess had mastered many a man like that.

Melindi put back her head and laughed. Then she lowered herself slowly, her feet sliding apart.

Anastasia knelt and raised the still-hard shaft. She pointed it up at Melindi's wide-spread crotch as the model did the splits. Gael blanched at the thought of that vulva, so tightly stretched as Melindi flattened out.

With a gasp of satisfaction, the girl engulfed the whole of him and sank down on his balls. They welled out momentarily, so pink against the supple Nubian skin. Then they were engulfed as well as the gaping vulva came to rest.

Melindi leant back. She buttressed herself with her arms. Her breasts were now moulded smoothly to the contours of her torso. She was stretched so tightly that Gael could see the penis bulging under her skin. She rubbed it slowly as she closed her eyes and grinned. It was her final act of conquest.

Then she rose elegantly. She eased herself from his impalement in one, smooth motion and sank back into the Chesterfield, her finger between her legs. She displayed her throbbing labia to him as he turned his head and stared at them. His shaft appeared to surge. And when Melindi ran her finger through her slit, his hand went to his own hard flesh. In unison they worked themselves. Melindi set the pace, her finger gliding through her slipperiness while her gaze bore into his.

With every upward stroke of the long, black finger, he closed his hand and pulled his foreskin up. With every downward plunge, he bared his glans and made it swell. As it appeared through his fingers, it coloured purple for a second before it was hooded by his foreskin once again.

They masturbated slowly. Nothing at all was said. The whole of the room's attention was focused on the masturbating hands.

Now he lay back against Anastasia's legs, her finger in her crevice too. But Markwell had no thought for her. His eyes were fixed on Melindi's crotch and the red-nailed, frigging finger.

He opened his legs, displaying to her just as she displayed to him. He showed her his balls and drove a finger deep into his scrotum as he rubbed his web with the fingers of his other hand.

In turn, she pulled her legs back, showing him her anus and the tightened membranes of her loins. The V between the woman's legs led his eyes to the pulsing-mouth. And likewise, the V formed by his legs led Gael's eyes to his balls and stubborn cock. Why the hell didn't he come? The scene was driving her to distraction. Her quim was throbbing for the need to be sucked or filled – preferably both, and soon. She was getting really randy.

The pace increased. The mischievous Melindi knew how to goad the man. She frigged herself deeper and more quickly. He worked himself in sympathy with her tempo, his strokes shorter and more urgent. At any second, Gael expected him to spurt.

Melindi came again. As rich nectar welled and ran, she spread it around her vulva to make it shine deep purple.

As he pushed his hips up and strained, Gael waited to see a copious shot of semen. But he let go of his cock and lay back on the floor.

They all knelt round and viewed the organ, stiff and rosy from the pounding it had had, but still devoid of semen at the little mouth that opened in the tip. A finger touched the web. Another stroked his balls, while others smoothed his belly and his thighs.

Boo raised his cock and worked it gently. Then she produced a condom from a pocket and rolled it on. She knelt astride him, showing him her labia and the tight ring of her anus. Her fingers came from between her legs and splayed her vulval mouth for him.

Suddenly he was up, scattering the ministering hands. He pushed against Boo's anus and was in it in a second.

The onlookers gasped. Fingers worked distended vulvas briskly.

Boo wriggled and pushed as he clawed her back and grabbed her hips to pull her tight. As Gael gazed down at the coupling, the view was the same as she had seen when she'd had Boo with the double-headed dildo. The difference was that this was real, hot flesh, not a rubber imitation. And it was buried in her bottom not her quim.

Gael couldn't stand being left out. She knelt and held his balls through his legs. She tightened his foreskin by pulling his sac to make him thrust deep into Boo.

Boo came with a judder and a little cry of relief. Gael could feel her contractions on the cock between her fingers. But still it didn't shoot.

As he turned to look at Gael, she came back to the reality of the situation. She recalled what came next. He'd had five of them in different ways and now it was her turn. She was the sixth and final woman in the dream.

Quickly, she rose. She turned and walked sedately from the room. She was halfway up the stairs before she heard him, his footfall heavy as he came.

She started to run.

He bounded up the stairs, two at a time.

She reached the top but stumbled. Unable to rise quickly enough, she started to crawl along the landing, but he caught her gown and ripped it off, leaving her naked apart from a minimal thong.

She crawled away again.

This time he caught her ankle. He gripped her hard and dragged her back towards the staircase. Her belly and breasts chafed on the carpet, her nipples swelling with the heat which the friction caused. The thong cut into her crotch, parting the lips of her purse, rubbing at her anus. She could feel her moisture running. She could feel the heat in her belly rising fast.

She grabbed at a table on the landing, but could not halt her slide. Her hips rubbed the edge of the topmost stair, her knees lodged a little further down.

The thong tightened in her crotch as he took hold of it. When he ripped it apart she felt the coolness of air on her naked purse.

Then she felt the pressure of his hands upon her buttocks. As he stood on a stair below, straddling her legs, the tip of his cock came level with her vulva.

She felt its heat, then felt his fingers open her widely. She moaned with the sensation of the swollen head of his shaft pushing between her vulval lips, his thumb penetrating her anus.

16

His Wildest Dreams Fulfilled

As Gael glanced around, she was aware of five eager faces looking up from the bottom of the stairs.

She was also aware of the triumph on the face of Hilton Markwell as he drove himself between her legs. As she felt the heat of his shaft push through the moistened fringes of her vulva, she closed her eyes and sighed.

It was difficult to breathe, her belly hard against the topmost stair, flattened to the landing. Her breasts rubbed on the carpet, her bottom on his thighs as he thrust into her. Then she recalled her role in the fantasy.

She wriggled. She pushed out at him to unbalance him but this only served to make him penetrate her deeper. She felt the hardness of his pubis against her anal ring. She wriggled even harder, managing to make him take his hands from her hips to stop himself from falling. It was all she needed to escape.

In a second she was on her feet and bounding along the corridor. Her heart beat fast and her breath rasped from her throat.

His heavy footfalls behind her told her he was near.

She hit the wall at a corner with outstretched hands, turned and sped on. But, in her haste, she passed her bedroom door. There was only one haven – the linen cupboard. Wrenching the door open, she fell inside. She hoped against hope that he would not have reached the corner before she'd closed the door.

The little room was black, the light switch on the outside. She stumbled on a pile of sheets dumped upon the floor. She swore at Sophie for being so untidy and hoped that Markwell would not have heard her fall. In the darkness she groped for a hand hold. But before she could get up, the space was filled with light as he flung the door aside.

On her back, she looked up at him, his eyes afire with lust. Her lightning glance took in his cock, springing as he breathed. Upon the tip a little bead of moisture welled. So he was near to climaxing at last.

Supine among the bedclothes, Gael was at a loss. For the second that he stood there, she knew that she was his.

The light was eclipsed as he closed the door, leaving her in darkness. Then she felt his knees on the insides of her own knees as he knelt between her legs. She felt his hands upon her ribs, the thumb and fingers cradling her breasts. And she felt the heat of his cock again, as it nosed into her cleft.

'Get off, you pig,' she rasped into the darkness. 'Get out of here, this instant.' She tried to wriggle free from him, but there was nowhere to escape to.

He said nothing as he thrust through her vulval lips. In the silence, she heard it sucking on his cockshaft as it slid in. His own silence added menace to the scene. Although she knew he wouldn't hurt her, the charade had taken a more sinister twist. But that stimulated her more than any loving treatment might have done. She wanted him so badly now. The stripping of him in the salon had fired her up. And watching him taking the girls one at a time had brought her to a pitch of readiness from which she could not retreat. If he took her protest literally, he would leave her with her need.

He held her in the blackness, his cock inside her

180

swollen, clamping sleeve, his testes brushing at her loins. Now as he thrust he pressed down on her ribcage, pivoting on his hands. He drove himself deep into her, letting out a gasp of satisfaction as his penis reached its limit, and her vulva squeezed its shaft. Gael gasped with the sensation of fullness.

But then he pulled right out. She felt his helmet barely touch her labia. It cooled for the second that he held it out and then it plunged in again. He was playing with her cruelly. He was feeling what her heat was like. He was enjoying that elation which she knew must come from the first touch on a woman's fleshy purse before he thrust his cock inside her.

She pulled her legs back hard.

He clearly thought that this was to give him deeper access. As he drove the curved shaft downward, she put her feet on his shoulders and pushed him back as hard as she could manage.

He went flying through the doorway and landed on his back. As she raised herself she looked between his legs. His shaft was wet from its foray into her sex. His balls rose heavily with his breathing.

Gael was up and out before he could respond. She vaulted over him and made straight for her room. Barging through spectators in the passage, she ignored their lecherous looks, too intent on her gambit to pay them any heed.

She slammed the door and locked it. She stood against the frame, her belly heaving, her breasts riding up and down. The nipples were almost painful in their hardness and tender from their chafing on the carpet. Her lower belly held a growing ache – the tension from her need to mate. She knew that would be soon, and the very thought of it drove her heartbeat harder.

The lock gave way as he barged through the door. Gael flew across the room. She landed on a deep-piled Turkish rug. He caught her as she went to rise.

She twisted and shook him off. 'Bastard,' she spat as she kicked at him. 'Let me go, you pig.'

For a moment she saw uncertainty on his face. A tiny smile from her dispelled his doubt. But she followed it with angry words.

'Touch me and I'll kick you where it hurts.' She rose and faced him angrily, her fingers clawed as she crouched to spring. He mirrored her stance and circled. She didn't take her eyes off his at all.

When he struck, he caught her powerfully. He meshed his fingers with her own. He twisted her and flipped her on her back. Now she knew that even with her judo training, she would be no match for him. He was too strong. He was too horny. He was intent on having her and nothing in the world would stop him now.

She didn't want him to withdraw. She was so horny too – she needed him badly. He threw himself on top of her, pinning her down with his weight. His knee came up between her legs and ground upon her vulva. She wanted to part her legs to feel it more. But she didn't. She knew she must resist him. Her climax would be greater if she did.

She was so slippery with her sweat and his that she managed to slip away from under him. She caught his arm and twisted it, then stood up, put her foot hard in the hollow of his back and pulled the arm up tightly.

A glance at the doorway showed five faces peering around the jamb. The eyes showed admiration. The mouths wore face-wide grins.

Gael threw her hair back haughtily. She looked down at her prize. His buttocks tensed. The muscles of his legs were taut, his testes bulging powerfully between them.

She saw the muscles of his legs go tight. He rolled aside, taking her down as she tried to hold his arm. Now he was upon her.

He slid on her perspiration and her nectar. He lost his grip as she wrenched her wrists away, but he moved his grasping hands up to grip her neck lightly.

182

'Get off, you brute,' she croaked against his hand. 'Get off.' She beat him with her fists and threw her head from side to side against the firmness of his grip.

Still he kept his silence. His eyes were wide, his mouth curved in a smile of certainty. He knew that she was his to have just as he liked.

'Bastard!' she gasped as she felt his cock between her legs again. 'Bastard,' she repeated as he thrust in with great power.

To every thrust, she rasped out, 'Pig'.

To every stroke, he gasped.

She squirmed and scissored her legs, not to get away now, but to feel his thrusting better. She wanted him deeper. Stronger. Longer. Harder. Even more brutally still.

Now he took her with such verve she knew how it would end. He wouldn't be thwarted by his dream this time.

She began to heave her hips.

He thrust and ground her nubbin with his pubis.

She growled out, 'Bastard'.

He gasped with every push. His eyes were closed, his teeth clenched hard, his penis pounding deep into the purse between her pulled-back legs. My God, he was a brute. He was such a horny beast that she wondered if she'd ever have another man like him. She prayed she would. It was absolutely marvellous.

'Bastard!' she screamed as his tempo rose.

'Whore,' he gasped, thrusting deep into her.

'You lousy rotten, fucking prick.'

'But you're loving every minute of it.'

'I hate it, you monster.'

'You're lying, you little whore. Feel my cock.'

She felt it. She felt every millimetre of it as he drove it up, hooking her, curving it inside her.

'Bastard,' she yelled and wriggled her hips, as much for the pleasure of the watchers as for herself.

As he stared into her eyes, she saw a look of triumph. She smiled for a second, goading him to greater passion still.

Each forceful drive made her belly jolt. Her breasts rode heavily, swinging to the sides. She pushed her pelvis up and set her head right back. She was coming. My God, she was coming and it was going to be terrific.

He increased the tempo of his thrusts.

His hips worked like an engine, his cock the piston driving in her lubricated sleeve.

'Bastard!' she shrieked.

'Slut,' he cried. 'You love it.'

'Get off.' She clawed his shoulders and his arms. She raked him down the face. But she wound her legs about his thighs and tried to crush his cock between her legs.

Her nectar flowed and her soft flesh felt his hardness as she squeezed.

That only served to make him take her more strongly.

Incredulous faces looked down as the other girls stood round, each one now quite naked. They formed a semicircle, their legs apart, fingers plucking at their breasts, others in their clefts.

Melindi held the whip. She smacked it in one palm. She grinned that wicked grin which Gael loved so much.

The whiplash landed on Hilton Markwell's back. It caught Gael's thigh and made it sting. She contracted the tightening muscles of her sex.

He groaned.

She squeezed again; not for him but for herself. She was going to come and damn him to hell if he didn't come as well.

He pinned her to the floor but let her pelvis rise.

Melindi struck again.

He bowed his back, making each thrust stronger still.

Gael rose up against him, sinking as he withdrew. She rose again, making him ram her nub.

The whiplash caught her bottom where her vulva met her anus. Then she felt the heat of his flush. She felt his semen trickle from her cleft. Suddenly she was slippery from quite a different source. It made her flesh more sensitive. It made her judder with the thought of his jism pumping in her, flooding her, setting her alight with the energy of lust.

'Oh God – not yet,' she cried as he withdrew, his semen spilling on her vulval lips.

He slid right up her body. He took her breasts and pushed them into mounds, then thrust his cock between them until it touched her neck. And then he came again, letting out a hoarse, triumphant cry. 'You whore. You fucking, lovely whore.'

Gael looked down between her breasts. She saw the phallus of the man tunnel through the valley that he'd made. She saw it spurt its fluid and opened up her mouth. She felt warmth upon her chin and liquid trickle down her neck.

A cheer went up around the room. The other girls clapped loudly.

Markwell rolled away from Gael and lay back on the rug. 'Fucking hell,' he gasped. 'Fucking, bloody hell.'

Fiona knelt and took his cock. She worked it gently with a slender hand. She squeezed it so its milk oozed out, and then she licked it slowly.

Sophie sat astride his foot and rubbed her vulva on his toes. They waggled through her furrow and made her wriggle more.

Melindi knelt by Gael. She massaged at her breasts. She worked the thick, white fluid like a masseur would work in oil.

Anastasia rubbed Gael's clitoris with great finesse. She ran her fingers down the fringes of her sex. She collected semen from Gael's thigh and spread it into the deepest inner folds of her vulva.

Gael did not come. She moaned. She needed the man, not Fi or Boo or Sophie or Melindi – not even the voracious Anastasia. She still wanted fucking hard.

Markwell sighed and pushed through Fiona's fingers. She stroked his balls as his penis spurted once. She licked it like a lollipop from his testes to his glans.

'Fucking hell,' he groaned again. 'Fucking, bloody hell. That was nice.'

'Is that all?' Melindi slapped his thigh.

'OK,' he grinned. 'It was bloody marvellous. I've never had a fuck like that.'

Gael leaned on her elbow, resigned now that she would have to wait her turn to climax. Perhaps she would take him to the chamber and have him there. She ran her finger around his hardened nipple.

'And is that how the dream ended?'

He sat up too, resting on his elbow to mirror her. 'I don't think it could have ended better. Christ, I love you all.' He kissed Gael lightly on the lips. 'But I love you the most, you wicked hussy.'

'Ahh. Isn't that nice,' Fiona sighed as she worked his foreskin slowly.

Gael scowled playfully. 'You randy bastard. I hate you. You didn't make me come.'

He took her mouth with passion. He lay her down and pressed his lips to hers. He placed his legs between her own and kneaded at her breast. Then he rolled on top of her, resting on his elbows, holding his weight off her. He slipped his cock inside her and began to fuck her slowly.

'I think we'd better go,' Fiona whispered. 'This is getting serious.'

17

A Cocky Fellow

An hour later, Gael stood in the foyer looking up at
Hilton Markwell. They'd played and rolled and sucked
and rubbed together on the bed. She'd had a little
climax, but the explosive tension between them both
had gone the minute that he'd come. She smiled and
brushed his cheek.

'Will you come again?'

He shook his head. 'I don't think it could ever be the
same again. I don't want the memory of it ever to
change, sweetheart. Sorry.' As he closed his eyes, she
watched a tear running down his cheek. She wiped one
from her own. Then the doorbell rang. It was the taxi
that she'd ordered.

She held out the keys of his Aston Martin.

He closed her fingers on them and shook his head.
'No – I said I wanted you to keep it. It's very precious
to me, but what you've given me today is priceless. I'll
send the papers in the morning.'

As he entered the taxi, she held out the keys for one
last time. He forced a smile and waved her away. 'Keep
it to remember me by. Anyway – I've got another two
at home.'

The week passed very slowly. Gael slouched around the
house, the excitement of the tea party leaving a vacuum

in its passing. Could anything ever be that wild again? Melindi had gone. Gael was pleased even though she missed her. Sophie had not returned to her former, loving self. She seemed either to be brooding about Melindi, or there was something else on her mind. She continued to make Gael's breakfast and clean the house as usual, but whenever she saw Gael giving Todd Flanders orders for the garden, her mood turned black and she wouldn't speak for hours.

Twice Gael saw them talking by the potting shed, Sophie smiling up at him. But his demeanour seemed to be as superior as ever. Gael's feelings of jealousy sparked into life. With no prospect of ever seeing Hilton Markwell again, she still needed a man for that explosive climax she hadn't had. She didn't need a woman at the moment. Certainly not Sophie. Not even Melindi. And unless she could have Flanders in her own way, she didn't want him at all. She would have to wait until the next party in a fortnight.

She turned her thoughts away from sex – at least from her own needs. There was still a fantasy to fulfil for the woman who wanted a man's cock but without the inconvenience of having the man. She was scheduled for the next day and Gael still needed to find a way to make the fantasy come true. She had the glimmer of a plan.

She was polishing the Aston Martin when she saw the reflection of Flanders in its bright red door. She looked up sharply.

He scowled at her over the bonnet. 'I suppose you think you've very clever, don't you, miss?'

'Clever? What do you mean, Mr Flanders?'

He nodded to the car. 'Nice little present. Worth opening your legs for?'

She slapped him hard across the cheek.

He simply grinned.

Now she stiffened as she blurted, 'It belongs to a friend, if you must know. Now – haven't you got some work to do?'

188

'I'm finished for the day.'

She looked at her watch and shrugged. It had just gone five.

Flanders didn't leave. 'Good, was he?' As he came closer she smelled his scent and felt a thrill go through her. Naked above the waist and dressed only in shorts and sandals, he was as provocative as ever, and he knew it.

'Good, was he?' he asked again, running his palm over the wing of the car just as if it were her thigh.

She threw her head righteously. 'I don't know what you mean.'

He closed right in and whispered, 'I think you do.'

She tried to ignore him and rubbed briskly at the coachwork.

'But he's gone away to Hong Kong, I hear. So you won't be having him again. Not for some time, anyway.'

Gael rubbed angrily. 'It's none of your damned business, even if it were true.'

'It is my business if you expect me to fuck you when you're horny.'

She spun on him. 'How dare you. What makes you think I . . .' Then she saw his smirk. He'd laid a trap for her and she'd fallen in head first.

He grinned and rubbed his bulge, then turned and sauntered towards his motorbike, standing black and shiny in the shadow of the coachhouse. Gael watched him in the reflection in the bonnet of the car as he sat astride the saddle and kicked the motor into life.

Damn the man. He was too cocky by half. But the thought of his cock set her trembling.

'I'll need you tomorrow,' she called out as she got into the car. 'Come to the house at eleven.'

He drove the bike up to the car, looking down on her. 'There you are – I knew you'd need this soon.' He rubbed his bulge again.

She glowered. 'I want you to help me with some maintenance – that's all.'

189

'What do you want me to maintain?' My interest in your cunt?'

'Don't be so crude.'

He shrugged. 'All right. Do you want me to maintain my interest in your vagina? What's in a name? It's the same warm, wet yawning place between your legs for me to slide my prick into.'

She knew that he was being crude just to annoy her. He was quite refined in some ways. In fact he was too well spoken and too articulate for an ordinary gardener. She wondered why he did the job at all. Unless of course it was for the perks he had with Sophie and Melindi.

Gael thought that Flanders seemed reluctant to go. Did he think that she wanted him after all? She did want him. She craved him wildly. But, remembering his challenge to have her where and when he wanted her, she was determined to resist him. She would have him in her own way – on her own terms.

He rubbed his palm over his bulge again as he revved the motor of his bike. 'I'll do you now if you don't want to wait till the morning.' His slight smile showed that he was joking.

She studiously ignored him as she started the car.

'Come into the potting shed, if you like, miss. I've got some sacks in there,' he said softly.

She glowered. He never gave up, even when he knew that it was hopeless. 'I think you'd better go home, Flanders,' she said icily. 'Come to the house promptly at eleven in the morning.'

He tugged his forelock. 'Yes, ma'am. Anything you say, ma'am.' Then he grinned at her. 'Shall I bring some handcuffs and a whip?'

She revved the engine and screeched across the cobbles backwards. As she roared out of the stable yard she narrowly missed him. She accelerated down the gravel drive, the wind pulling at her hair. Then she saw him in the mirror. She slammed on the brakes as he passed and did a sliding turn at the gate. Then he made the bike rear like a cowboy's horse before he roared away, grinning widely.

'Damn,' she swore as she drove sedately through the gateway. Why did he get her so tuned up?

She knew why. She had been so horny since the tea party for Hilton Markwell. The experience had been too violent just to ebb away. Now the more she denied Flanders, the more her tension rose. She refused to let him know that she wanted him because that would feed his damned ego and put her at a disadvantage. But that would soon be remedied. She had definite plans for cocky Mr Flanders in the morning. She would kill two birds with one stone – fulfil the fantasy and sate her own needs without him being able to do a thing about it.

18

Standing Up for Her

Jannine Wellington-Moncrief was stunning. The smart suit she wore was obviously couture. As she stepped out of a chauffeur-driven Rolls, she looked alive and very chic.

'Hello.' She put out her hand demurely to Gael as they met on the steps. 'I've told my driver to wait. I hope that's all right with you.'

'Of course. Do come in.' Gael found herself speaking in the same clipped way and tried to walk as elegantly as she could.

She looked at the long-case hall clock just as it struck eleven, and showed her visitor into the salon. 'We've just a couple of things to arrange before we carry out your wishes. Would you like some coffee or some tea?'

Surprisingly Jannine pulled a hip flask from her bag and took a swig. Clearly she was not so calm inside as she appeared. But Gael was experienced enough to know that behind many a smooth exterior there were churning currents of desire which when let loose could tear a girl apart.

In the kitchen she found Flanders drinking coffee as he toyed with Sophie's breast. She slapped his hand as Gael ordered her to take a tray of coffee to the salon.

Gael looked Flanders up and down. Good – he wore only his usual shorts in the heat of the summer day.

Motioning him to follow her, she led him down the basement stairs.

'Where are we going? To some secret place where we can play without being disturbed?'

Gael didn't turn. 'You'll see in good time. Come on. I haven't got all day.'

He whistled with surprise as she opened up the chamber.

'Don't say a word,' she warned.

'Didn't say a thing, miss,' he returned, his eyes scanning the implements which stood around the space.

She didn't put on all the lights in the darkness of the secret room. She didn't want him to see too much. Nor did she want him to get ideas about how he might use them on her.

Pointing to the ceiling, she handed him a light bulb. 'The light just there has gone. I want you to replace it, please. It's too high for me to reach.'

As he stepped on a low, padded bench just below the light, she smiled at the memory of him stopping her from falling as she'd climbed the ladder in the scullery. Now the tables were about to be turned.

It was nearly too high for him to reach. She had calculated carefully that it would be. As he stretched, she took some padded shackles and snapped them on his ankles. As he screwed the lamp in, he was blinded by its light.

Quickly, Gael wound a handle of a winch at the end of the bench. As the ropes attached to the shackles began to pull, he realised what she'd done.

'You witch,' he snarled. 'You scheming bitch.' The winch pulled him off balance and he fell. He tried to undo the shackles but without a key it was useless. The outcome was now certain as she winched the ropes in tight. His feet were drawn towards the foot end of the bench.

'It won't do you any good,' he snarled. 'I won't play your game.'

She shrugged matter-of-factly. 'You don't have to do anything except lie down.'

He laughed. 'You can go to hell. You won't get any fun from me.'

Now it was Gael's turn to laugh. 'Isn't that what I said as you strung me up in the hay-loft? You thought you were so clever as you licked between my legs. Now it's your turn to see how it feels to be strung out helplessly.'

'And I said I'm not playing your game, you witch.' He pulled the ropes but could not make them give.

'But surely you haven't forgotten your challenge, Mr Flanders? You said I could have you in any way I wanted if I caught you.'

'So what. You can't make me do anything if I don't want to.'

She shrugged again and went behind him. He didn't look round, seeming to refuse to play her game. But it was his undoing. She slipped a leather halter over his head and wound a handle at the top end of the bench.

His hands went to his throat as she had planned they would. She'd rehearsed this whole manoeuvre several times. As he tried to release the halter, she snapped another padded cuff on one wrist. Now he was wise enough not to let her capture the other, but she reeled him in steadily. There was nothing he could do to stop her. Soon he was stretched out along the bench, one arm pulled above his head, the collar tight about his neck, but not too tight to hurt him.

He lashed out with his free hand but she dodged him. She held the shackle out. 'Give me your other wrist.'

'Not on your life, you slut.' He lunged again.

'All right. Please yourself.' As she gripped his balls tightly, his free hand shot down to protect them. She snapped the fourth cuff on and stood back quickly, grinning with elation.

He let out a long growl of frustration. 'I'll get you, you hussy. Don't think you'll get away with this.'

'You're in no position for making threats, Mr Flanders. Now lie still.' She wound the handle which pulled the second hand above his head. Now his belly was flat and his armpits hollow with the tension of the rack. He struggled to no avail.

Gael felt totally safe as she calmly ran the zip of his shorts down. He growled but she took no notice.

His penis was limp but large inside a pair of pristine briefs. He protested loudly as she took scissors and sliced through the legs of his shorts and let them fall away. Then she pulled the remnants from under him. She ran a finger up the inside of his leg until it met the bulge of his testicles. She thought she saw his penis move as he growled and glared at her.

Now she cut away the underpants. As she bared his penis, her fingers trembled violently. Her thighs began to quiver, transmitting little tremors of delight up into her vulva.

He lay there naked now. Perspiration beaded on his forehead. But was it because he was frightened? Or was he just as excited as she was?

She whispered in his ear, 'I'm not going to hurt you, Flanders. But I am going to teach you a lesson, you conceited pig. Now, if you lie still and behave yourself, I'll give you a treat you won't forget for years.'

'I'll catch my death of cold stretched out like this,' he hissed, the pressure of the traction making it hard for him to speak.

'Then I'll cover you up.' She took a large black velvet sheet which she'd prepared the day before. She covered the whole of his body, and the winches and the bench. There was a hole for him to breathe through. She adjusted the position of the sheet, making sure that a second hole came right about his crotch. She pulled his penis and his scrotum through the aperture. His testicles lolled heavily on the black material. And although his penis fell to one side, Gael was sure that it was becoming hard.

'You can stop that, you hell cat,' he croaked. 'It's no good touching my prick, I won't cooperate. But if you let me go, I'll give you the screwing of a lifetime.'

She laughed. 'I've already had "the screwing of a lifetime" from the man who gave me the car. But thank you for the offer all the same.' She raised the sheet at the head end and kissed him on the lips whispering into his mouth, 'Now, just in case you won't be quiet, I'm going to have to gag you.'

He protested loudly as she stuck a strip of sticky tape across his mouth. She tied the collar firmly to the bench to stop him raising his head and then replaced the sheet.

Pleased with her handiwork, she switched out all the lights. Then she went quickly to the salon where Jannine was sipping coffee and flicking nervously through *Vogue*.

Gael sat and poured a coffee for herself, her hands shaking and her heartbeat banging loudly. Then she stared into the woman's dark brown eyes. 'Tell me again about your fantasy, Jannine.'

The woman gulped. 'It – it's just that I crave for a man's hard bits, but don't particularly care for men. I would give anything just to have a warm, hard cock to play with but not to have to bother about him, or what he'd do to me.'

Gael gave a reassuring smile and held out her hand. 'Then your fantasy is about to be fulfilled.'

As she opened the door to the chamber, hot air rushed out to meet them. She led Jannine in and closed the door. Then she whispered, 'Don't be afraid. I won't be far away. Just enjoy your fantasy.'

As she switched on a solitary spotlight, a disembodied, sun-browned penis seemed to float in the darkness. Its testicles welled roundly in their sac.

Gael guided Jannine forward so she could study it closely. 'Don't be afraid of it,' she whispered. 'But don't hurt it. If you treat it nicely, I'm sure it'll reward you with whatever you desire.'

Flanders was so quiet that Gael wondered for a moment what had happened. But then she heard his breath and she saw his penis move. He had probably heard her whisper to Jannine and decided to play along.

'Strip me,' Jannine whispered. 'I want to be naked before I touch it. I want to feel its skin against my own.'

With shaking hands, Gael removed her jacket. As she slipped the buttons of the blouse, she felt the taut, round breasts well out with nothing to restrain them. The nipples were already hard, the belly undulating deeply as Gael released the waistband of her skirt. When she felt the curly hair of the woman's prominent mons, Gael realised that she wore no panties. She smiled at the thought of the woman stepping so genteelly from her Rolls without her knickers on.

Jannine Wellington-Moncrief had a most exquisite body. She was a brown-pink version of Melindi. Her breasts were large, but not too big to be unwieldy. The sturdy nipples stood up hard, the little bumps of their nimbuses like tiny nipples too. Her pubic mount had a mat of thick and curly hair. And, as she stood before the bench, she pushed it out as if to say, Look at the secret place at the apex of my legs.

Gael saw her lick her lips as she looked down on the apparently discarnate penis. She knelt beside it, studying it carefully. 'It's very soft,' she whispered. 'I thought it would be hard.'

Gael knelt beside her. 'You can make it hard if you touch it. You can lick it if you want to.'

Flanders' belly heaved but he didn't make a sound. He probably thought Gael would hit him if he did, and he was in no position to retaliate.

Jannine put her lips to the limp cock. She kissed the foreskin lightly, then ran a series of little licks down the whole length.

'I think it's coming to life,' she whispered, her voice sounding excited as the cock began to swell.

She kissed the balls, making them retract. Then she licked deeply between them and up the centre of the growing shaft. It burgeoned before their eyes, like the sped-up motion of a growing plant. The head swelled from the foreskin as the supple flesh rolled down.

Now Jannine put her tongue-tip to the web which tightened as she touched it. The head swelled more as the shaft began to stiffen and to curve.

The woman gathered confidence. She flattened her tongue against it and lapped at it hard. Turning to Gael she grinned. 'My God – look what I've made it do. I've never had one do that before. The only cocks I've seen have already been hard. And I've never felt one with my hands or kissed one quite like this.' She lapped at his balls again and sighed.

'Why haven't you touched one?' Gael asked softly as she stroked the woman's arm.

'Because they've been too keen to get them up my fanny. So I've just lain back and waited till they've finished.'

'That doesn't seem much fun.'

Jannine sighed and kissed the glans again, making it swell fully. 'I've liked the feelings it's made as it's fucked me. But the men have been brutes. That's why I wanted this.' She stroked it as gently as she might stroke a kitten, pulling back the foreskin so it stretched.

'Well, I hope you like it.'

She smiled. 'I do. I hope it doesn't mind me playing with it.'

Gael smiled too. 'I don't think it does. It wouldn't be as hard as this if it didn't want to be played with.' She stroked Flanders' web and made his penis jolt. As he sighed, she jabbed him in the side without Jannine noticing.

The woman looked at Gael with a query on her face. 'What shall I do now?'

'You could try working it through your fingers.'

198

'How exactly?'

Gael ringed Flanders' cock and masturbated slowly. When Jannine had a go, he flinched.

'Gently,' Gael whispered, as she took the cock from her and worked it with the tips of her fingers. 'You can only be rough with it when it's straining to spurt.'

Jannine's eyes went wide. 'But how will I know when it's going to spurt?'

Gael smirked and tapped her nose. 'You'll know. When he thrusts out his hips, it'll pump up hard.'

'Like I push my cunt out when I want to come?'

'Just like that. Do you come easily?'

She shook her head. 'I've only come once, and that was with a dildo which vibrated.' She ran her fingers up and down the cockshaft.

'Then I'm sure you'll love this one. It'll spurt strongly into the air if you work it up enough.'

'I've never seen one spurt. I've only felt them in me.'

'Then you're in for a surprise.'

'What does the spurt look like?' She took the head of Flanders' cock and mouthed it, closing her eyes and sucking on it gently.

'You'll see what it looks like soon enough.'

'What does spunk taste like?'

Gael shrugged. Just play with it. You can taste it when it spurts.'

'It smells divine.' She sniffed it hard. 'It makes my pussy hot inside. I'm getting rather wet.'

'Good. Perhaps it's time to feel it between your legs.'

'May I?' Her eyes went wide again.

'It's your fantasy, Jannine. You can do what you like with it.'

Jannine stood astride the man, the bench just the right height for her to do so without her vulva touching his penis. She sank down on it and rubbed herself up and down its length. It was fully hard now and rising from his belly.

199

Jannine rose on her toes, pulled the shaft up to vertical and eased down on its length. Her breathing slowed as she felt it.

Gael watched it disappear into her sleeve with a rush.

Jannine sat there with it deep between her legs and smiled contentedly. 'Bloody hell, that feels so wicked.'

'Good. It's the wicked times which are the most fun.'

The elegant woman began to spring. With each rise and fall the cockshaft worked like a well-oiled, curving piston. With every thrust her tempo rose until she was riding him fast. He began to thrust his hips. Gael jabbed him in the ribs but it didn't stop him thrusting.

Now Jannine turned around to face his feet. She took him in again. But her body shaded out the light. Prepared for any eventuality, Gael brought out a torch and shone it between Jannine's legs. The woman's sexual mouth was huge, the lips long leaves of supple flesh. As she sank down on the object of her desire, they spread out on Flanders' thighs leaving imprints of their wetness when she rose. Jannine watched with fascination as she rode her steed. She opened her vulva wide by putting her feet up on the bench. Now she tried to engulf his balls, pulling the leaves of her sex aside with her fingers, letting them enclose his sac.

He moaned as he felt the heat.

Gael prodded him sharply once more.

Now Jannine began to pant. As she plunged, the supple flesh of her cavernous purse sucked at his cock. She leaned forward and clamped his thighs. Bracing her arms so she could pivot easily, she looked between her legs to watch herself engulfing the long, hard shaft.

Gael took a breath as she saw it disappear. Watching a strong penis plunging deeply into her own body always made her come just that bit faster and more violently.

Jannine thrust back her head. She closed her eyes as her belly tensed. She pushed her breasts out and squeezed them.

Now Gael stood astride the gardener's legs facing the panting woman. She plucked at Jannine's swollen nipples as the exquisite creature took in the man's hardness. His penis slid in easily.

Jannine came in a series of juddering contractions. She sank down on to the shaft and held it deep inside herself.

When she had quietened, she rose and drew it out. She sat again, holding it to her mons, rubbing her nubbin gently up and down its root.

He came with a spurt which reached her breasts.

She looked down at it with surprise. And when the second spurt shot up to her lips she licked them with relish. She worked him gently, milking him until his pumping beats quietened to a tick. Then she rubbed his pearly semen into the skin of her breasts. She coated her belly with its moisture. When this was done, she eased back on his chest and lowered her mouth to kiss his cock.

In the light of the torch, Gael watched the last drops overflow as Jannine squeezed him. Then she put her mouth over the still-stiff shaft and took it in.

When Jannine had sucked the foreskin up and let it slide right down again, she looked up and wiped her mouth with the back of her hand and sighed.

'My God, that was incredible, Gael. It was absolutely marvellous.' She licked it like a greedy child attacks a lollipop. This made him hard and thrust again and soon he came once more. This time she made him spurt into her mouth, closing her eyes and sucking as his penis pushed in. She studied it as it made its final little ticks, and then she lapped his glans and kissed his web.

Together they played with Flanders' balls, delighting in making them move. They licked each side of his shaft together and giggled as their tongues met, fenced and departed down the shaft again. They smeared his glans with honey and sucked it from him slowly.

'I'm told that it's wicked in your bottom,' Jannine sighed as she sucked a glob of honey from his scrotum.

'It's excruciatingly nice,' Gael grinned. 'Perhaps you'd like to try it if we can get him hard again.'

Flanders groaned.

This time it was Jannine who dug him in the ribs. 'Who is it?' she whispered, her face bright with excitement.

Gael grinned. 'Nobody at all, really. It's just a big prick.'

They shrieked with laughter as they looked at the 'nobody's' cock, and rubbed it with their palms until it stiffened and spurted once again.

After Gael had dressed Jannine and taken her to her car, they kissed. She looked radiant and alive. The chauffeur pretended not to be amused as he closed her door. Then the Rolls hushed across the gravel forecourt and Gael returned quickly to the chamber, her heart pounding as she approached the tied-up man.

19

Taking a Very Firm Stand

Gael stood with her back to the closed door of the chamber. Her labia were throbbing and her clitoris was hard.

Before her floated the disembodied penis in the darkness. She closed her eyes and took a long deep breath. Then she went to the bench. She drew back the sheet and removed the gardener's gag.

He had his eyes closed as if he were savouring his experience. When he opened them he smirked, saying, 'Christ, that woman had a cunt like a boxer's glove.'

Gael slapped his shoulder hard. 'You're the crudest man I know, Todd Flanders.'

He grinned. 'But you like me talking dirty.'

'Dirty and crude are different.'

'Are they? Give me an example of the difference.'

'You're incorrigible.'

'It's being so incorrigible that makes me so attractive to women.'

'Don't kid yourself. You're just another prick to most of us.' She pulled his penis hard and made him wince.

'Now who's being crude?'

She wrung the foreskin over the glans. 'It's true. You are just another prick. The lady had the right idea. If I could have this without your boorish behaviour, life might be a little quieter around here.'

He pushed up through her fingers. 'But you can't have my prick without me, I'm afraid, miss.'

'Want to bet?' Gael wrung the hardening shaft and smiled widely even though he couldn't see it in the dark. He groaned as she began to work him up.

'You can stop that, you whore. I'm getting cramp trussed up like this. Let me go so I can screw you properly. You know you want it.'

She bit his arm and breathed deeply at the hollow of his armpit. A man's sweat always drove her wild for some quite unfathomable reason. She breathed again, letting the scent send little waves of energy through her body. She could already feel her labia engorging as it reached them. She sniffed again.

'You're just an animal really, aren't you, miss?' he whispered. 'Why don't you kneel and push your quim out for me. I'll do you like a ram would.'

She slapped him hard.

'Hitting me changes nothing,' he hissed. 'Why don't you stop pretending that you don't want my cock between your legs.'

She slapped him hard again and threw the sheet back over his face. 'OK, OK. I admit it. I do like it. Now shut up while I give myself a treat without you interfering.' Now she stood astride Flanders' face, facing his feet. Covered in the black velvet sheet, all she could see were his genitals, highlighted by the spot lamp. His penis was quite limp, his balls mobile.

Immediately below her she knew there was a hole in the cloth to enable him to breathe, even though she could not see in the darkness. She felt his warm breath as it sidled in and out between her legs. It warmed the opening of her vulva and made her close her eyes with the pleasure that this created.

She heard him breathe in deeply and knew that he was smelling her. This surely would make him horny once again. Now she set her feet wider apart to lower her vulva closer to his mouth. The bump of his nose beneath the sheet pushed between her labia. His breath on them was hotter now. She watched his penis move, but it didn't stiffen. Then she felt the slightest touch as the tip of his tongue came through the breathing hole. As she felt it skim one lip of her vulva, she adjusted her position to let it find her nub.

The tongue-tip licked again, the barest touch skimming through her furrow. She felt herself moisten and put her head back, her hands spread on her hip bones, her breasts pushed out. She set her feet even wider apart, and closed her eyes. This was bliss. It was heaven. It was marvellous to have the ministrations of the tongue while its master was bound and could not retaliate by grabbing her and eating at her, avidly.

Flanders pushed his tongue-tip through the stretched mouth of her purse. He flicked his tongue like a snake, titillating her nubbin, making it swell. It throbbed steadily now, with that little tingle that preceded the swelling of her vulva running up through her belly until it reached her nipples. She plucked at them gently, sending their own pulses of excitement back down to her clitoris to swell it even more.

Flanders blew hot breath through her furrow. He ran his searching tongue along the inside edges of her vulval lips. It tickled at the hairs which had colonised the fringes again.

She spread her fingers on his chest and buttressed herself so she could move effortlessly on his tongue. But he withdrew it through the hole.

'Don't stop,' she whispered. 'That felt so nice.'

He let a little laugh out through the breathing hole. 'It would feel nicer if you lay on your back and let me lick your pussy properly.'

She wriggled on his covered face but she could not make him lick her. Damn him – he had done it to get her going, expecting that she would succumb and release him from the shackles.

Gael moved to sit astride Flanders' thighs. She could just see his cock resting on his belly below her. She inched forward so that her stretched vulva barely touched his balls. She loved the way the soft and hairy sac tickled on the edges. She needed harder contact but his penis was still limp despite her stimulation as he'd tongued her. She took it in her hand and held it lovingly. Even though she got angry with the man, she had no quarrel with this. Jannine had been very wise in wanting only the parts of a man which alone could give her pleasure. Why bother with the rest? The rest was often boorish, conceited and insensitive. If only one could have a man like she had the gardener now, it might be a refreshing relief. Of course, to be honest, she wouldn't want that all the time. A man who had humour and flair in the way he took a woman could be infinitely more exciting than this, no matter how pleasant it might be at the moment. Flanders had a wit which made her laugh at times. And he had shown a touch of sensitivity when he had saved her from falling off the ladder. He was so impetuous too. How much better to have a male who would sweep you off your feet when you were least expecting it. She smiled at the memory of finding herself strung up by the ankles. That had been so exhilarating. Of course she'd shown him anger. With a man like Flanders one didn't just lie there saying, *I love the way you've strung me up to lick my pussy. Now fuck me with your tongue.* She couldn't have said that even though it might have been more honest than pretending that she had hated every minute. The way he'd knelt and rubbed her with his balls until she'd squirmed had been quite a new experience.

She looked down again at his balls between her legs. But, this time, she was on top and he was strung out helplessly. She rubbed her moist purse over the little hairs, making them shine. She tugged at his penis slowly, pulling the foreskin down until it was fully

206

stretched. This made the head swell, but not too much. The thing seemed not to be very interested in being brought to hardness. Had she worn it out at last?

He snored.

She slapped him hard across the belly.

He snored louder.

She pulled his cock but it made no difference, so she squeezed his balls gently.

'Ouch. You she-cat. That hurt.'

She rubbed them tenderly. 'Sorry. But I'm not letting you go to sleep on me.'

As he laughed, she realised he'd been pretending to be asleep. He'd caught her out again.

She slid back down his legs, his shins hard inside her thighs, delighting in the feel of the velvet cloth in her slit. Taking his penis in her mouth, she sucked it slowly. It showed no signs of hardening, but it was better than a rubber one. It was so alive even though recumbent.

She kissed the tip and licked its little hole. He trembled slightly. Now she simply took the whole of it into her mouth, warming it, pressing it with her tongue, sucking it very slightly. It grew gradually, becoming thicker and longer as the seconds passed. Now it was at the back of her throat. Running her lips over the glans, she pushed the foreskin down, which made it stiffen faster.

With her forehead against his lower belly, Gael kept the penis in her mouth. His belly rose and fell with his breathing. It was so peaceful, so free of tension.

As his cock grew stiffer, she realised that she was making love to him. She was being tender and caring instead of taking him wildly as she had intended. But she'd had some really wild sex in the past days and it was perhaps time to relax. She certainly had to take advantage of having Flanders tied. There was no way he would be fool enough to let her catch him out again. But as she lay there with the limp penis stiffening so that

207

she could thrust it between her legs, she wondered what the next few days would bring. Would he be angry and storm off? Would he strengthen his resolve to have her in any way he wanted, at any time and place? A thrill went through her at the thought. She knew that that was really what set her alight. The fight and the eventual submission would set her labia pulsing and drive that tension in her belly to an almost unbearable level of need before she climaxed.

Although he was stiff enough now for her to take him into herself, his lack of participation had robbed her of the fun of it. Watching Jannine having him had been amusing. Knowing that he was helpless to stop his cock rising and spurting had been exhilarating. But now the fun had ebbed away.

She lifted his cock and sank down on it until the tip just nosed between her labia.

He sighed and began to whisper, and as she rose and stretched her cunt, he felt her yank his cock up. Then he felt her heat as she sucked it in. She moaned as she felt his knob ripple up inside her.'

Gael slapped his belly to stop his commentary, putting into words what she was feeling. 'Shut up, Flanders,' she hissed. 'I want to do this without any input from you.'

He laughed, the sheet billowing around his face. 'What do you think you've got in your cunt but "input" from me?'

She ignored him. That feeling of being opened out as a thick, hard cock burrowed through her labia never ceased to make her thrill.

'And then she felt his bollocks, rasping at her bottom,' he whispered. 'And the lips of her quim sucked his prick.'

She punched him hard and made him wince, but he laughed again.

'And then she got angry,' he rasped, 'and she began

208

to pound up and down on his dick, willing it to come so she could feel his spunk shoot inside her.'

She punched him again. The repartee was adding that tension into the affair which had been missing. It had been too cold and calculated before. Now he was goading her again and stirring up her anger. She realised that she needed to compete with him and she needed him to fight back. Having him helpless and at her mercy had not been enough. She brought her knees up to the bench. As she rose and fell, she looked down through her crotch to see what the spotlight showed. She couldn't see the mouth of her sex, but she could feel it widely stretched as the long shaft of the gardener slipped between its lips. Each time she engulfed it, the black, curly hair of her mons blended with his golden hair. She rode him hard, feeling his hair rasping at her nub and his scrotum tickling at her bottom.

She turned to face his feet and shone the torch between her legs. As she sank on him, she watched his balls. Their sac tightened as she put her pressure on his cock, squeezing it as hard as she could, feeling the head right inside her body. The testicles welled out then disappeared between her thighs. She strained herself open, trying to take them in but she was not as big as Jannine.

Gael had to be content with feeling his scrotum against her clitoris as she took the slack skin between her fingers and rubbed her nubbin gently with it. Then she spread the cheeks of her bottom with her fingers and rubbed her anus on his pubic mat. This sent trickles of excitement up into her body.

'She was a slut,' he whispered, 'in the way she made her cunt lips gobble at his prick. She moaned as she rubbed her arsehole on his hairs.'

She slapped his legs but it didn't stop his commentary.

'Her cunt,' he said softly – even romantically, 'was

throbbing from the sensation of having a real man's horn at last. She begged him to fuck her like no other man had done.'

She hit at his side with her fist. 'Shut up, you.'

'And you shut up, you slut,' he laughed. 'Shut your quim and squeeze my cock.' Then he said in a treble voice, 'Oh, darling, that's absolutely marvellous.'

Despite his taunting, Gael's passion was rising. She would not be put off. As she sprang and plunged, his cockshaft was as huge as she'd ever seen it.

She turned and faced his head, even though she could not see it under the cloth. Now she sprang in little motions, imitating the short strokes of a masturbating man.

He began to pant. He strained his hips in an effort to make himself spurt. But Gael had become too intent on her rising orgasm to pay any heed to him.

His breath rasped as he whispered, 'And as she squeezed him with her quim, he came in a fountain of hot, thick spunk which filled her first then trickled down her legs.'

As she felt his semen pumping she screamed and beat his chest. 'You bastard! You lousy, rotten bastard. Don't you dare go soft before I've finished.'

He juddered under her as his penis pumped. She felt the heat of his ejaculation filling her, just as he'd described it. Then she felt his semen trickle down her thigh.

Now she rode him hard and he cried out with every thrust, but she didn't care. She needed to come. She couldn't stand her tension any longer. But he lost his erection and she had nothing to push down on.

As he slipped out of her, he sighed. 'That was very nice. Thankee kindly, miss.'

She worked herself over the limp penis but it didn't make her climax. 'Damn,' she swore loudly. 'Damn you to hell, Flanders.'

210

She sank forward on his chest, her energy spent, even though her tension had not broken. With his ribcage undulating beneath her breasts, she let her body ride. He was so warm, and, despite her anger at him, she still wanted him. But she was tired of the sparring. She wanted him to come into her room, strip her naked and lie beside her, his stiff cock hot against her leg. Then he would take her mouth with his. She would feel his hand between her legs as he kissed her passionately. He would coax her nubbin into life as she spread her legs for him, and make her pussy moist. Then he would roll over her and take her strongly. She would wind her legs around his hips and let him plunge down into her while she squeezed him. And she would come quickly with wonderful surges of energy, heating him with her fluids, making him shoot his hot, thick jism deep into her body.

Gael shook herself out of the fantasy. There was no way he would ever behave like that.

She stood beside the bench, the spotlight showing the disembodied cock. She drew the velvet sheet off him and unshackled his hands.

He lay grinning up at her, his eyes triumphant as he whispered, 'When can we do this again, miss?'

Clearly he thought he'd bested her. He was magnificent stretched out naked. She wanted to kiss him all over, but she was too tired.

'Here's the key,' she croaked, throwing it at his feet. 'You can undo the shackles on your ankles. I'm going up to take a shower.'

20

In the Maiden at Last

The next days sped by. Gael had parties to arrange. She spent hours on the phone talking to caterers, wine merchants and dressmakers. But now she had her last fantasy from the first party to fulfil. The man was scheduled for the next day. His fantasy of having three women at a time, in a way that he had specified very particularly, had not been too difficult to arrange. Fiona would be there supported by two young models; a voracious creature called Celine and a platinum blonde called Mandy.

Gael had decided not to include Sophie. The house-maid had been too petulant since the incident with Flanders in the chamber. She had seen Gael emerging from the basement and had scowled. When Flanders had followed, completely naked, she had fumed and hit him hard. Now she was hardly speaking to Gael as they went about their business. But Gael had noticed that the girl was still not freezing Flanders out. She'd caught them both in a tête-à-tête. They had looked amused when they'd seen her and she was sure that Flanders was planning some revenge for the way that Gael had used him. The challenge was still on since neither of them had called a truce.

Gael took her mind off the gardener and the maid. There was the fantasy to see to on the morrow. They would take the man to the chamber. The three participants had their own needs too and Gael had made a promise that as soon as they had fulfilled the man's desires, they might indulge themselves.

Gael sat back in the study chair, her finger tucked between the legs of her jeans. She still had a need to climax properly. Her dildo hadn't been enough. As she moved the finger, she thought about the chamber. There were several things she still hadn't tried, particularly the infamous 'Maiden'. She hadn't plucked up courage for that yet. Perhaps she would give it a go that evening, when the servants had gone.

Sophie stood in the doorway and snapped out, 'There's a van outside.' Then she turned on her heels and went back to the kitchen.

Gael went quickly to the stable yard. Two men in aprons were unloading a large, ornately carved armchair she'd bought. They carried it to the basement under Gael's strict supervision, and set it down outside the chamber. She tipped them heavily then dragged the chair into the chamber herself. With a spotlight on, it looked like a throne.

As she turned, Gael looked at a wooden box with a very thick glass lid. As large as a coffin, it was painted black inside and out. With the light shining from above, she couldn't see into it at all. She lifted the lid to find a black mattress in the bottom. She had puzzled over this box since she had first seen it, but still hadn't decided what it might be used for.

Gael shivered as she glanced at another black box – the Maiden. Named after an infamous instrument of torture, this particular Maiden had been specially designed to give the occupant the most exquisite sexual stimulation. Melindi had said it was the best device she had, but not for the faint-hearted.

Later, when Sophie was just about to leave, Gael went down to the basement again. Flanders had usually left by this time, so she judged that she was alone in the house. The answerphone was on.

The chamber was in darkness. Gael put on one spotlight over the Maiden and gingerly lifted the lid to peer inside.

The original Maiden torture device had been a box like this, but full of sharp metal spikes. When the victim was forced inside, the spikes in the lid and back skewered him. Nobody ever survived.

In this particular Maiden, the spikes were made of rubber. They were floppy like the fingers of a glove and the points were well rounded. In the bottom they looked like a bed of nails. Then there were larger rubber protuberances at various points. When Gael switched a switch, a motor whirred somewhere underneath. She took hold of a remote control with explicit diagrams, then dropped her kimono to the floor and stood naked, trying to pluck up courage to get in. Eventually she eased herself down gradually in the way she would enter a very hot bath. The rubber protuberances lay flat beneath her weight. So far, so good.

She closed the lid.

The protrusions on the lid hardly touched her body. Some pressed at her back but not too hard. There were none about her face; only from her shoulders down to her shins.

Now she was in pitch blackness. She couldn't hear a sound. She took a deep breath and pressed a button on the remote control.

Now the bottom and the lid began to expand like an inflatable dinghy blowing up. The protuberances inflated too. They pressed into her back. Those in the lid bore down on her, all over. She stopped the inflation when the pressure was just a little more than comfortable. Then with bated breath she pressed another button. The protuberances began to vibrate. The ones around her breasts worked in little circles, titillating her

214

delightfully. Those between her legs seemed to move to and fro, sweeping up the insides of her thighs. Those over her belly pressed down hard, pushing into her navel and the tense flesh just above her mons.

When she pressed the next button, the rubber fingers began to work in waves which travelled up and down her body. God, it was nice. The ones underneath massaged at her bottom, working between its cheeks. Those on top worked her torso. When she pressed the final button, she juddered with the sensation which that brought her.

A large protrusion grew between her legs, pushing them apart. As she widened them and pushed down, it vibrated delightfully between the open lips of her vulva. There seemed to be a small finger which trembled near her anus. She moved to press her anal ring against it.

Now the whole of her body vibrated slowly, not an inch of her torso untouched. She pumped the rubber fingers harder so they pressed into her flesh. 'My God, that's so incredible,' she whispered to herself. Already she was almost on the brink of climax. Immersed in a sea of sensation, she cried out, 'Yes, oh yes. Eat your heart out, Flanders. I won't need your prick any more.'

'I think you might, miss.'

Gael was so lost in the tingling sensations she didn't register that the motor had been switched off. It was the bright light which made her open her eyes. Flanders grinned down on her. Then he bent and lifted her out. 'I think you'll be screaming for me in a little while, miss,' he whispered in her ear.

She beat at his chest. 'Let me go, you moron.' She struggled but he was too strong for her. Then she felt herself falling. He put her down on something soft. In the darkness she saw the reflection of the spotlight as he shut the glass lid and fastened it. He'd put her in that other box. She pushed at the lid, but it didn't give. She hammered on the sides but couldn't escape. When the

215

light went out, she nearly panicked. The bastard was going to leave her. Was he teaching her a lesson for shackling him and leaving him in the dark? But what on earth could he do with her shut up in a glass case?

She lay there breathing steadily whispering over and over, 'Don't panic. He won't hurt you. He's only playing with you. You knew he'd try to get his own back on you for what you did with him.'

But how had he found her? How did he know about the Maiden? Then she recalled that she had left him in the chamber to undo his shackles. He must have had a look around before he'd left.

As Gael lay wondering what he planned to do with her, she heard voices. Straining to identify them she stiffened as she heard Sophie's treble tones.

'Why do we have to come down here, lover?' she whined. 'Can't we go and find a bed?'

Flanders laughed. 'I thought it might be a bit more exciting to play with you down here. You've never wanted me to do you in a bed before. Now, be a good girl and take your knickers off.'

'Shan't.'

Gael could picture Sophie pouting. She was being awkward with Flanders too. But why had he brought her to the chamber? Surely he didn't think that he was going to have both of them? Perhaps Sophie didn't even know she was in the glass-topped box. Were they going to screw while Gael was made to listen? No – that wasn't Flanders' style. He was more ingenious than that. More devious.

'Take them off, I said.'

'And I said no. Why don't you love me nicely like other men do?'

'You haven't had other men who loved you nicely. You told me so.'

'So – I can hope, can't I?'

There was a tearing sound, then Sophie's high-pitched voice. 'You brute. That was my best blouse.'

'Then you should have taken it off yourself, shouldn't you. Drop your jeans.'

'If I must.'

'Yes, you must. I want you stripped.'

'You're not stripped. I want you naked too.'

There was a pause. 'There. Is that naked enough for you? Now hold my cock.'

There was a longer pause.

'Now suck it.'

Gael lay trembling through the next long pause, imagining Sophie as she knelt to suck on Flanders.

'Take your knickers off,' he growled.

A bright light shone down on the glass. Gael blinked. Then as her eyes became accustomed to the glare, she found she could see through the glass, up to the ceiling. Two figures loomed above her. Flanders sucked on Sophie's breasts as she palmed his curving cock.

'Now are you going to take your knickers off,' he whispered, 'or am I going to rip them off?'.

'Why?' She was giggling now.

'Because I want to see your quim, you little tramp. I want to see how wet you are.'

'Take them off yourself,' Sophie giggled. 'And if you want to see it, you'll have to force my legs open first.'

Gael knew it was an invitation rather than a protest.

There was a gasp from Sophie when she landed on her back on the cold glass lid. As Gael stared up she could see between the girl's legs. A pair of lacy panties were drawn into her crotch. Then Gael saw Flanders' hands. They pushed the girl's legs back and ripped her knickers down. Now Gael was looking straight up at the housemaid's vulva as he spread her legs and pushed them back.

Gael's heart thumped. The lips of Sophie's purse were only inches from her face. The coppery hairs around the lips shone brightly in the light. The moistness on them showed that she was aroused. She was probably more

217

aroused than if he'd taken her to some bed and had her 'nicely'.

Gael saw Flanders, poised above, but he didn't look at her. It was as if she weren't there. Then Gael recalled how she hadn't been able to see into the box from the outside. Sophie wouldn't see her either.

Now Gael began to see what the rogue had planned.

Sophie wriggled and tried to close her legs. He forced them wide apart.

Gael could see his penis as he stood with his shins against the box. It loomed above her, looking huge against the light. She could see through the mat of his pubic hair, up over his belly to his mouth, grinning widely as he knelt on the glass. He placed the tip against the housemaid's cleft and seemed to hold it there for rather longer than necessary. Gael knew that he was goading her.

'Don't muck about,' Sophie whined. 'Do me properly if you're going to do me at all.'

Flanders withdrew. 'Perhaps I won't fuck you after all.'

Sophie sat up, her labia squashing on the glass. 'Pig. Why did you bring me down here if you're not going to do me?'

'Because I like to play with you, my sweet.'

'Well, you can go and play with your dick.' She tried to rise but he pushed her down. He pressed her legs so wide that the membranes of her loins hollowed. These pulled the lips of her sex apart and showed Gael a clear view of her clitoris, standing proud at the top of the long, lush slit.

When Flanders put his lips to it and sucked, Gael trembled. She recalled sucking on that nub herself.

Sophie wriggled. She pushed down on Flanders' mouth.

He thrust his tongue out and drew it through her cleft.

Gael's hand went down between her legs, her own purse wet and swollen with the stimulation of the game. Flanders was a cunning swine but she admired his ingenuity.

Sophie began to writhe on his tongue, but he withdrew it from her as soon as he realised she liked it.

'No,' she cried. 'Don't stop now. I want it in my pussy.'

'Then you're a lewd and wicked girl and I'm going to spank you. Turn round and kneel.'

Sophie knelt on the glass. She spread her legs and pushed her bottom out, the purse of her sex pouting between its cheeks. What man could resist driving his cock into that? Gael wondered.

But Flanders resisted it. He spanked her instead. She yelped and pushed her bottom out for more. As he spanked again and again, the cheeks of her bottom grew quite pink. The lips of her vulva swelled out more. And as the tips of his fingers caught it lightly, it began to open and close as the muscles of her vaginal walls went into little spasms.

Gael frigged her nubbin in little circles, trying to bring herself off, desperate to release her tension. She knew that if she didn't, she would be left strung out again. Then Flanders would gloat. He would walk away and leave her unfulfilled, just as he had done each time they'd clashed before.

'Fuck me, Todd,' Sophie whispered. 'Fuck me properly or I'll scream.'

'The mistress might hear you.'

She sneered. 'Don't be stupid. She wouldn't hear me down here.'

'She might be closer than you think.' He slapped her bottom hard and made her yelp.

'Do me, Todd.' She put her hand through her legs and pried the lips of her sex apart.

Gael breathed hard, trying to control herself. Her

fingers frigged her nubbin. And as Flanders knelt and spread the housemaid's vulval lips, she trembled, knowing what he would do next.

As his cock came up to Sophie's bottom, he thrust it out to show Gael just how hard it was. He made it nose between the lips, held open by his thumbs. Then he eased it into the gaping hole and buried it inside.

Gael could not climax. Hard as she tried, her tension would not break. She needed what the girl was getting. She needed it now. There was nothing like a strong, hard cock to make her tension break. As she looked up through the glass, her view was of Todd Flanders' balls, swinging as he pushed to the limit of Sophie's ample depth.

He began to charge into her slowly.

Gael rubbed her nubbin faster.

The tip of his cock came right out of Sophie's vulva, rubbed on her clitoris and drove back in.

Gael rubbed the whole of her vulva with the flat of her hand. She wanted to feel every millimetre of its pulsing flesh. She was so wet that her hand slipped easily. She rubbed it hard, hoping that the heat and the friction would bring her off at last.

Flanders was fucking the girl fast and hard now. His balls were swinging wildly, his inner thighs tense. He held her fully open, looking down to watch his cock being engulfed by the sucking mouth between the stretched-out thighs.

Gael watched it too, fascinated at the sight, desperate to feel it herself. Would he do her that way when he'd finished with the girl? Perhaps he wouldn't climax. Then he might need another succulent place to drive his cock and . . .

Once again, she stopped herself fantasising. This was no time to be having those kind of dreams. He was a bastard, and if he thought she would beg him to take her after he'd finished Sophie, he was wrong.

As Flanders thrust in the ravening hole, the redhead

pushed back. Her large breasts swung heavily to every ardent jab. Now he slapped her bottom each time he thrust. Then he tensed as he gripped the housemaid's hips, pulling her vulva hard on to his shaft.

Gael tensed as well. She watched his belly tighten, expecting him to spurt. But he pulled right out and ran his penis over Sophie's anus, rubbing his balls on the puckered ring, pushing his cock so hard that the glans swelled hugely and the veins sprang out. Then he gushed, spurting high into the air.

Sophie cried out, 'No. You bastard. I haven't come.'

He smacked her on the bottom and worked his penis with his hands, squeezing it just as Gael would have if she'd been above the glass.

Gael closed her eyes and took a deep breath. Normally she would have had her mouth over his cock by now, sucking the last drops.

Sophie turned. She knelt up and glared. Then her hand struck him hard across the cheek. 'You prick. I'm never going to let you fuck me again. Never.'

He put his head back and laughed, his hands on his hips, his penis wagging as his belly shook. 'You say that every time, my pet, but you still come back for more.'

She struck him again, her breasts bouncing with the effort.

He held his cheek this time, clearly stung by the force of the slap but Gael thought that his ego would be more hurt, particularly since she was watching.

Sophie left, banging the door noisily.

Now Gael was alone in her glass prison. She was a captive to the man and he could probably do anything that took his fancy. No one would hear if she shouted out. No one would come running to her aid.

When he didn't open the box, Gael was surprised. As he sat on the lid just above her face with his legs apart, she was annoyed. It was as if he was pretending that she wasn't there.

221

When he began to masturbate, he knew that she was watching every stroke. His balls touched the glass as he pulled at his cock. The man was a stallion, already hard again. His cock was curving as strongly as it had only a few minutes before. But why was he doing it? Was he one of those men who liked to flash at women; to show them how big his balls were and how horny he could get? But she knew how big and horny he was. She'd seen that cock many times now, flushed with the pressure in it, urging as he pushed it out to touch her.

The thought was cut short as he stood and opened the glass lid. Hinging it back, he looked down on her with a wide smile. She looked at his balls then over the shaft, his belly and his chest, to see the light of lust in his blue eyes. There was no point in resisting him now. So she pulled her legs back to bare her vulva, spreading it wide with her fingers. She was through with being coy. They both knew what she wanted.

He looked with approval between her legs and smiled again. Then he lowered himself on top of her. Without a word he drove his cock inside her, smoothly.

She felt the hilt press against her nubbin and moaned with the pleasure that it gave her.

'And now, miss,' he whispered, kissing her lightly on the lips, 'I think I'll go to bed.'

21

A Judge of Sensuality

Gael was furious with herself for being seduced by Flanders. While her mind had told her not to be influenced by his erotic display on the glass-topped box, her body had not obeyed. She had pulled back her legs the instant he had opened the lid, his cockshaft straining with its pressure.

Now she stormed about her room, kicking discarded knickers to the side. How dare he do that to her? Then she recalled how she had contributed to the act by her acceptance of his challenge. But now that he had had her in that box, would he lose all interest in having her again?

She flung herself upon her bed, looking at the mirror on the ceiling. Her breasts were full from the tension he had wrought. Her inner core still ached with a need to be fulfilled, he'd brought her to such a pitch of readiness. She had half decided to go to him, to make him finish what he'd started. Then she realised that she didn't know where he lived. In the village somewhere? In a flat? With a wife or girlfriend? She didn't know anything about the brute except that she wanted him more than she had wanted any man for months. Then she persuaded herself that it was simply a need to get even. She hated being bested, particularly by him.

She pulled up her knees and viewed herself in the

dressing mirror at the bottom of the bed. Her pubic hair had grown quite thick. The long lips of her vulva, swollen from the titillation in the Maiden and then the glass-topped box, hardly showed through the curling beard.

She took out her biggest dildo. She peeled apart her labia and rubbed the cock between them. The mushroom form slid easily through the moist sleeve of her sex. She pushed it in as far as it would go. Then she pumped it up to make it swell. A bulb around the root of it pressed against her, widening the entrance to her core. And when she switched the motor on, the vibration it imparted was nice – but only nice. She needed living flesh, and a man to drive it in.

Slowly she pumped the dildo in and out, but it did no good at all. She was in no mood for toys, even though her tension was still high.

She showered, then dusted her breasts with pink-tinged powder and viewed them in the mirror. They hung round and full. The reflection showed the nipples standing hard, the nimbuses raised fully, dark pink against the paleness of the mounds. If only there had been someone there to suck them. But there wasn't – so there was no point in wishing. Tomorrow would bring relief. There would be three other women in the house, as well as the man who would come to have his fantasy fulfilled.

Flanders behaved as if nothing had happened between them. When Gael bumped into him while taking an early walk, he stood aside politely, saying, 'Good morning, miss' in that deep and husky voice she'd come to like.

She looked at him hard, uncertain as to whether he was being facetious or polite, but his smooth face showed no laughter. The dark eyes looked down warmly, and his mouth remained quite straight. The smile which often churned her stomach wasn't there. Was his challenge finished as she'd feared? Perhaps he thought he'd won. Would there be nothing more between them in the future but polite exchanges as she gave him orders for the garden?

Sophie stamped about the kitchen when Gael went in for breakfast. Where was the rapport they'd had? The time when Gael had sat and sucked the siren's breasts and they had whispered naughtily over croissants, seemed long past.

Time dragged until the doorbell rang. Gael headed Sophie off and reached the door before her, but the housemaid hovered sulkily, pouting as she looked to see the caller. When she saw Fiona, she turned and stomped back to her work.

With ginger hair shining in the evening light, Celine arrived soon after with Mandy, the fourth girl for the fantasy. Gael had chosen Mandy very carefully. Her antics at the party when she'd had four young men together on the stairs had been the best credentials she could have. Blonde and very beautiful, Mandy was quite stunning as she flashed her clear, blue eyes and pursed her lips.

Gael took them quickly to the chamber, where she gave them strict instructions. Their eyes were wide as they viewed the room with all its opportunities for fun.

'You can play later,' Gael said sternly. 'For now, just get undressed. He should be here at any time.'

On cue, the doorbell rang.

Gael scampered up the basement steps. Sophie had gone home and the house was very still.

Bradwell Ainsely-Jeaves was tall. He towered over Gael as she took his hand and kissed it. His grip was firm – too firm perhaps, and his look was somewhat hard. She saw a glint of lustfulness in his dark and searching eyes. They discussed his fantasy in minute detail, then she led him to the basement. Outside the chamber door, she showed him all the garments she'd obtained to meet his needs. Then she went in on her own.

The other three were eager to get started so Gael turned down the lights. Only the spotlight above the ornate chair was left.

They waited tensely in the darkness. Fiona held Gael's hand. 'How old is he?' she whispered as if he might hear.

'Late thirties, maybe,' Gael whispered back, the tension getting to her too. She needed this fantasy to be successful. As someone in the high court, Jeaves was an influential man.

'Is he a brute?' Fiona asked. Then before Gael could reply, she added, 'I like a brute between my legs when I'm in the mood.'

'And are you in the mood?' Celine hissed over her shoulder.

Fiona gave a tinny little laugh. 'I'm always in the mood for a really horny dick. Aren't you?'

'Make that two really horny dicks, and I'm all ears,' Mandy joined in, with a giggle. 'In fact, make it three or four, and I'm anybody's.'

Gael frowned. 'Shhhh, ladies. Try to take this seriously.'

'But we've only come for the fun, darling,' Fiona whispered hoarsely.

The exchanges were cut short as the door swung open. The dark-eyed man moved to the spotlight by the chair. He sat and peered into the darkness, his face set hard, his eyes alert.

'The court is now in session,' he boomed fiercely, and banged a wooden gavel on the chair. 'Let the first defendant come forward and plead her case.'

Gael looked with pleasure at the result of much hard work hunting around theatrical costumiers. Dressed in scarlet robes, a long wig to his shoulders, Bradwell Jeaves looked like a judge presiding at his court.

Nobody stood forward. Then Gael pushed Fiona. Dressed in long, black stockings, a pair of skimpy panties and a bra, she faced the 'judge'.

'You stand accused of being a wanton hussy,' he growled and scanned her closely as she stood a few feet from his chair. 'How do you plead?'

'Guilty, your honour,' she smirked.

Gael poked her hard in the back to make her be more serious.

'And what have you to say in your defence?'

'Nothing, your honour, except that I like the feel of a strong, hard cock in my sex. I can't help it if I get the hots when a man drops his pants and thrusts it out at me. It makes me go all funny. I suppose I'm just an addict, your honour.'

'Then I sentence you to be chastised, my girl. You will have your hands tied. Your knickers will be taken down and your naked bottom will be soundly spanked. Stand down.'

'Yes, your lordship. Thank you for your kindness, your lordship.' Fiona smirked, did a little curtsy and retreated from the light.

'And ten hard slaps for impertinence,' he growled into the blackness.

Gael pushed Mandy forward, wearing nothing but a black thong and stockings high up her thighs. The thin strap of the thong was tight between her buttocks making them swell out. Gael could imagine how it rubbed on Mandy's anus and pulled deeply between her legs, stimulating her with every long-legged stride.

Mandy thrust her breasts out at the man. Gael hadn't seen them before. Well proportioned but very large, they ballooned above a slender waist, her belly brown and freckled. Her pubis was prominent, her bottom firm. A bush of golden hair frizzed out between her legs.

'And how do you plead?' the judge asked, peering down intently at her breasts.

Mandy pushed them out at him and rubbed the nipples. 'If having big tits is a crime, m'lud,' she said in a husky voice, pouting her lips at him, 'then I'm guilty. Do you want to suck them? You can rub your prick between them if you want to.'

He scowled. 'I shall reserve judgment when I strip you naked to examine you more closely. Then I shall decree a suitable punishment.'

'What kind of punishment, m'lud?'

'What kind of punishment would you dislike the most, you siren?'

'I hate the taste of cock, m'lud,' Mandy piped up brightly. 'I tremble when some fellow puts it in my mouth.'

'Then I sentence you to suck my penis until you see the error of your ways, girl. Stand down.'

Celine stepped eagerly into the searching light. The coppery hair of her mons shone through the hole in crotchless panties. Her pure-white bra had holes for the nipples to poke through. This made the nimbuses look swollen. She pushed her hair behind her head, and pouted at the judge.

'You are accused of tempting men, girl. How do you plead?' He stared down at her crotch as she pushed her hips at him. Then his gaze rose to her nipples, poking through her bra.

'I plead not guilty, your worship.'

'And what is your defence, girl?'

She shook her head, the coppery coils sweeping her slender neck, her breasts swinging to the motion. 'I've got the biggest pussy most men have seen, your worship. Is it my fault they want to fuck it as soon as they get a glimpse of it?' She turned and pushed her bottom out at him, the lips of her vulva pressing through the crotch hole of her panties.

He stared between her legs and licked his lips. 'That's no defence, girl. And stop trying to influence my judgment with your lascivious behaviour. Turn around and face me.'

Celine turned, looking at him coyly.

'Now explain something to me,' he said, standing so they caught a glimpse of his stiff shaft through his robes. 'Tell me how men could possibly see your – your . . .'

'My pussy, m'lord?' she giggled.

He coughed. 'Yes – how could they see that if you were properly dressed?'

'They lift my skirt and pull my knickers down, your worship. No one can resist it when it purses its lips at them, but it really isn't my fault.'

'That's a very serious accusation, girl.'

'But it's true, your honour.'

'I'll be the judge of that. I remand you in custody for inspection of your . . .'

'My pussy?'

He cleared his throat. 'Quite so.'

'But how will you inspect it, your worship? I don't drop my panties lightly.'

He scowled. 'You will be restrained first. Then your knickers will be removed.'

'And if I don't let you take my knickers down?'

'Then they will be ripped off, girl.'

'And if I resist the inspection?'

'Your legs will be held apart ready for my inspection. And for trying to influence me so wantonly, I sentence you to a sound spanking to run concurrently with the inspection.' He peered into the darkness to locate Gael. 'Custodian? Step forward.'

Gael did as she was ordered.

'Take these women and prepare them for their punishment. I shall retire and return shortly to investigate their – their cases further. The punishments I have decreed will then be carried out.' He rose and swept out of the room, his robes flowing out behind him.

The three 'convicted' women laughed aloud. Gael

silenced them with a scowl. 'Come on. We've got work to do. Don't stand here tittering.'

She pulled forward the wooden framework she'd had made. It was a pillory – a board with three sets of holes for neck and hands fixed just above waist height. The three had to bend deeply as Gael clamped them in. Now they were captive, unable to move their heads or arms. They were forced to thrust their bottoms out and place their legs apart. Gael had set three spotlights to highlight each straining crotch and three lights on their faces.

They started to giggle, but Gael stopped them just as Bradwell Jeaves entered imperiously. The red robes wafted apart showing that he was naked underneath. His belly was taut, his cock hard. She turned up the lights on the women's faces. From the blackness where she stood to oversee the scene, Gael thought she saw his penis swell as he walked along the line.

The captives tried to look up, but they could only see him from his belly down, his cockshaft rearing just before their faces.

Gael quickly focused the lights so that their mouths were lit brightly. Everything else was in complete darkness.

With Mandy in the centre, he faced her squarely. 'Ah yes. I believe it's you who has a dislike for sucking on a man.'

'Yes, m'lud,' she sniggered. 'I hate the way his cock swells in my mouth.'

He flexed his shaft and pulled the foreskin tight. 'Then I'll punish you, you wicked creature.' He placed his glans against her lips. 'Open your mouth, girl.'

Unable to retreat, Mandy opened her lips just wide enough to let his helmet in. He pushed, easing the thick shaft between her lips. She sucked it, gobbling on it eagerly. He smiled as he pushed and felt her heat.

She closed her eyes. She savoured him. She sucked his

230

penis slowly and with passion, making it glisten in the light. The he pulled it out of her mouth and made her lick his balls. He held them hard against her face and flexed his knees.

She licked him lasciviously in long, full strokes.

As he went behind the frame, Gael switched the lights. Now all the man could see was a trio of female bottoms bending in a line, the twin lips of their vulvas pursed and proud inside their panties.

He took a flail with leather thongs and flicked Fiona's crotch, her black hair showing clearly through the lace of her panties.

She whispered, 'Yes,' and pushed her bottom out.

He flicked her harder. 'Quiet, girl, or you'll be chastised until you cry for mercy.'

'Oh yes,' she whispered hoarsely, pushing out her bottom even harder.

Now he came to Mandy, bands of soft, pale flesh showing where her stockings met the V shape of her thong. The pink lips of her sex were plain beneath the see-through lace. The curly hair which fringed them bristled out.

He whisked her bottom and her thighs, making her squirm with the pleasure that it gave her.

Now he reached Celine. The hole in the crotch of her panties showed the moist lips of her sex, shrouded in ginger hair. Gael thought he tarried longer at Celine as he scanned the insides of her thighs. He whisked her with light strokes, making sure that the tails of leather caught the hollows of her loins. Her labia swelled and pulsed, moistening more and more. He whisked again, reddening the pale pink of her bottom.

She moaned again and spread her legs.

Gael took a deep breath and slipped a hand between her legs. She could feel the warm leaves of her purse, slippery as she moved. She wanted to take her panties off and show him her quim as well. But that would not be fitting. She was the fulfiller of his dreams, not his toy to play with. Even so she wondered just how long she could keep up a neutral position. As she studied the three bottoms and the sexual parts between the spread-out legs, her heart beat like a drum.

The judge now paced along the line, whisking at each bottom, making his captives squirm with sheer delight. He felt the soft cheeks of Fiona's buttocks, running his hand over them and between them. He slipped his fingers down between her legs and stroked her. Tight in the see-through panties, her labia were firm. Gael imagined how they would be pulsing, needing to feel the coolness of fresh air.

Now he touched up Mandy, running his hand up the inside of her legs until it reached her crotch. She wriggled as he spanked her hard. He stroked her really slowly, palming her sexual purse, feeling its sultry heat as he pulled his foreskin gently with his other hand.

He moved then to Celine, the lips of her vulva bare. He ran his finger through them to see how moist she was. Then he took his finger to his nose to smell her with a long, deep breath. Slowly, he eased her knickers down. He bared her inch by inch. She set her legs together as he drew them slowly off then stepped out of them quite daintily. Widening her stance again she worked her vaginal muscles very slowly.

His eyes lit up as her vulva opened and then closed. 'Ah – I believe this is the one who said that she had the largest . . .'

'Pussy – m'lud?' She giggled again.

He murmured with approval and divided her vulval lips, studying how they quivered to his touch. 'But size is comparative, my dear,' he whispered as he spread them wide. 'How big is your pussy compared with the other two?' He lay his shaft against her cleft, parting her ginger hair. Then he moved along to Mandy, in the middle of the three. Slowly he eased her knickers down, leaving the paleness of her bottom stark against the blackness of her stockings.

Gael gulped.

Celine giggled with excitement.

With Mandy exposed to his ardent gaze, Jeaves knelt between her feet. Gael's heart began to thump as he tongued her crevice slowly. Gael worked her hand between her own legs, pressing her nubbin gently.

The judge held his shaft and placed it between the leaves of Mandy's purse, measuring again from her anus to her nub. He rubbed it through the moistened flesh, nodded wisely and passed on to Fiona.

As he studied Fiona's twin-lipped bulge, he nodded with approval. Then he took hold of her panties and ripped the seam apart. The rent exposed two cleanly shaven leaves. Between them poked the inner lips, dark pink folds of supple flesh. Gael wanted to press her mouth to them. She wanted to feel the smoothly turned-in skin against her tongue and suck on the inner folds. She wanted to sniff Fiona's scent and take the risen nubbin in her mouth. She watched as Jeaves breathed deeply. His tongue stroked lightly through Fiona's naked sex, feeling the slickness of its lips, forcing them to open as it passed.

Fiona murmured, 'Yes. But lick me harder. Wriggle your tongue about.'

He slapped her hard and made her jump. He put his mouth against her nub, pulling it and stretching it until she moaned again. He slapped her bottom as she moaned and ate at her with passion. He ran his palms up the insides of her thighs, skimming the flesh he'd made so wet, trailing a finger around her pushed-out anus.

Gael stripped off her gown and let it fall. She worked her nubbin hard.

The man took the measure of Fiona, pressing his cock between her labia. He stood right back and viewed her.

Then he went back to Celine, feeling deeply between her legs. Now he worked a thumb inside her. Then he turned round with a frown, saying thoughtfully to Gael, 'I can't quite judge which is the most appealing, the shaven one or this one with ginger hairs. I like the way they tickle, but the other is so smooth.'

'What about mine?' Mandy asked. 'Don't you like blonde?'

He slapped her hard. 'Speak when you're spoken to, girl. I didn't ask your opinion.'

Gael was stuck for words. But when he took her hand and placed it on Fiona's cleft, she trembled.

'See what you think, guardian,' he said to Gael. 'Try her with your finger.'

Gael felt the softness of Fiona's sex. As she eased her finger in, Fiona clamped down on it hard. Gael began to work it but the man drew her away.

'And now try this one,' he whispered conspiratorially, as if the captives couldn't hear. 'It's a great deal larger, and the lips pout more, but is it quite as tight?' He held Gael's hand against Celine, who clenched her muscles and made her labia move against Gael's palm. Gael's belly tightened. She never ceased to be aroused by the softness and the lushness of the flesh between a woman's legs.

He took Gael's finger, aimed it and pushed it slowly into Celine. As Gael felt the pressure on her finger, she moved it in and out. Celine tried to clamp on it.

'See how strong she is,' he whispered. 'and see how the fringes of her pussy move as she tightens around your finger.' He traced the long leaves of Celine's sex with the tip of one finger, then ran it round her anus.

Gael stood back, her legs turning to jelly. Before her in the spotlights the sexual parts of three women worked in unison. She closed her eyes, almost unable to withstand the temptation to kneel and take each in her mouth.

'Now,' he said, pulling Gael close again. 'I think this one is largest.' He put his shaft against Celine, and spread her wide. 'Look how she enfolds my cock when I stretch her and release her.' As he let go of the leaves of Celine's sex, they closed about his penis.

Celine sighed as the shaft slipped inside her.

He began to work in long, slow strokes, pushing hard against her buttocks, stroking her anus with a thumb. This made her wriggle and squirm upon his shaft. It made him close his eyes and gasp.

Then he withdrew and growled, 'Before I make my final judgment, I'll try the others fully.'

With his penis shining in the light, he moved along to Mandy. He held his shaft against her, seemingly sensing her heat, working his glans between the lush leaves of her vulva. The he placed one thumb in each taut hollow at their sides and eased them apart, exposing her pale pink sleeve. He slid his penis in. He worked her slowly for a while as he appeared to be judging how she felt in contrast to Celine. Then he tried Fiona.

Fiona's sex was swollen now. Their nakedness made them seem more prominent than the others in the line. Gael focused the spotlights sharply. Now all that could be seen in the blackness of the chamber were three pulsing female forms, each one seeming to be inviting the man to push his straining phallus deep between their leaves.

Soon buried deep in Mandy, he leant back, pushing his hips out to drive his penis home while he worked the other two with searching fingers. His motions were much faster now, his cock making shorter thrusts. He clawed the buttocks of one girl then thrust his thumbs inside the other two. They all began to writhe, three bottoms working in circles.

Gael sensed that he was about to come. But then he knelt to suck on Mandy. He licked the insides of her thighs, the hollows of her loins and up around her anal ring. She wriggled as he tickled it with his tongue. After a while he stood then slapped her buttocks hard, and declared, 'You're acquitted, miss. I've tried all of you fairly, and I find that you have the biggest, tightest, most inviting pussy I've ever seen. You're free to go.'

Gael turned up the lights.

Jeaves released the bar which held the three girls in their bending pose. 'And as for you two,' he growled, cupping each one's purse one final time, 'you've had your punishment. You're free to go as well.'

They stretched their arms and thrust out their breasts. Then, before Gael could restrain them, Celine picked up the scarlet robe and drew it on.

'And now,' she said, pushing her breasts out through the robe, and baring her coppery mons, it's time for another trial.' She turned to the others. 'I think we'll see just how good he is now we're all unshackled.'

They turned to Jeaves and Celine smirked. 'You stand accused of working us up but denying us satisfaction. How do you plead?'

He looked at Gael quickly. She gave him a shrug as if to say, I didn't plan this.

Celine took up the flail and flicked at his thighs, making his shaft spring as his muscles tightened. He tried to push past her, but she blocked his way, her breasts coming against his chest.

Fiona and Mandy each took one arm and twisted. They forced him to his knees. 'How do you plead?' Celine rasped, her breathing tight, her breasts heaving heavily.

'Not guilty. Now let me go or . . .'

'Or what, m'lud?'

He dropped his eyes.

'Do you deny that you've worked us up?'

He shook his head.

'And do you deny that it's unjust to leave us wanting satisfaction?'

236

He shook his head again.

They made him bend, with his forehead to the carpet. Then Celine took the flail and whisked him lightly. He flinched at every stroke. But when Fiona knelt, put her hand between his legs and cupped his scrotum, she looked up and grinned. 'The bastard's hornier than ever, girls. I want him first.'

They pushed him on to his back. Fiona sat astride him. She pulled his phallus up and sank on it in one, smooth movement. Gael gulped as the naked lips of Fiona''s vulva spread out around its root.

Celine straddled him as well. She knelt above his face and spread her knees. As her vulva touched his mouth, he groaned. 'Lick,' she commanded. 'Lick until I come.' She lashed at his belly and wriggled on his face.

Gael saw him licking at the redhead's sex. Then Mandy joined the game. She knelt astride his foot. She made herself as wide as she was able and sank down on his toe. 'Wriggle it', she hissed, 'but gently.'

He wriggled the toe, sweeping it through the valley that it touched.

Gael gaped. This wasn't what she'd planned. But he seemed to be enjoying it. He was eating at Celine and pushing up his hips. Fiona rode him strongly, thrusting out her breasts and clawing at his belly with long nails. She came with little judders, her breasts shaking with each one.

'My turn,' Mandy gasped, almost at her climax from the working of his toe. She pushed Fiona off, sinking on Jeaves' shaft as Fiona landed on her back beside him.

Fiona took his hand and made him flex his fingers in her sex, keeping the pulses of her orgasm going as long as she could.

Mandy rose and fell on him. She ground her sex against his sac, sliding around on him, trying to get more friction for her nubbin. She plucked at her teats and rubbed her breasts. She set her head right back and gasped aloud, 'Yahoo. You horny bastard. I've got your cock. Now fuck me.'

He bucked and threw her in the air. Her large breasts bounced and swung, and then she came as well.

Mandy lay back too. She pulled her legs apart, the lips of her vulva rosy with the friction of her ride. Then she took his free hand and drew it through her legs, making him feel how wet she was, and how her sex lips pulsed.

Gael needed desperately to come. Why did she always get left without satisfaction? Then as Celine took him, Gael saw her chance. She knelt over his face, and widened her knees very, very slowly. She could feel the membranes of her loins stretch tightly, pulling the lips of her sex apart. She always loved that feeling. Then she felt his breath. She felt his tongue as he extended it to skim the valley of her sex. She wriggled for more contact. Now his tongue-tip touched her nub and sent a thrill right through her. She stretched herself so he could lap at her firm clitoris more easily. She rubbed it on his tongue, but he moved his head and licked one long leaf of her purse. Then he rasped the other side. She flexed her hips, trying to make the delving tongue touch her where she wanted most to feel it. That was so much nicer than a finger, but she craved his cock even more. She couldn't wait much longer.

The others played their part now. They brought a bench and leant Celine across it. They made Jeaves kneel, his cock coming level with her sex. Mandy and Fiona ran their hands around her buttocks then down between her thighs. Their fingers eased her flesh apart, showing him the target for his thrust.

Gael would not be left out. She slipped a hand around his hip, then took his penis and guided it to its mark. She wiped the tip through Celine's nectar, making sure that it was slippery before she pushed him in.

Celine swore as they pulled him out, rubbed him on

her anus and pushed him back again. 'Hell, you two. Don't muck about. Make him do me properly.'

They pushed it in until the whole of it was swallowed. But now he took control. Kneeling close against Celine, he gripped her by the hips and took her hard.

'Fuck her,' Fiona whispered. 'Make her come. We'll spank you if you don't.' Gael slapped his thigh, making him thrust in strongly. She spanked again and made him push in once more. Now they built a rhythm. She spanked each time he thrust, as Celine cried out, 'Yes. Oh yes. Hit him harder. I want to feel him pump.'

Gael stopped. She wanted him herself. 'It's my turn now,' she growled. 'You've had him long enough.'

Celine scowled. 'Piss off, Gael. I want to feel him come.'

Gael pulled him off her. The others cheered.

'Bitch.' Celine turned on Gael and caught her hair. 'I'll fight you for him.'

Gael yelped as Celine tugged her hair. Their fingers locked and they sank down on the floor, their legs entwined, the heat of Celine's vulva on Gael's thigh. Celine heaved on top, her hands around Gael's neck. When someone slapped her bottom hard, she tensed. Gael rolled on top, pressing down on Celine. Slippery with their sweat, their nipples rubbed together.

Celine hissed, 'I want him first, you cow. You said we could play with him after he'd had his way with us.'

Gael pressed Celine's shoulders to the floor to stop her getting up. 'I said you could play here in the chamber. I didn't say you could have him.'

'But he's loving every minute. His cock's up like a telegraph pole.'

Gael glanced round. The man was on his knees, rubbing at his penis.

'I'll have the winner of the fight,' he laughed. 'Christ, Gael, this is better than I asked for.' He fell on top of Gael as she held Celine down. Gael felt the heat of his

239

cock between the cushions of her bottom, then felt him open her up. She gasped as he thrust in. Her tension and the fighting had made her far more horny than she had been for ages.

Celine wriggled under her, tears running down her cheeks. 'You bitch. You bloody double-crossing bitch. He's mine.'

With the man's weight bearing down on her, Gael pressed her conquest to the floor.

Celine bit her neck.

She yelped and drew away.

Celine writhed and pushed a knee up hard between Gael's legs. As Jeaves thrust into Gael, she could feel him rubbing his scrotum against Celine's intruding leg. He was getting double stimulation from the struggle.

With a superhuman effort, Celine threw them off. Now Jeaves was under Gael, his penis still inside her. His hands came up around her breasts. In a mirror on the ceiling, Gael could see herself impaled on his hard length.

Celine straddled her. She braced her hands upon Gael's belly and worked her vulva firmly on Gael's mons.

Mandy squatted above Gael's face until her sex lips touched Gael's mouth.

Fiona slipped her hand between Jeaves' legs and held his balls while he pleasured Gael.

They formed a knot of heaving, sweating bodies. They pulled and sucked and wriggled. Then Celine took them all off guard. She dragged Gael from the man. She pulled his shaft up roughly and drove it up inside herself, giving out a cry of satisfaction. 'Got you, you lovely prick,' she squealed as she watched it sink between her legs. 'Now fuck me.'

The others could do nothing as Celine rode the man, her red hair flying as she threw her head from side to side and clawed his belly with red-nailed fingers.

Suddenly, he rolled her off. He threw Gael on her back, hissing, 'Show me your cunt, you hell cat.' He pushed her legs apart until her vulva gaped. The he was on her, and in her, his bottom pumping hard, his testes bulging out between her legs.

Mandy raised the flail and whipped his back and sides, just hard enough to make him flinch. The whipping sped his action, and made him take Gael more avidly. She cried out, 'Yes. Ahh, Yes,' as someone chanted, 'Fuck her.'

Another voice joined in as well. 'Fuck her. Fuck her. Fuck her.'

He took her hard, pounding at her pelvis with long and powerful motions.

Mandy whipped her as she writhed. The lashes on her shoulders and the tight flesh of her thighs made her wriggle more. Her breasts bounced to his thrusting as she heaved him on her hips.

Lithe hands slipped around her waist. Long fingers pulled at her nipples. They took her breasts and made them rise and fall.

Fingers scored her belly from her navel to her breasts. She moaned and pushed up harder, opening her vulva to the man. But he withdrew his penis from her purse. He knelt between Gael's legs working at his foreskin with short, fast strokes as he watched her vulva spasm. Then someone knelt behind him, circling his shaft with long, seductive fingers which pushed into his scrotum. His penis swelled, the glans growing ever larger. Gael rubbed her vulva as he watched, desperately trying to bring herself off. The she let out a cry of disappointment as a jet of semen shot into the air, followed by a second and a third. They landed on her vulva and trickled through her furrow.

The fingers around his shaft worked slowly as he beat.

Other hands spread semen over Gael's tingling vulva lips, rosy from his rubbing, shining with his milt.

Gael had lost all track of who was supposed to be doing what to whom, her mind in a daze. She needed urgently to come and yet the man was spent.

That night Gael lay in a deep, hot bath. She spread the soap suds up and down her belly as she thought about the scene. It had been completely wild – much wilder than she'd planned. The way she'd fought to gain possession of Jeaves' cock had been totally irrational. But the last of the fantasies from the first party had been fulfilled. The diary was full for the next two months. Organising two major parties would take a lot of time. A few more fantasies would use up any slack.

Despite the relaxation of the bath, Gael's urge to sate her own need was torturing her. If only Flanders were less cocky and more loving, she would have a ready-made solution to her needs. But it was his potency and bravado which drove her senses wild as soon as she even glimpsed him. He only had to touch her to make her body tremble. She would hardly have to look between his legs before her nub would start to tingle. Her sexual lips would pulse. They would become so sensitive that she could feel them every time she turned and walked away from him. Fuck him. Yes – fuck him. That was really what she craved. She needed him to take her in the way that she liked best – pinned down and helpless as she wriggled. Either way would do. On her back with her legs open wide, or on her belly while he thrust between her thighs.

But he seemed to have stopped goading her since their encounters in the chamber. Now she didn't know if he would spring on her at any moment or never try again. She had purposefully walked in the garden and the woods. But he hadn't appeared from behind some tree to pin her to its bark and rip her knickers off. She thought that might be too unexciting for him now. If he was going to do anything, it would certainly be creative.

He would be most unlikely to come into her room, strip the duvet off her and open up her legs. He might bend her over the kitchen table as he'd taken Sophie, pulling down her panties and driving into her without a word. No, he wouldn't do that either. It had been done. He seemd to need novelty. He seemed to want danger and daring and a fight.

A fight always stoked up Gael's passion. The fight with Celine had been that way. Now she was suffering from the consequences.

She stroked a finger idly through her labia. But even though she was as tense as hell, she wouldn't frig herself tonight. If Flanders was going to make a move on her tomorrow or the next day, she wanted to keep her tension so that when the dam that held it in finally burst, it would flood her in such a torrent of sensation that she'd quiver for an hour. And if he didn't come after her again, someone else would do. Sooner or later some man or woman from the parties was sure to do her in the way she loved the most.

Gael shook herself, bringing her attention back to the steamy bathroom. She had been fantasising again. Now she wished that she had someone she could tell her fantasies to and have them enacted, just as she arranged to enact the dreams for others.

She ran some more hot water and soaped her breasts. Then she closed her eyes, swishing a tide of the warm and soapy fluid up between her legs. The heat was so nice there.

As she dozed, Gael thought she heard the engine of a motorbike. She listened carefully, trying to make out where the throaty throbbing came from. It sounded as if it were in the stable yard. No – it couldn't be. Flanders had gone home at five. She'd seen him roar off down the drive. He'd worn no crash helmet, and was dressed only in a T-shirt and his scanty shorts, his hair streaming out in the balmy breeze. She would have liked to have been his passenger, with her arms about his waist. She might even have dropped them to his crotch and rubbed his penis while he roared down the country lanes.

She stretched her arms above her head, making her breasts hang heavily. Then she sank into the water. It felt so nice to let them bob, but it was even nicer to have them lifted by strong and passionate hands.

Gael stopped her thoughts again. Daydreaming would get her nowhere. She knew she might as well make up her mind to find another man.

She heated up the water, then dozed.

'Wash your back, miss?'

Gael smiled. She was even imagining Flanders' voice now. She held her breasts and touched the nipples gently.

'I asked if you wanted your back washed, miss. Or perhaps you'd like your boobs soaped. I do it very well.'

She turned abruptly to see Todd Flanders standing by the bath.

22

Ridden Hard and Fast

He towered over Gael. As she sat up sharply, her face came level with his penis. It was long though limp, but she was sure it wouldn't take more than a touch of her fingertip or a few well-chosen words to make it stiffen.

'Get out,' she whispered hoarsely, covering her breasts with her hands. 'How dare you come in here when I'm . . .' She stopped as he knelt beside the bathtub.

Trailing a finger through the suds, he drove warm water up between her legs, making waves against her crotch. 'I've come for you,' he whispered. 'Are you going to let me dry you? Or are you going to make me drag you wet and screaming to the bed?' He kissed her shoulder lightly and ran his finger up her belly to her breast, toying with the dripping nipple.

She didn't pull away from him. This time she wouldn't fight. She was tired of squabbling with the man. Apart from that, she wanted him too much. His manner was softer than of late, his eyes lit with passion.

'I think you ought to go,' she said softly, folding her arms about her breasts.

He shook his head. 'I don't think you really want me to go.'

'How do you know what I want?'

He smirked. 'I can read you, miss. All the signs say, I want you, but I'm too proud to admit it.'

'And what makes you such an expert on human behaviour all of a sudden?'

He smiled widely now. 'I have a master's degree in psychology and I'm doing my doctorate thesis right now. Do you think I simply sit at home at night, pulling at my prick as I think about you lying naked on your bed with your finger here?' He ran his finger between her legs, spreading her labia.

Gael was surprised – not at the way he touched her, but about his academic prowess. She stared at him closely, trying to discern if he were playing games with her again. But she couldn't detect any hint that he was lying.

She half closed her eyes. 'I don't believe you.'

He shrugged. 'Believe what you like. Did you really think I was just a country bumpkin content to tug my forelock to a virago like you?'

'I don't know what you mean.' She sniffed haughtily and threw her wet hair back.

'I think you do.'

She bristled just enough to let him know she wasn't pleased. He thought she was a shrew – bad-tempered, at best, a masculine, controlling type of woman at the worst. What should she do? Be bad-tempered or put on her female charm?

'I am not a virago.'

'Have it your own way.'

'I shall.'

Now he grinned widely. 'And which way do you want it? Tied to a tree like Sophie, while I lick between your legs? Over the kitchen table with your knickers round your ankles? Or trussed up on your hands and knees while I fuck you from behind?'

She slitted her eyes tighter. 'You know damned well that I didn't mean that.' Then she realised that her protest hadn't made things better. She couldn't help a smile escaping on her lips.

246

He picked that up and whispered, 'So what way do you really want it?' Now his cock had risen. He stroked it.

She closed her eyes. He was too close and she was too vulnerable. She could have reached over the rim of the bath and taken his penis between her fingers to make it fully hard in seconds. Why didn't she? Because, she rationalised, that would be too provocative.

The initiative was removed from her as he pulled the bath plug.

'What are you doing?'

'I'm going to dry you. You're getting goose bumps.'

'What business is that of yours?'

'I'm making it my business, miss. I don't like my women cold. I like them warm and soft and very compliant.'

'I thought you liked a fight with a woman.'

He grinned. 'I like them to be compliant after I've won the battle to strip them naked.'

'You're just a chauvinist.'

'Perhaps I am. But at least I know what I want.'

She looked into his eyes as he pulled her to her feet. She didn't fight – the fighting was over and he'd won. And he had her naked, even though he hadn't stripped her himself. But she wouldn't be as compliant as he wanted her to be. She still had a little bit of pride left.

'And what is it that you want, Mr Flanders?'

As he enveloped her in a large, hot towel, she held his gaze with hers.

'You know I want to fuck you, miss,' he whispered as he rubbed her belly with the towel.

She sighed and raised her eyes to show that she was bored with crass remarks like that.

He grinned again. 'But I want to fuck you in a way you've never been fucked before, and probably never will be again.'

Now she knew that she'd been right about him being

247

devious. She had guessed that if he did make another move on her, he would have something quite extraordinary in mind. She knew he wouldn't hurt her. The games he'd played with her had stopped just short of pain. Now he was being so provocative that it set her skin tingling. She loved the way he rubbed her through the towel. He had her breasts now, making the softness of the towel brush gently at her nipples. Whatever the devil planned to do with her she would find it difficult to protest.

He dried her face, patting her cheekbones gently, his warm breath flirting with her mouth. And when he bent and kissed her, she closed her eyes and almost swooned. But he withdrew his lips and passed the towel between her legs, sawing it through the valley of her bottom, chafing at her anus. She loved to feel his touch there. She wanted him to kiss her ring, to lick it then to touch it with the firm tip of his cock. She wanted to feel his penis nudge her and then push gently in. She wanted to feel filled by it while his fingers worked between her legs and brought her to fulfilment.

Gael snapped her thoughts back to the scene and widened her stance to give him better access to her sex.

Perversely he stopped drying her there. He seemed to love keeping her on the edge of coming. What did she have to do to make him take her as she wanted? Should she kneel and take his penis in her mouth? Should she lick his balls, or make him lie back on the bed while she rubbed herself over his cock? No – that would be too ordinary, no matter how much she wanted it.

He went to the bathroom cabinet, seeming to be searching for something. When he turned with a smirk on his face, he was holding a knobbly condom. He thrust his cock at her and rolled the condom on, watching her watching it as he pulled it tight.

Without a word he took her in a fireman's lift.

She squealed and tried to wriggle free. 'Let me down, Flanders.'

He slapped her bottom hard. 'I'll let you down when we get to where we're going.' At her dressing table he scooped his fingers through a jar of moisturising cream and smeared her anus and the wide-stretched purse of her sex, working the cream around the lips. He smeared the condom too before he strode out with her slung over his shoulder.

'Where are we going, pig?'

'I'm taking you on a journey of delight, my sweet.'

She slapped at his back. 'I'm not going down to the chamber with you.' It was a useless protest as he started down the stairs, each step jolting her, making her breasts jar against his back.

'We're not going to the chamber, my sweet. Our destination's much more exciting than anything down there.' He laughed theatrically, his chest pumping against her mount.

Balmy night air fanned her bottom as he strode into the stable yard. The cream around her vulva felt quite cool.

He swung her down and sat her across the saddle then climbed behind her quickly, before she could escape. As he bent her forward, he made her grip the steering bars, her breasts hanging heavily over the warm tank.

She felt the heat of his penis hard between her buttocks. It slipped through the cream and nudged her anal ring. Then it entered her so smoothly, it didn't hurt at all. As it slid in she whispered, 'You're a bastard, Flanders. I hate you.'

'But do you hate this, my pet?' He drove his shaft up tight into her bottom. It made her gasp. Now she was half sitting on him, half on the seat. His penis impaled her, while her nubbin rubbed the saddle leather.

He turned on the engine. Now she heard that motor-cycle engine once again, throbbing in the still, night air. Her heartbeat raced and her body thrilled with sheer anticipation. The vibrations, transmitted by the hardness of his cock, shot up into her deepest core and made her belly throb.

He revved then flicked the gear change and started off around the yard.

The sensation of bumping over the cobbles was exquisite. Gael gripped the handlebars with such force it made her knuckles white. Her arms were ramrod hard, vibrations from the front forks, shuddering through her shoulders, making her breasts quiver to every little movement. The penis in her anus thrust with every bump – not because he moved it, but with her weight upon its length. The man was a devil. He had devised the finest torture, but it tuned up each nerve cell of her body, forcing wide her anal ring, and making her push down.

He stopped circling the yard and roared towards the lawns. She gripped the handles fiercely. Every undulation in the lawn made her rise and fall.

'Do you like it?' he shouted against a rushing breeze.

She couldn't answer. The motion took her breath away. Each rise and fall made her belly churn. The full lips of her sex were cooled as they sliced the air. And, in the centre of her bottom, his cockshaft worked persistently.

He took his hands off the handlebars and clamped them on her breasts.

She shrieked as the bike veered. She yanked the steering bars to take control, swerving one way and then the other. All he did was knead her breasts.

'You bastard,' she shouted over her shoulder. 'You lousy bastard.'

He laughed and tugged her nipples. 'I told you I would fuck you in a way you've never been fucked before.'

'And never again,' she whispered to herself. My God, it was incredible.

She screamed as the bike sped towards the trees. As

the summer-house then the chapel passed in a blur, she took the path towards the lake, unable to slow her pace.

Leafy branches brushed her skin. They scraped her thighs and grabbed her hair. She squealed at every one, but still he held her breasts.

Gael swerved along the lake shore, water hissing at the heated metal, spraying up her legs and wetting her thighs. She turned the bike back through the woods. They emerged into the moonlight on the lawns but careered towards the summer-house.

He bit her neck and tugged her nipples gently.

She threw her head back and thrust her breasts hard into his palms.

When he let go and took the handlebars, she was almost disappointed. But as he steered in circles, she pressed down with her feet to rise and fall upon his shaft. Now she was lost in a sea of hot sensation. The circling of the bike made her dizzy. She was almost in a trance when he stopped before the summer-house. Coupled to her, he gripped her waist, lifted her and took her in, the atmosphere still warm from the heat of the day. Now he lay her face down on the cushions from the wicker chairs, clearly having arranged them earlier.

As her bottom stuck up in the air, he pressed his hands into the hollow of her back. Using them to hinge on, he took her with great strength, but with a gentleness which made her moan, each knobble of the condom bringing her great pleasure.

The tight ring of her anus contracted on his penis. She tried to push her bottom out against his weight.

His strokes were long and slow now, his testes dragging at her inner thighs, their hairiness tickling at her labia.

'Yes, oh yes,' she whispered.

'Yes what, miss?'

'Yes, you're the biggest bastard I've ever known.'

'And yes, I've got the biggest, hardest cock you've

ever had?' He pushed in deeply, the hairy root of his penis rasping at her anus, his scrotum brushing her labia as he forced her legs apart. The knobbles on the condom rippled deep inside her, adding to the feelings he created.

'I've had bigger cocks than yours, you brute,' she wheezed.

'But not like you're having it tonight.' He compressed her with his weight and worked her even slower.

She couldn't answer back. She didn't want to. All she wanted was to feel the wonderful sensation the brute was creating in her. She knew that if he didn't change his stroke, if he didn't abandon her like he'd done before, she would come soon. She would have the biggest climax of her life.

Despite the cooling night, Gael was boiling hot, her breasts warm against the cushions. She rubbed the nipples, then wriggled her bottom, contracting on the penetrating shaft.

'Do you admit I've won our contest, miss?' He drove in deeply and held there, making her expel her breath quite violently.

'I'm hardly in any position to deny it, am I?'

'Good.' As he withdrew abruptly from her, she swore. He was going to abandon her again. He was going to keep her strung out just so he could control her and make her plead with him to bring her off.

He rolled her on to her back. He spread her legs apart, kneeling up between them, pushing with his knees till she was stretched. Then he stripped the condom off. He placed his hands upon her ribcage, spreading his fingers widely. As his back bowed, his penis curved downward. He nosed its head against her vulva to let her feel its warmth, then he drove it into her with one expert thrust. It filled her full, pressing against the top of her vagina. It rippled up her sleeve, opening her out, making the mouth of her vulva suck at its root.

She took him in. She wound her legs about his hips. She pulled him as hard as she was able to.

'Fuck me,' she whispered. 'Please. Don't leave me on the brink again. I just can't stand it any more.'

With his cockshaft fully in her, he flexed his hips, lowering his mouth to press on hers. He kissed her long and gently, then he said, 'Admit that I've won our contest and I'll fuck you until you come.'

'Promise.'

'I promise. But admit defeat.'

'All right. You've won. I'm beaten.'

'And admit that you've wanted me to fuck you ever since you stood by the chapel that first morning, eyeing up my cock?'

'All right. I admit it.'

'And you wanted me to lick you between your legs ever since you saw me licking Sophie by the lake?'

'All right. I admit it. But there's no need to rub it in.'

He laughed, transmitting a tremor to his penis. 'But there is a need to rub this in.' He worked his penis gently.

'Ha, ha. Very funny,' she hissed, quite out of breath. 'But if you do it as gently as that, I won't come before the dawn.'

'So you want a good, hard fucking, do you?'

She nodded.

'Not good enough, miss,' he smirked, pushing up to the limit of his length. 'Tell me in words exactly what you want. Talk dirty to me and perhaps I'll give you what you've wanted for so long.'

She closed her eyes, trying to wriggle to get more sensation from the flesh between her legs. 'All right. I need to feel your bollocks bouncing on my arse. I need you to rub your hairs against my clit.'

'And do you want to feel my spunk inside you? Or shall I pump it over your tits or in your mouth?'

She whispered, I want to feel your spunk pumping in my cunt. It makes my muscles tighten, but only after

253

I've come. Don't you dare shoot before I've come, or I'll never let you do me again, you pig.' She was aware that her normal inhibitions with words was gone. She didn't care. She needed to stop this verbal fencing and make him do her hard.

'OK. I'll try not to come too soon,' he said, starting a series of slow strokes.

'You'd better. You can look for a new job if you come before I do.'

He kissed her lightly again. 'I'm leaving anyway, miss. I've got to finish my thesis. I only took this job to help with expenses. Now I can't spare the time to come here every day just to play with you.'

Gael's heart sank. Did that mean that she wouldn't see him again? Before she could ask, he kissed her tenderly and began to push into her, the root of his shaft pressing wonderfully against her nubbin.

'Harder,' she whispered.

Now he took his mouth away. He bowed his back strongly and began to thrust. He flexed his hips, drawing out of her fully before driving in again.

His motion sped up. His tension became greater.

Gael squirmed to wring as much sensation from the act as she could get.

Now he fucked her fast and hard, making the whole of her body jolt.

She tightened her legs around his hips, presenting herself widely to his penis, making it possible for him to drive down into her with force.

She scratched his arms as he sped faster and faster.

He closed his eyes and whispered, 'You wanton creature. Squeeze your cunt.'

She squeezed, clamping her muscles on him each time he rammed into her, opening herself as he withdrew.

She clawed at his belly.

He pressed her ribcage hard, his thumb and fingers circling her breasts, kneading them.

She made her vulva suck him. The lips were so engorged that she could feel every millimetre of his veiny flesh as it drove in past their fringes.

'Fuck me harder,' she rasped, hardly able to catch her breath.

He sank down on her. He slipped his hands under her buttocks and lifted her from the cushions. Now he could bear down on her harder, and thrust into her even deeper. And, as he took her with greater strength, her tension rose.

'Harder,' she rasped, heaving her hips up as he drove down. 'Harder, you animal. Fuck me. Oh God, fuck me. I need to feel your cock. It's so beautiful.'

'Then feel it, you horny creature.' He pounded into her, stretching himself in her. She could imagine how taut the foreskin of his cock was, how swollen the glans as it pushed so urgently inside her, desperate now to spurt.

But would it spurt before she came?

She threw her head from side to side. My God, it was so wonderful to be had so brutally at last.

She shrieked with pleasure as he drove his finger hard into her anus. She racked on the finger and squirmed on his cock.

'Bastard!' she cried. 'Deeper. I want it deeper.'

'Slut,' he gasped and twisted her sideways.

On her side, she held her lower leg straight against the cushions. He bent the other up so her knee touched her breasts. His hands curled under her buttock and lifted, opening her up. One middle finger drove deep into her anus. A finger of his other hand worked her nubbin. She could feel his scrotum rasping at her inner thigh as he pushed through her yawning purse. His pubis rammed against his finger, driving it deeper into her anus. She'd never been had sideways before, and it was marvellous. It gave him access to every part of her that she needed to be rubbed or penetrated.

He moved a hand to her breast, the other staying in her anus. He put his head back, bowed his body and closed his eyes as he thrust, again and again.

'Harder,' she cried as she put her hand between her legs and began to rub her nubbin. Now she could feel his cockshaft sliding past her frigging finger.

'My God, I love your cock,' she groaned.

'And you've got the tightest cunt I've had for months,' he croaked. 'Squeeze my prick.'

'I don't want it to shoot. Fuck me, for God's sake, I'm coming. I'm coming.' She wriggled, twisting and turning her hips to get even better contact. 'Ram me, you horny bastard. I said ram me.'

He rammed her powerfully, making her free breast jolt. The shock of it went right up through her body. Then she came with a gasp as she sucked the night air deep into her lungs. His thighs tightened and he gave one almighty thrust and held at full extension.

He turned her and pressed her to the floor. He pushed her legs back so hard she was stretched as wide as she could be. Then he pushed again.

She felt the heat of his semen, pumping up inside her. She felt him beat.

She came again with a tightening of muscles so hard that she cried out with the pain. Then it turned to heat. The heat rushed up from the parted lips between her crabbing legs. It filled her belly which held the man's extended cock. It rushed up to her breasts. When it had filled them full of fire, it spread up to her cheeks and rushed out to her ears.

She sobbed as she racked on the pulsing cock. She squirmed for harder, closer contact with his flesh, letting out a cry of anguish, letting go all the accumulated tensions of the past few weeks. Her body arched, her breasts thrusting hard against his chest.

He sank down on her belly, his penis still inside her. She wanted it there. She wanted to keep it and to feel it for as long as she could. His semen was easing warmly from her sleeve. She could feel that and her own rich nectar warming the hollows of her loins.

She made her vulva suck his cock.

'Hussy,' he rasped, still trying to catch his breath. 'I'll have to fuck you again if you keep on doing that.'

She smiled demurely as if to say, Yes please.

After some minutes he withdrew from her. He stood over her, his legs astride, his penis jutting strongly still.

She rose and licked him from his testes to his glans.

'Harlot,' he grinned.

'And you're a randy dog.'

'But you liked it.'

'I loved it.'

'Will you do me like that again?'

'What – already?'

She knelt and mouthed his cock. Sucking on it hard, delighting in the salty taste of his semen as she milked it. Then he pulled his penis from her mouth and rubbed his balls over her face. He held her by the ears to make her tongue rove over his shaft, between his legs and up under his scrotum.

She took his cock in her fingers and began to masturbate him slowly. He bent his knees and pushed it out at her. Speeding her strokes, she made them shorter, squeezing him harder, pulling his foreskin tight.

He closed his eyes and pushed into her hand.

She felt him tense and plunged her mouth over his cock, gulping on it as he gushed again. He was a stallion in the way he hardened and came so quickly.

She held him in her mouth until he'd stopped beating and began to soften.

They lay for some time in the warmth of the summer-house and the heat of their orgasms. Listening to the rasping of Flanders' breath, she gazed up through the glass at a full moon high above her.

Eventually he put his lips to hers, licking his semen from them. 'Harlot,' he whispered.

She grinned. 'So I'm not the goody-goody you thought?'

'You're the hottest bit of stuff I've had.'

'Good,' she giggled and closed her eyes as she fondled and kissed him, sucking on his tongue. She wanted it again already. 'Take me to bed, Flanders,' she whispered.

He kissed her tenderly, making her close her eyes. 'I've got to go. I've got an early tutorial in Oxford in the morning.'

When she opened her eyes her spirits sank with disappointment to see that he had risen. She sprang up as he walked out to the bike and kicked it into life.

'Todd?' she called desperately. 'Todd, I need you. Please don't leave me now.'

He shrugged. 'But I've got to go, miss.'

Her bottom lip began to quiver as she flew to his side and held his arm tightly.

'Don't go,' she whispered.

'I must.'

'Fuck me again.' A tear ran down her cheek.

'Not now.'

'But when will you come back?' She pressed her mons against his knee and held his penis tightly, not knowing quite how to make him stay. 'When will you come to fuck me again?' All her inhibitions had gone. 'When?'

He shrugged. 'The next time I come upon you in the woods and pull your knickers down before I bend you over a log. Or perhaps when I come into the kitchen, lay you back on the table, rip your knickers at the crotch and push this through the slit.' He curled his fingers around hers, making her masturbate him for a few, slow strokes before he whispered, 'Or maybe I'll come in the night. You'll wake up to find me pushing back your legs to bare your quim so I can push this between its slippery lips.'

He made her strip his foreskin back and rub his glans. Then he put her fingers to her nose.

Gael breathed his scent. Then she gasped sharply as he slipped a finger between her legs and stroked it through her furrow.

'Keep this warm and slippery for me, miss – won't you.' He grinned, rose from the saddle and pushed his cock out hard.

She cupped his balls and pushed his scrotum back, making the glans swell large and shiny in the moonlight. He thrust into her hand one final time. Then he roared the engine, making the bike rear up before he sped away.

NEW BOOKS

Coming up from Nexus and Black Lace

There are three Nexus titles published in December

The Schooling of Stella by Yolanda Celbridge
December 1997   Price £4.99   ISBN: 0 352 33219 0

When English rose Stella Shawn wins a coveted scholarship to Castle Kernece, Scotland's sternest training college, she plans to fulfil her ambition of becoming a schoolmistress. More than a college, Kernece is a way of life, a fierce arena of dominant and submissive females where punishments are frequent and taken 'on the bare'. Only by her own total submission to the rules can Stella learn to dominate.

The Reward of Faith by Elizabeth Bruce
December 1997   Price £4.99   ISBN: 0 352 33225 5

Faith returns from her training to be claimed by her Master and ready to be instructed in the arts of carnal pleasure. Yet her new-found discipline will be severely tested as she enters Alex's decadent world in which Masters and Mistresses have Pleasure Slaves to serve their every sexual need. Faith joins the select ranks of the Chosen, where she has her taste for bondage and submission fully explored as she enjoys bizarre new extremes of humiliation.

The Training of Fallen Angels by Kendal Grahame
December 1997   Price £4.99   ISBN: 0 352 33224 7

Lisa and Janet are two teenagers who are driven by their insatiable libidos to discover new ways to satisfy their depraved desires. They become servants of the enigmatic Mr Gee, who lures them to his rural manor. But there is something sinister happening there. Lisa and Janet are blind to the danger they are in, intent on exploring new realms of debauchery – will they realise the risks before it is too late?

Emma's Secret Domination by Hilary James
January 1988   Price £4.99   ISBN: 0 352 33226 3
In this, the final instalment of the *Emma* series, Emma returns to
London only to fall back into the clutches of her cruel former mistress Ursula. Realising that she has missed the bittersweet delights of
lesbian domination, she begins finally to enjoy Ursula's attentions –
but this only serves to anger and humiliate the prince, who is still her
master. How will he administer the discipline she deserves?

'S' – A Story of Submission by Philippa Masters
January 1998   Price £4.99   ISBN: 0 352 33229 8
When 'S' answers an advert which seems to promise an escape from
her dull life, little does she realise that her fantasies of total submission are soon to be fulfilled. Entering into a secret world of domination, subservience and humiliation, she explores the bounds of her
sexuality, finally realising the depravity of her darkest desires.

Lake of Lost Love by Mercedes Kelly
December 1997   Price £4.99   ISBN: 0 352 33220 4
Princess Angeline lives on a paradise island in the South Seas. Married to Prince Hari and accepted into the native culture and customs, she has a life of ease and debauched sensual delights. When Prince Hari's young manservant is kidnapped and used as a sex slave by the cruel and depraved female ruler of nearby Monkey Island, Angeline sets about planning his rescue.

Contests of Wills by Louisa Francis
December 1997   Price £4.99   ISBN: 0 352 332 239
In Sydney, Australia, in the late 1870s, lascivious young Melanie has married a man old enough to be her grandfather. When their honeymoon is cut short by his sudden death, his will is contested by his grandson, the louche and hedonistic Ric Lidell, and his promiscuous half-sister. Ric's dark satanic looks draw Melanie to him like a magnet – but Melanie's kinky former lover is unwilling to let her walk out of his life.

Sugar and Spice – *a collection of Black Lace short stories*
December 1997   Price £6.99   ISBN: 0 352 332 271
This is the long-awaited first anthology of Black Lace erotic short stories. Testament to the wildness and originality of the untamed female sexual imagination, there is a variety of settings and characters here to suit all tastes – from the icy tundra of Siberia to the more familiar locations of the office and library. Only the most arousing and erotic stories have made it into this anthology.

Unhallowed Rites by Martine Marquand
January 1998   Price £4.99   ISBN: 0 352 332 220
Twenty-year-old Allegra di Vitale is bored with life in her guardian's Venetian palazzo – until temptation draws her to look at the bizarre pictures he keeps in his private chamber. Her lust awakened, she tries to deny her powerful cravings by submitting to life as a nun. But the strange order of the Convent of Santa Clerisa provides new temptations, forcing her to perform ritual acts with the depraved men and women of the convent.

Nexus

NEXUS BACKLIST

All books are priced £4.99 unless another price is given. If a date is supplied, the book in question will not be available until that month in 1997.

CONTEMPORARY EROTICA

THE ACADEMY	Arabella Knight	Oct
AGONY AUNT	G. C. Scott	Jul
ALLISON'S AWAKENING	John Angus	Jul
BOUND TO SERVE	Amanda Ware	
BOUND TO SUBMIT	Amanda Ware	Sep
CANDIDA'S SECRET MISSION	Virginia LaSalle	
CANDIDA'S IN PARIS	Virginia LaSalle	Oct
CANDY IN CAPTIVITY	Arabella Knight	
CHALICE OF DELIGHTS	Katrina Young	
A CHAMBER OF DELIGHTS	Katrina Young	Nov
THE CHASTE LEGACY	Susanna Hughes	
CHRISTINA WISHED	Gene Craven	
DARK DESIRES	Maria del Rey	
THE DOMINO TATTOO	Cyrian Amberlake	
THE DOMINO ENIGMA	Cyrian Amberlake	
THE DOMINO QUEEN	Cyrian Amberlake	
EDEN UNVEILED	Maria del Rey	
EDUCATING ELLA	Stephen Ferris	Aug
ELAINE	Stephen Ferris	
EMMA'S SECRET WORLD	Hilary James	
EMMA'S SECRET DIARIES	Hilary James	
EMMA'S SUBMISSION	Hilary James	
EMMA'S HUMILIATION	Hilary James	
FALLEN ANGELS	Kendal Grahame	
THE TRAINING OF FALLEN ANGELS	Kendal Grahame	Dec

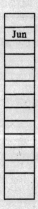

BEATRICE	Anonymous	
CHOOSING LOVERS FOR JUSTINE	Aran Ashe	
DEAR FANNY	Aran Ashe	
LYDIA IN THE BORDELLO	Philippa Masters	
MADAM LYDIA	Philippa Masters	
LURE OF THE MANOR	Barbra Baron	
MAN WITH A MAID 3	Anonymous	
MEMOIRS OF A CORNISH GOVERNESS	Yolanda Celbridge	
THE GOVERNESS AT ST AGATHA'S	Yolanda Celbridge	
THE GOVERNESS ABROAD	Yolanda Celbridge	
PLEASING THEM	William Doughty	

SAMPLERS & COLLECTIONS

EROTICON 1		
EROTICON 2		Jun
EROTICON 3		Sep
THE FIESTA LETTERS	ed. Chris Lloyd	
MOLTEN SILVER	Delaney Silver	
NEW EROTICA 2	ed. Esme Ombreaux	

NON-FICTION

HOW TO DRIVE YOUR WOMAN WILD IN BED	Graham Masterton	
HOW TO DRIVE YOUR MAN WILD IN BED	Graham Masterton	Jul
LETTERS TO LINZI	Linzi Drew	